Manda Scott is a veterinary surgeon, writer and climber, not necessarily in that order. Originally from Scotland, she has spent the best part of the last decade in rural Suffolk sharing her life with a lurcher and an assortment of wildlife. *Hen's Teeth* is her first novel.

HEN'S TEETH

MANDA SCOTT

First published by The Women's Press Ltd, 1996
A member of the Namara Group
34 Great Sutton Street, London EC1V 0DX

Copyright © Manda Scott 1996

The right of Manda Scott to be identified as the author of this work has been
asserted by her in accordance with the Copyright, Designs and Patents Act 1988.

British Library Cataloguing-in-Publication Data
A catalogue record for this book is available from the
British Library

ISBN 0 7043 4496 3

Phototypeset in 10.5 on 13pt Goudy by Intype London Ltd
Printed and bound in Great Britain by BPC Paperbacks Ltd

For my Family, with Love

ACKNOWLEDGEMENTS

As is ever the case, the list of those who deserve my thanks is far greater than the space allowed. There are those, however, without whom *Hen's Teeth* would simply not have made it to publication and this is their place.

My thanks first and foremost to Jane, the world's most supportive agent; for unwavering faith, for unending patience and for continual good advice. Thank you, Jane.

Thanks also to the clinicians, lay staff and final year students at the Cambridge Vet School for giving me the space, time and encouragement to start and, similarly, to David and all at Frontier for the freedom to finish.

Chloë provided a writer's perspective and encouragement, Dick kept me in touch with the things that matter in the veterinary world and so kept me sane. Shirley, the inspirational climber, introduced me to, amongst other things, the joys of Welsh limestone and dragged me out on to the rock when 'word-processor-cramp' was becoming permanent. Penny and Stat took me out with the dogs and opened up the dawns again, Pat and Pat made their farm a home and a model for the place I would most like to live. Caroline made magic with acupuncture needles, Sue simply wove magic and Päivi came along near the end with love and a magic all her own. To all of these, my thanks.

Finally, for Debs, Tony, Mike and Robin, my reference points in a changing world, thanks are never enough – but are better than nothing. Thank you.

CHAPTER ONE

It was shortly after midnight when the phone rang.

I was lying in bed at the time, counting Artex ridges on the ceiling as a creative alternative to sheep and trying not to think too hard about life, the universe or anything.

Janine, who never lets the vagaries of our relationship interfere with her sleeping patterns, reached across me without waking and ripped the phone cord from the wall. The bedroom sank back into silence and the answering machine in the living room was left to take the call.

It's only ever Janine who gets calls in the wee small hours: a random array of journalistic crises that, invariably, will wait until morning. I lay back and listened with a kind of vacant curiosity. At that time of night a human voice, however strange, is better company than an Artex sheep.

'Kellen, are you there? It's Caroline.'

What?

I rolled out of bed, wide awake, jammed the line back into the socket and grabbed the receiver all in one go.

'Hi, Caroline. It's me. What's up?'

'Bridget's dead.'

Bridget? Mentor, teacher, friend and, a long, long time ago, my lover. The only one who ever counted.

9

She can't be dead.

Not Bridget.

'Kellen, are you still there?'

'More or less.'

'Could you come over? Please? The police are on their way. I need someone here.'

Don't we all?

'Will you come? Please.'

'I'm on my way.'

It's not far out of Glasgow along the Great Western Road over the switchback through Bearsden to Milngavie and out to the Campsies beyond. The last mile or two from the village to the small farmhouse at the foot of the Ben are slow; no street-lights and a single-track road make for tentative night driving unless you happen to own a four-wheel-drive Land Rover, which I don't.

The police did. Two, and both of them in a great hurry to be at the farmhouse ahead of me. I pulled into a passing place after the second one tried to push me off the road and waited for a moment, listening to the late-night news on the radio.

A black 7-series BMW nosed along a few minutes behind the others. The green emergency light sat askew on the roof just above the driver's-side window, flashing dysrhythmically. The local GP.

I opened my door and stopped him as he tried to squeeze past. Not a popular move. A mid-thirties golfing executive with a sharp suit and an expensive tan glared at me from behind the wheel. Stravinsky conducted *The Rite of Spring* on the car CD. The window beside me slid open just far enough for me to catch the closing bars. His voice followed, carrying easily in the sudden silence.

'Move.'

It's a long time since anyone spoke to me like that.

I leant down and peered through the gap in the window. 'I'm sorry?'

'Get out of the way. I'm a doctor. I need to get past.' He enunciated each word with unnecessary care and then, when I didn't jump into action, he shoved the car into gear and let it grate forwards until the bumper touched my door.

I listened to the faint tap of the impact, estimated the size of his insurance compared to the value of my car and did nothing.

He stopped, cursing. He jabbed one foot on the clutch and gunned the engine with the other.

'I'm a friend of Caroline's,' I said carefully. 'She called me.'

Wrong password.

I watched him while he categorised me: designer dyke, opportunist lover, 'friend' with sewn-on inverted commas. I could have told him that I was a therapist, but I wasn't sure it would cut much ice.

Try again. 'I was Bridget's partner in the business,' I said. 'I own half the farm.'

'I see.' Categories dropped. 'You better come down then. There's been an accident. Apparently Ms Donnelly's had a heart attack.'

'You've examined the body?'

He toyed with the clutch again and the car shuddered under my hand. Members of the lay public do not question the given truth.

I kept my face at the window and smiled my best professional smile. He humoured me.

'Not yet,' he said, 'but the police were quite specific.'

Jolly good. Diagnosis by constable.

'Thanks.' I kicked my car door shut to let him move on. 'I'll follow you down.'

I gave myself five minutes to cool off before I pulled out and eased my tired Escort down the last half-mile to the farm. Time to lose the aftertaste of bile that went with the BMW and to wonder how in heaven's name a man like that gets to enter the caring profession.

The guard lights flicked on as I drew in and lit up a yard empty of cars except for Bridget's old maroon Rover. There were a lot of skid marks though; someone had been playing handbrake turns in the gravel. Outside the gates, two police Land Rovers and a black BMW sat in a tight phalanx, grouped ready for mass escape.

The back door to the farmhouse hung open. Inside, the kitchen smelled of wet dog and peat smoke. It always did. The rusty knife of nostalgia twisted in the old reminders of home and I stopped for a moment just inside the door, to take stock and to check for the changes inevitable after four years' absence.

The newspapers on the breakfast counter were new. And the walking boots stashed under the bench by the fire. Surprisingly little else.

Half a dozen empty mugs cluttered the Rayburn. The cats, displaced from their rightful space between the hot plates, lay in a furry pile on the flagged floor. Black limbs mixed with tabby-white and a single four-set of smoke grey. I crouched down and spoke to the king head on top.

'Ashwood, where's your mother?'

One amber eye opened briefly and the brow whiskers twitched. Not here.

There were voices somewhere, separated by two or three sets of lath-and-plaster but not difficult to trace. Caroline: low and musical as ever, but with an edge of controlled hysteria audible even through the walls. Two others: one male, one female, both unknown, possibly the law.

I followed the sound upstairs, negotiating the creaking floorboards with the instinct born of long practice, and paused outside the half-open door to the bedroom.

Caroline was there, standing stiffly by the bed. A fragile

12

marionette waiting for a new pull on the strings. Odd shadows patched the delicate bones of her face, hiding whatever was there. Her fine, blonde hair turned to mouse in the soft light of the bedside lamp, except at the ends, where it caught in her mouth and she chewed it into dark rats'-tails. A slim gold chain at her throat, half-hidden beneath the open collar of her shirt, rippled to the rate of her pulse. A fast pulse. Too fast for comfort.

Opposite her, on the other side of the bed, four uniformed police officers performed perfect examples of the elevated ostrich manoeuvre – if you don't look, then what you can't see doesn't exist. Their eyes travelled blind circuits of the room, avoiding the dead woman on the bed, the live one opposite them and, above all, the series of prints and pencil life drawings on the walls. Too many likenesses. Too many boundaries broken.

The WPC was coping better. She sat on the edge of the bed, her eyes on Caroline's face and a hand on her arm, forming a bridge from living to dead.

The dead. Bridget. She lay on the bed, fully dressed. Ready to go and feed the chickens or clean out a loose box. Peaceful. Still. Untouched by the ridiculous tableau around her. I could see her face clearly from the door, the strong cheekbones enhanced by the light and by the odd falling of flesh that happens with death. Her short, dark hair was stuck to one cheek as if she had just turned over in her sleep.

At her side, his nose on her shoulder, lay Tan, the tricolour border collie we exhumed together from the living death of the RSPCA pound a lifetime or two ago. All he had to do was swipe his tongue across her cheek and wake her up. We could have got rid of the rest then, and sat on the bed and sorted things out. Except he didn't, so she didn't and we didn't. But I was waiting for it all the same.

Reality returned abruptly in the form of the adenoidal executive

13

sneer of the BMW-driving GP speaking from the other side of the door.

'Ms Leader, a preliminary examination would certainly suggest a cardiac arrest. Your ... ah ... "friend" ...'

You have to be joking. This is the 1990s, for gods' sake.

I stepped in sideways through the doorway.

' "Partner", doctor,' I said. 'She was her partner.'

Brilliant. I should have been in the theatre. People wait lifetimes to make an entrance like that. Tan was ecstatic. He left the bed at shoulder height, a black and white and gold heat-seeking missile, intent on coating me in dog drool. I crouched down to absorb the onslaught and watched while the six people around the room recovered from the sudden intrusion.

Caroline, predictably, was first. 'Kellen!' Her voice was raw. 'My God, Kellen! What the hell are you playing at? Tan, *leave!*'

The dog let me go and returned to his post.

I joined his mistress by the side of the bed for a quick hug. 'Sorry, C. The man's an idiot. I couldn't resist.'

The four representatives of the law developed goldfish eyes and looked hard at spots on the far wall. The doctor stared daggers and his jaw muscles worked overtime, gritting his teeth. The artificial light reduced his tan to an interesting shade of terminal jaundice and the suave flick of dark brown hair flopped less suavely over one brow.

I produced my best professional smile. 'Everyone dies of cardiac arrest in the end, doctor. It doesn't often happen spontaneously. Any ideas what triggered this one?'

He slicked back his hair and pasted on a lopsided smile of virtuous but nevertheless waning patience. 'A very large number of things may cause the heart to fail, Ms ...?'

'Stewart, Kellen Stewart,' I said and offered him my hand.

'*Dr* Kellen Stewart,' added Caroline helpfully, waving a hand to include the group in the general introduction.

The medic stopped in mid-shake, rearranging his

preconceptions again. His eyes narrowed as he tried to work out where the 'Dr' came from.

'PhD. Ancient Mongolian architecture,' I lied. He knew it.

'Edinburgh?'

'Glasgow.'

'The Royal?'

'The Western.'

It's a social ritual. Like dogs sniffing under tails. Three things matter when medics meet. Where did you qualify? Where did you do your house job? He was two up on me, but I knew his answer to question three: What do you do now? My ace in the sleeve. He was a GP or he wouldn't be there. I had no intention at all of letting him know what I did for a living.

I released his hand and turned to the policewoman on the bed. Somewhere along the line she had taken off her hat and let her hair fall, straight and dark, below her ears. It turned her back into a human being, young but dependable. When I walked in, she was focused on Caroline, sheltering her from the invasion, providing good, basic, unconditional support. By the time I finished bickering with the doctor, she was staring at me with the kind of frozen frown that is either utter distaste or a desperate attempt not to laugh. Impossible to tell which.

I nodded at her and raised a smile. 'Is there an obvious cause of death?' I asked.

She shrugged. 'There is no evidence so far to suggest that Dr Kemp's initial assessment isn't accurate – '

'That's ridiculous. She was forty-one, for God's sake! Nobody dies that young for no reason . . .'

It's a long time since I heard Caroline that close to the edge. Or with that much sheer frustration running under the surface. The WPC heard it too. At least, she frowned again and reached out a hand. Then she looked at me and took it back again.

15

'We'll get a post-mortem in the morning, ladies. That'll tell us what we need to know.'

We jumped, all three of us. It was the eldest and the most senior of the three police officers behind the bed. A wrinkled, sun-beaten man with peppered grey hair and a gorgeous West Highland accent. He would have looked a great deal more at home hauling in creels in a lobster boat than he did in a uniform in a dead woman's bedroom.

He looked at Caroline. 'Are you the next of kin?' There was sudden compassion then, as if we'd crossed the line into real life, part of his patch after all.

'Aye. I mean, yes. There's a will somewhere . . .' She pushed a hand through her hair and her eyes flicked around the room. 'Downstairs, I think . . .'

He shook his head. 'No need now. It's a bit late in the day for that.' He looked at me. 'You can take care of the lass tonight?'

I nodded. 'That's why I'm here.'

'Good. There's an ambulance on its way. It'll be here any minute now, so you won't have to stay in the house with – ' He broke off and stared distractedly towards the door, stroking the side of his nose. 'In the meantime,' he said, his gaze focusing back on me, 'perhaps we'd all be better downstairs, where there's a fire and a kettle.'

And no bodies littering the furniture. What an amazingly good idea.

He shepherded us in an orderly flock out of the bedroom and downstairs, to where the kitchen was filled with the warmth of the Rayburn and the sleepy opportunism of the cats.

The three young constables crowded round the fireplace and played inexpertly with the peat bricks and kindling. Lazy puffs of peat smoke filtered out into the room, thickening the atmosphere and adding to the late-night sense of dreamy unreality.

The young WPC joined Caroline at the Rayburn. Between them they made enough coffee to keep us all awake for the rest of the week and then began arranging a year's supply of biscuits neatly on the breakfast tray.

The doctor removed himself to the far end of the room and hovered by the door, staring at me poisonously through the haze, as if I reminded him of someone he'd rather forget.

'D'you no think the lad needs company?' The voice at my shoulder glowed with rounded vowels. The weather-worn police inspector stood beside me, a full mug of coffee clasped in either hand.

I shook my head. 'If he does,' I said, 'it isn't ours. I think you'll find he's leaving.'

'No, no. He'll not be gone before the ambulance is here. We may as well make ourselves popular.' He held out his hand. 'The name's MacDonald, Stewart MacDonald,' he said, 'and our friend over there is David Kemp. *Dr* David Kemp.' A pair of hairy brows rose above a set of very balanced, very thoughtful sea-grey eyes. 'Since he's a colleague of yours,' he said, 'I think we owe it to him to share a drink. How do you suppose he takes his coffee?'

'Neat,' I said. 'By intravenous drip. With the serpent blood.'

'You reckon?' He tilted his head, giving the idea due consideration. 'I'd have said black, no sugar. Stimulation without the calories.' He gestured towards the door with one of the mugs. 'Shall we see who's right?'

We both were, oddly enough. The coffee went down like sewage down a sump, but the doctor wasn't staying to make polite conversation. Or even to say thank you. The dialogue was minimal, monosyllabic and uninspiring, and the BMW was gone in a violent spurt of gravel before anyone else's coffee was drinkably cool. Not quite the kind of man to inspire confidence in the open-hearted tendencies of the medical profession.

The ambulance arrived a good ten minutes after he left. They parked it in front of the gates and Inspector MacDonald

17

borrowed the keys so that they could carry the body out the long way: through the hallway to the living room and out of the front door, thereby avoiding the kitchen. The policemen carried her, all three of them, clattering downstairs in their duty boots, making not quite enough noise to wake the dead.

We followed them out on to the drive. Not for any more concrete reason than to see her go. A last goodbye. Something to fix the fact of death when all of it felt like a passing nightmare. I drifted out in Caroline's wake, aware that the young WPC was beside me. For support, perhaps. Or to see that I didn't do anything untoward.

Both of us watched as Caroline, the most obviously bereaved, stood on the tailgate of the ambulance and slid her hand under the blanket to ruffle the tangled hank of oak-dark hair that hung over the edge of the stretcher.

It wasn't, on the face of it, a particularly emotional gesture, but the blue flare of the emergency lights spun round as she did it and so my last memory of Bridget, whether I like it or not, is an upside-down ghoul-white grimace framed by a regulation NHS blanket. The kind of thing to haunt dreams for eternity.

I left Caroline with the policewoman and withdrew to the warmth of the kitchen. The other two followed me in a minute or so later and we shared yet another silent cup of coffee, each of us lost in a world of remembered death.

Inspector MacDonald came back in as the ambulence left. He stood in the kitchen doorway, where the dithering firelight pushed age and the time of night into the crags beneath his eyes. His voice was brisk all the same.

'Right then, ladies. That's it for tonight. I'd appreciate it if you didn't move anything from the bedroom. We'll be back for a wee look round first thing in the morning.' He bent down to pat the dog, his eyes on me. 'I take it you can see that the lady here gets some sleep, Dr Stewart?'

Maybe.

'I'll do what I can.'

'Good.' He nodded. 'I'll be off then. Don't worry, I can see myself out.'

He did just that and a moment or two later we heard the two Land Rovers grumble to life and grind their way up the drive towards the village.

We waited, riveted by the noise, until the last exhaust crackle had faded into the distance. I reached out then, giving her contact, trying to make the real unreal, to make the world all right. Caroline stood stiffly in my arms, her face set, holding tight to the edges of self-control.

'The ponies,' she said, 'they need feeding.'

And so, at somewhere around two a.m., kitted out in boots and old jackets, we went out to the barn to feed the ponies.

Nothing had changed. Nothing ever did. Eight years on and it still smelled of creosote after the crazy summer when the four of us took the cow byre and turned it into the best set of loose boxes this side of the Clyde. There were still centuries-old cobwebs in the corner where the power hose didn't quite reach. The streaks of bird shit and patches of dried beet pulp on the walls were possibly a touch thicker than they had been, but not so that you'd really notice.

The ponies were still in the same places, still with the same smell and the same feel. Perhaps a little more grizzled. Midnight had turned into a pale grey dawn. Tarquin had acquired a few more saddle marks and a couple more over-reach scars on the backs of his legs, and there was a new Connemara filly where Rain had been. I took time to make friends, feeding her a scrap of Polo Mint from the lining of the jacket pocket.

We worked together, a full displacement routine, filling over-full water buckets, retying bulging hay nets and feeding a barn full of ponies already somnolent after at least one late feed. They nuzzled warm half-questions into my hair or my pockets or the small of my back and I patted back a non-answer or rubbed it in under the base of the mane as each one wanted. 'Nothing for you. Keep peace. Be kind later.'

And please don't get colic. Just this once, take a change in routine and don't throw a gut ache. Please.

I had just reached the end of my line when I realised that Caroline had gone.

I looked round for her, wishing desperately for the charade to be over so that we could go inside and talk. And cry. And find out what really happened. And begin to put the world back together.

'Caroline?' I called into the shadows outside the box. 'Are you there?'

'The bantams have gone.' Her voice was tight, like a cheese wire.

She was there, somewhere in the dim light of the forty-watt bulb at the end of the barn, oddly ethereal in the shifting shadows. Her body never quite followed her mind in the transition from town girl to farming woman.

Chickens came very low on my list of priorities.

'Forget it. We can find them in the morning. It's time you came inside.'

I bolted the last door in a hurry and got to her just as the control broke, the hard lines on her face folding finally, turning her back into the woman I used to know.

I took her back to the kitchen, made her coffee, then sat with her on the floor by the fire, holding her, keeping her boundaries solid while the first real waves of grief pulled her world apart.

It was a pattern set in a childhood long past, when my house was the one at the top of the hill and hers was one of the huddle in the valley. It snowed one Sunday morning, the first real white-out I remember. Everyone under the age of fifteen and a fair few over forty were out on the slope, making the most of the glass-packed snow. Caroline Leader was an iced-blonde waif, another anonymous kid in the mass of sliding figures. Our plastic-bag sledges rammed head-on half-way down the slope and she rolled the rest of the way to the bottom in a slither of mushed grey snow. She grazed her knee and cried on my shoulder. Her mother was out, because her mother was always out, and so it was me that washed the knee clean, wrapped it with a torn-up tea-towel and then took a new friend home for tea. I was five years old at the time, her senior by eighteen months.

Later, at school, she cried over the passing boyfriends and consoled herself with the problem pages of the *Jackie* filched from my school-bag. Later still, when it wasn't boyfriends any more, she followed me through the identity crisis and out the other side, dry-eyed and peaceful, trusting me to lead the way safely. And then afterwards, when the first new experience crumbled to nothing, I still provided the shoulder and she still cried on it. Lovers may come and go, but your friends are with you for ever. Something like that.

So it was easier than it might have been, to sit there with my back against the big chair, rocking her gently back and forth, listening to her grieve over the woman who was my lover first.

Now and again, I fed another peat brick on to the fire so that I could keep my eyes on the flames and not have to think.

We slept there, in the kitchen, in the end. There seemed no need to wake her when the place was warm and lacked any immediate ghosts. I found spare bedding in the airing cupboard, banked up the fire and held her curled up tight in my arms as she cried herself out and then slept.

The cats slid down from the Rayburn and came to form a cordon, keeping the ghosts at bay until the dawn came and the siren call of the local rodent population drew them back out to the fields. Quite a long time after they left, I let go of the crowding memories and fell into a cramped and uneasy sleep.

A cold nose behind my ear and a blast of dog breath on my face brought me back to time and space.

I reached out and found fur. The nose shoved again, more urgently, and a mass of dog hair draped across my eyes. Tan. He has a way with words.

'Time to go out, huh?' I spat out a mouthful of collie hair and was half-way through inching myself out of the tangled mass of bedclothes when I realised that I was alone.

'Caroline?' I looked blearily around the room.

'Here.' She sat on the tall stool by the Rayburn, dressed in clean jeans and a fresh white shirt with a towel slung round her neck and her hair still damp from the shower. The gold necklace lay quietly along her clavicles, no longer a useful index of a pulse.

The dog began to wash behind my ears. Very sweet, but not quite what I needed just at that moment. I slid back under the covers.

Caroline watched, faintly amused. 'Ignore him. That's his alarm clock routine.' She snapped her fingers. 'Tan, get lost.'

The collie gave me one last wet smacker and then retreated sedately to the foot of the stool.

I writhed out of the clutches of the duvet, feeling each of the joints in my spine as they uncreaked, and then wandered over to stand with my back against the Rayburn, warming out the knots while Caroline produced a mug of coffee.

'How are you?' I asked after the caffeine had filtered though to my brain.

'Better. Better than last night anyway. I've been up to the bedroom and had a look round.'

Gods. Could I have done that? 'And?'

'And . . . all sorts of things.' She stared at me hard, the fine blue patches under her eyes tightening up. 'I need your help, Kells,' she said eventually.

Good. Very good. Too many think they can cope on their own for too long.

I waited, trying to decide if I was too close to offer useful, objective therapy.

'She didn't just die, Kellen.'

Oh dear.

Some things are obvious beyond words. And sometimes curiosity overrides common sense – in answering late-night telephone calls, for instance. There is the odd occasion, however, when common sense wins hands down and this is one of them.

If the rest of the world wants to know how Bridget Donnelly died, then the rest of the world can do the finding out. I know my limits. In this case, I am a therapist and nothing else.

I reached out, finding her hand, and squeezed her fingers. 'Caroline. Love. Denial's a first line of defence, but – '

She jerked her hand away. 'Don't give me that therapy shit, Kellen Stewart. I am not one of your fucked-up clients. She's dead and it wasn't an accident. I called you last night because I thought you might still care enough to help. If you don't, that's fine, you can get the hell out of here . . .'

I didn't say a word but she stopped anyway, a thin line chiselled across her brow.

Perhaps I wasn't the best person to call.

'Oh, shit, Kells. I'm sorry.'

'Don't be.'

I turned and looked out of the small leaded window over the sink. A waddling mallard led a late brood of ducklings in single file to the pond under the hawthorn hedge. Even the ducks hadn't changed.

I took a deep breath and turned back. 'I'd better go.'

She let me hunt down my jacket and dig my shoes out from under the bench and sat there without moving. It wasn't until I reached the kitchen door that she turned and slid off the stool.

'Kellen?'

'Yes?'

'Please don't go.'

I could have opened the door then and gone out. Out into the sunshine and the early morning frost. Away from the ghosts of the night and the past. Free.

Only 'I need you' said my long-lost childhood friend.

And what woman was ever born who did not need to be needed?

And so, finally, we talked. Caroline made another pot of coffee, built up the fire and took me though the events of the previous day. It was an average mid-September day: three treks of varying lengths in the foothills of the Campsies – mostly late-season tourists and the odd local schoolkid with 'time off' from school. None of them had been out of her sight for long enough to go to the house and back.

The farrier had turned up late in the afternoon to shoe one of the ponies and so it was dark by the time she had realised that the rest of the herd had not been fed and that her lover was not around. That was about six o'clock. It took her less than five minutes after that to find the body. She called me after midnight. In between, she lost six hours sitting with her fingers on a pulse, trying to make it go. Time does odd things sometimes.

The police had been overwhelmingly courteous and were obviously well acquainted with the domestic arrangements before they arrived, which says a lot for the value of village gossip. The GP with the fake tan and the designer haircut was not someone she recognised – an extra hand on loan from one of the big Bearsden practices, filling in while the local doctor was off on maternity leave. He had performed a cursory examination and confirmed the fact that Bridget was dead, but that was about as far as he got before I walked in and brought the show to a close.

'What do you want from me?' I asked when Caroline had ground to a halt.

I thought she hadn't heard, but then she disappeared into Bridget's office at the back of the house and came back with a cardboard folder. She hunted through it, pulled out a scrap of paper and tossed it across to me.

'Read that.'

It was a page roughly torn from a pocket diary dated the first week in August. An untidy hand had scrawled across it in black biro: 'Bride: Look after these for me. Please. Back soon. Thanks. M.'

Even had I not recognised the handwriting, there was only ever one other person in the world besides me who called her Bride.

I looked up at Caroline. 'Malcolm?' I asked.

'Mmm.' She sat down carefully in the chair by the fire and busied herself teasing knots out of the dog's coat. 'He turned up out of the blue on a Saturday afternoon a month or so ago. I was out with a ride and Bridget had gone into the village to get some batteries for the radio. He passed me on the lane as I was coming back. He couldn't drive past the whole ride and pretend not to see us, but I don't think he wanted to stop. He looked . . . strained . . . preoccupied. A lot worse than I've ever seen him. All he would say was that he'd brought us some hens for the farm and he'd come back later to explain what was happening. When I got home, there were six bantams in a basket in the porch and the note was on top.'

I tried to imagine Malcolm deliberately dumping half a dozen chickens on his sister. The mind boggled. 'I bet Bridget was thrilled about that.'

'She was all right. She doesn't . . . didn't . . . hate chickens as much as she used to.'

'And has Malcolm been back to explain yet?'

'No. And he won't be coming now.' She gave up on the collie's coat and stood up, shoving her hands in the pockets of her jeans. Her voice, when she spoke, had a new edge.

'He's dead, Kellen. Malcolm's dead. They found him in his office the morning after he was here.'

'*What?* Caroline, no!' I found myself back at the window, counting mallard chicks and breathing too fast. When I turned back to the fireplace, all I could see was the back of her head.

Bridget's brother was the driving force behind most of my professional life. From the night when he chaperoned me through my first full twenty-four hours as Junior House Officer on duty in his medicine ward, he had been there: a steady baseline, a friend in the camp, an icon of sanity in the insane world of hospital medicine. He made me coffee and taught me medicine. He brought me sandwiches late at night in the wards and taught me politics. He opened the magical doors into research so that I could walk away from the clinics and still be a doctor if I wanted. And, in the end, he was one of the few people who had really understood when I pulled out of medicine for good. To have him dead and for me not to know was, quite simply, unthinkable.

I stayed by the window watching the wind play across the surface of the pond. Caroline had retreated into the depths of the armchair, hugging her knees to her chest and chewing a rag-end of hair. She looked about fifteen years old and very scared. I caught her eye this time and held it.

'When did he die?'

'The twelfth of August.'

I don't believe this.

'That was six weeks ago, Caroline. Why in heaven's name didn't you tell me before this?'

'You were out of the country, Kellen. There was no way we could get hold of you.'

'Did you try?'

'Of course we did.' Her voice was a fingernail on glass. 'Bridget spent hours on the bloody phone trying to track you down. We had the consul all ready to put out a radio message for you, but we'd run out of time by then. You wouldn't have been able to get back in time for the service. She cancelled it just before the broadcast.'

I kept my eyes on the pond and counted the leaves floating on the water.

'It wouldn't have taken much to leave a message at home,' I said eventually. 'The machine was always on, even when we were both away.'

'And would you have wanted to come home to a voice on a machine telling you that Malcolm was dead and you'd missed his service and all that was left was a stone? Would you? Really?' She shoved herself out of the chair and across to the window, making herself a silhouette against the morning sun.

'You've got to believe me, Kellen. We spent more time talking about that than anything else. Bridget was going to offer to stay away from the service so you could go without having to meet her if that's what you wanted.' She spun round to face me, her features animated more by pain than by anger. 'Have you any idea what that would have cost her?'

I don't want to think about that.

'Well?' Her voice was like a cat's, sharp and full of accusation. 'Have you?'

'I can guess.'

'Right. So back off.' Her lips were a thin-drawn line. 'Where the hell were you anyway?'

'In Oregon. I needed space.'

'So you got your space. Maybe it was better like that. The service was at the Tron. There's a stone at the family ground in Blairgowrie. You can visit any time you like.' She ran out of steam suddenly and leant back against the window sill, tired and drained again.

'This is your kind of thing. We were going to call you as soon as we heard you got home ... but Bridget ...' She looked up at

27

the ceiling and through it to the empty bed in the room above. 'She didn't want to disturb you until we were sure.'

'Sure about what?'

'Sure about what happened to Malcolm. She didn't believe that he died by accident. She wanted to get you to find out what happened, but she didn't want to call you until she'd got as much information as she could.' Caroline spun the folder towards me. It skidded across the floor and came to rest against my foot. 'Everything she found is in here.'

I let the stuff lie where it was.

'What did the medics tell you?' I asked. 'About Malcolm?'

'That he died at work. He'd been in working over the weekend and they found him at his desk when they went in on Monday morning.'

'Was there a post-mortem?'

'Of course. The report said that he'd had a heart attack. Stress. Overwork. All the usual medical bullshit. He was working an eighteen-hour day and a seven-day week in a job that he hated without enough money to finish the project. It didn't seem completely unreasonable at the time.'

It never does with medics. Overwork goes with the job. If you don't hit the bottle, something else will crack in the end. Except that Malcolm didn't seem the type to crack.

I looked across at Caroline. She was chewing a tail-end of hair, looking at me as if I was the only hope left.

Some hope.

'So why didn't Bridget believe it?' I asked.

'I don't know.' She shook her head. 'She did at first. She would have believed anything, I think. We were so stressed out with organising the service and then trying to find you . . .' She bit her lip, stopped and changed direction. 'It wasn't until afterwards that we had the time to think. Then she started asking questions . . .'

Quite.

It is, after all, what lawyers are trained to do. It's just that most of them don't die as a result.

I took my mug and went to sit on the back step, looking out towards the pond and the fields beyond.

A young kestrel fought a thermal, trying to keep position over the muck heap, then closed its wings and dropped twenty feet in fewer seconds. It missed the mouse and flicked upwards again for a second try.

If I had a camera here, I could do something useful.

The dog pushed past me and came to sit at my feet. Caroline followed and stood leaning on the doorpost at my side, the folder hanging loosely from her fingers. All three of us watched the bird make another fruitless stoop. Two – nil to the rodents.

I took the folder from her hand and held it on my lap. 'So what did she find?' I asked.

'Nothing.' Caroline shook her head, her eyes still on the bird. 'That's why we didn't call you.'

I opened the file and flicked through the contents. There was a long, printed letter from Malcolm from a year or so before. When I knew him, he used to write once a fortnight, but Bridget, as a matter of general policy, never kept the letters. Something about not acquiring unnecessary clutter in her life. This one must have escaped the weekly clear-out. I ran my eye down the page and my name jumped out. I didn't stop to read it in detail.

Underneath the letter was a list of journal references written in Bridget's fine, angled script, detailing her brother's most recent publications and a list of the names, home addresses and academic positions of his close colleagues. None of the names was familiar, but then I had been out of medical academia for a good eight years, more than enough time for all the relevant personalities to change.

I read the reference list and tried to understand where Malcolm's work had taken him in the past few years. Somewhere into the stratosphere of high-tech molecular biology, a long way beyond my understanding.

Lastly, there was the scruffy note that had come with the basket of bantams. And the bantams had gone.

I looked up at Caroline. 'Have you found the hens yet?'

'No. They're gone. They were locked in the shed, Kellen. Someone had the key. The door's still locked and they're not there. Whoever murdered Bridget took the hens too.' Her voice frayed at the edges. She sat down carefully on the edge of the stone water-trough by the back door and kept her eyes fixed on the hawthorns beyond the pond.

I stood up and put my hand on her shoulder. 'What makes you sure it was murder?' I asked.

She didn't turn round. 'Instinct,' she said shortly. 'I wasn't sure about Malcolm, but I'm bloody certain about Bridget. Heart attacks don't happen in pairs. Not this pair anyway.' Her eyes flickered at me and then back to the pond. 'You don't have to stay if you don't believe me.'

'I know.'

I don't have to stay even if I do. I've kept away for the past four years. There's no real reason to change now.

I looked at the spiders' webs, wet with dew, strung out between the reeds of the pond and remembered a promise I made a long, long time ago. 'But I have to say goodbye first.'

Once a long time ago, I stood in the kitchen doorway and promised that I would come back and say goodbye.

It was three o'clock in the afternoon of Saturday 21 October. The rain hammered, unrelenting, on the window. Neither of us wept.

I carried out the final suitcase to the pile on the porch. Caroline was there, somewhere in the background, helping me pack. She helped me with everything then.

Bridget sat by the fire, watching me go, Tan at her feet and the cats ranged about her like a bodyguard.

'Are you going to say goodbye?'

'Not yet. I'll come back later.'

'When?'

'I don't know. Later.'

'You will say goodbye, Kellen?'

'Of course. Just not yet. It's too soon.'

Later. Not now. Later, I will come back and say goodbye. I promise.

And this is later and I still haven't said goodbye and it is still too soon.

It felt strange going back in daylight. Upstairs, the house still echoed with the awkward silence that goes with death. Even the floorboards creaked more quietly.

I let myself into the bedroom and stood just inside the door, getting my bearings and trying to let go of the odd sense of unreality that had hit the night before. The room looked much as it ever did. The only difference was the bed. None of the men had thought to touch it after they'd lifted her body and so the duvet still held the shape of her, like a thumbprint on soft clay, and the dip in the pillow still showed where they'd lifted her head. The rest of the bed was as smooth as when it was made. Whatever happened to Bridget Donnelly, she hadn't moved from the moment she lay down.

Nasty.

But I'm not here to start looking for answers. I'm here to ask questions.

I took my eyes off the place where she had been and let my gaze drift upwards until her eyes caught mine.

There's a black and white print on the wall behind the bed, centred over her pillow. A high-contrast, grainy shot pushed hard to make the most of the late evening light and hand-printed on the big enlarger in the darkroom we set up in the attic.

It's the best shot I've ever taken of Bridget. She's sitting on top of the grave mound near the cairn in the beech wood. One knee is pulled up to her chin and her head is cocked to one side as she smiles down into the lens of the camera. Her smile is warm and relaxed. Her eyes are alive with the spirit of the time and the place. Her whole body radiates a vibrant, ethereal energy.

Nobody could possibly believe that this woman was ready to die.

Except that somebody did. And I don't know who or how or why. And if I want to find out, I am going to have to go through this kind of thing again and again and again. I am going to have to start searching the diaries and reading the letters and talking to the friends I haven't seen or spoken to since the day I left. I am, in fact, going to have to do all of the things I haven't got around to in the last four years and which I really, really quite definitely don't want to do.

Or I could just walk out, go home and let somebody else sort it all out.

I looked up at the print again.

It's her eyes that catch the soul and hold it. The sharp, ironic, intelligent eyes of a woman who loves. The eyes of a woman who doesn't give up.

She was never one to give up easily, Bridget.

Downstairs, Caroline was still sitting on the kitchen step with the dog.

I slid past her and walked across the yard, listening to the crunch of her feet on the gravel as she followed me across. We reached the barn together.

'Are you leaving?' she asked.

'No.' I hauled the door open. A warm wash of horse breath

flowed out over the pair of us. 'I was going to help you feed the horses. I thought they might need it by now.'

'And then you'll leave after that?'

I lifted the lid on the feed bin and breathed in the smell of bran and pony nuts. The smell of home.

Caroline was watching me, holding her breath.

'No,' I shook my head. 'I'm staying. And I'll do what I can to find out what happened.'

She smiled then. Almost a real smile. It rose up as far as her eyebrows and then turned sideways into a frown. 'Are you going to tell me why?'

I smiled back. It felt real.

'Because I promised I would.'

CHAPTER TWO

Caroline had a ride to lead at nine. We had a row over that, which cleared the air if nothing else. I wanted her to stay and help me sort things out; she wanted to escape and pretend nothing had happened for a while. So I told her that she couldn't possibly take a bunch of schoolkids pony-trekking and she told me that it was the disabled riders, as if that pulled any weight at all. At ten to nine she pointed out that it was too late to cancel and I had to help her groom and tack up six ponies and Balder, her lead horse, in less than two minutes each.

I enjoyed it.

Then, while Caroline spent the morning messing about with horses in the brisk September sunshine, I moulded the portable phone to my shoulder and set about increasing Telecom's profits for the day by a significant margin.

A brief call to the answer-phone at home with an outline of the problem, a profuse apology and a vaguely estimated return time took care of the wavering domestic front. A second call, this time to the Sauchiehall Street Counselling Centre with news of a death in the family, secured me the rest of the week off work. The one advantage of working with bereavement counsellors is that they understand the need for plenty of time off after the death of an ex-loved-one. The various clients are rarely quite as understanding, but I don't work on reception so that's not my problem.

Next, I called up the university switchboard and dialled my way through the various levels of hospital administration to reach one Dr Lee Adams, late of the University of Glasgow medical school, erstwhile obstetric surgeon and current University Pathologist in the Department of Clinical Medicine (Strathclyde Area Health Authority).

Lee and I went through medical school together in the dim and distant past, when I still believed in the power of science and she still believed she could buck the system. We were both wrong, of course, but by the time we had found that out, we had forged a partnership that carried us through the houseman's years and out into the real world beyond. She's one of those people who's guaranteed to be there in an emergency. Once in a while, she creates the emergency and then life becomes seriously interesting. Either way, she's the single most useful person I know in a tight corner and I have trusted her at least once with my life, liberty and vestiges of sanity.

It took five minutes to reach her, but I was put through, eventually, to the depths of the pathology cold room and caught her at the start of clinical rounds, with a dead body lying on the steel table in front of her and a bunch of students hanging on her every word. The conversation was rather more truncated than I would have liked, but we both understood the essentials and she agreed to meet me later after work in the usual bar. She also agreed to conduct the post-mortem examination personally, provided I could clear it with the local GP.

No problem.

No problem at all.

The phone pad on the table had the names of the local medical practices, one of them highlighted in fluorescent yellow. The receptionist was well trained to keep outsiders at bay but the

Donnelly name proved an effective key and I was transferred after only a minute or two of shocked commiseration. Bridget, it appeared, had been widely known and widely liked, possibly even loved, by her neighbours.

Dr David Kemp, when he finally deigned to respond to the call, sounded exactly the same over the phone as he did in real life and anger did nothing to improve the irritating sinus whine. The sound of it cheered me up enormously. I sat back, put my feet up on the Rayburn and prepared to enjoy myself.

There is a basic technique taught in assertiveness classes known as the 'broken record'. Find your groove – in this case, 'I have arranged for Dr Adams to do the post-mortem' – and stay there. Repeat at any pause in the flow of invective from the other side. Played right, it has its place, although it usually works best against those with a low boredom threshold. Dr Kemp either had a very high boredom threshold or he knew the game and thought he could outplay me.

I kept to my groove. He kept to his, which was that he had already arranged a post-mortem with another colleague and there was nothing I could do about it. My memory of medical law is not wonderful, but I was fairly sure he was talking bullshit and eventually said so.

We were on the downward slide to a particularly cathartic slanging match when there was a crunch of gravel outside the door and a blue police Land Rover pulled up. The man with a heart from the previous night and his dark-haired minion hopped out.

I grinned triumph at the phone and held it out so that he could hear the footsteps on the gravel. 'It's the boys and girls in blue, Doctor. I think we could get ourselves a legal ruling on this, if you'd like to hold on for a moment.'

He didn't. By the time the uniformed duo had come within earshot, the line had gone dead. Very disappointing.

I hung up, feeling smug, and kicked a rock over to hold the back door open. 'Are you coming in?'

'If you're sure it's all right.'

Inspector Stewart MacDonald slipped past me into the kitchen with a nod, as if we were one of his regular coffee stops. He looked far more sprightly than he should have done, given that he can't have had much more sleep than I had.

His colleague followed more slowly, pausing on her way across the yard to talk to one of the cats sprawled under the hawthorns by the pond. She hesitated, standing warily in the doorway as if waiting for the right password to cross the threshold. 'Is Ms Leader not here?' she asked.

'No.' I fished around in the sink, looking for three readily cleanable mugs among the heap from the previous night. 'She's gone out with the horses. We didn't have time to cancel today's rides.'

'Aye,' said Inspector MacDonald, pausing in his investigation of Bridget's desk diary, 'I thought that was her we saw going through the village. The wee lad with the orange jacket on yon grey thing's not going to stay on top long if she takes them up over the moor.'

Donald James. Caroline told me about him while we were tacking up.

'It's all right. She knows. He's got cerebral palsy. She'll hold Midnight in at a walk for him when the rest have a canter.'

'Fair enough. I said she'd be fine.' He nodded amiably, his mind elsewhere. His eyes were already strip-searching the room.

'Coffee?' I offered.

'Fine. Thanks. White. Two sugars. WPC Philips there – ' he tipped his head back towards the door – 'takes herbal tea if you've got it.'

No calories. Not even stimulants. They get on like a house on fire, you can tell.

WPC Philips favoured him with a look that would have

curdled milk at fifty paces and didn't bother to switch it off when she turned back to me.

Astonishing.

The spark of humanity from the previous night had snuffed out in the cold light of the morning. In its place, I faced a pair of the most startling green feline eyes. Eyes that flared with a kaleidoscope of compressed emotions. Totally riveting. She didn't look like that in the bedroom last night. But then, she wasn't being wound up by her superiors last night.

She caught me looking and the stare transformed into something slightly less dangerous. More of a long-distance iceberg, designed to ward off all comers. Particularly me.

I kept my head out of the firing line and hunted through the pantry until I found a box of fruit tea in the cupboard. A relic from the days when Lee used to be welcome at the farm. I made the lass a mug and offered her a seat by the fire. She accepted both with a trained professional politeness, but she was not, absolutely not, going to indulge in trivial conversation for the sake of it.

Oh, well.

MacDonald took his coffee and made a vague circuit of the room in a discreet but none the less methodical examination of the magazines and the letters, the wall calendar and the desk diary, and the litter of old recipes, vet's bills and farmer's invoices that were impaled on the letter spike beside the kettle.

His sidekick and I sat in disconnected silence on either side of the fire and waited until he came full circle back to the breakfast counter, where Ashwood was using Bridget's leather-bound address book as a pillow. They regarded each other carefully for a moment and then he turned away to sit back by the fire. The address book stayed exactly where it was.

'Anything interesting?' I asked.

'You never know.'

I don't. But I would be surprised.

'Upstairs?' I suggested.

'Aye,' he nodded peaceably, 'good idea.'

The two of them followed me through the narrow hallway to the stairs and we began a detailed tour of the upper floor. The bathroom, the spare room and the airing cupboard yielded in quick succession to the prying eyes. A systematic probing of things personal that were never meant to be probed. I tried to imagine how I would feel watching strangers sift through the trivia of my life and was grateful, for once, that Caroline was not around.

The big bedroom was last and MacDonald, with a degree of sensitivity I wouldn't normally have associated with an officer of the law, stood back to let his colleague do the work. I stayed with him by the door and together we watched Elspeth Philips, neat in her ordered uniform, straighten the dimpled duvet as she passed the bed. A small, unconscious gesture of tidiness and respect for the dead. Or for the living, perhaps. Her hand hovered by the glass of water on the bedside table and then withdrew as she passed on.

The Inspector let out the breath he had been holding and nodded to himself.

'Are you going to take fingerprints?' I asked.

He shrugged. 'I don't know,' he said. 'Not if we don't have to. You'd not believe the mess it makes. Why?' He turned to look at me. 'Do you think I should?'

Depends.

I shrugged. 'You have a practising GP who will tell you it's a waste of time.' I smiled to let him see I wasn't joking and was surprised to see a momentary deepening of the crow's feet.

'You don't trust our bright young friend?'

'I don't trust anyone who drives a BMW on an NHS salary.'

'Oh, it's that, is it?' His eyes widened in mocking discovery. 'And there I was thinking it was a touch of professional jealousy.' He turned to gaze for a moment through the window, thinking.

'We'd best wait till we've had the post-mortem,' he said, turning back. 'If there's anything out of the ordinary, I'll come back with the powder and the brushes and we'll see how Ms Leader likes her home done all in white.'

We finished on the bedroom without turning up anything worth telling and after that it was a matter of minutes to take the pair of them back downstairs and lead them round the dusty, unused living room at the front of the house and then the drawing room at the back.

Neither held anything of interest and they departed a short while later. I saw them both out to their car, holding the driver's door open for MacDonald.

'Let me know if there's anything else you need, won't you?'

'Oh, we'll be in touch. Don't you worry. These things are never as simple as they might seem.' He swung up into the cab, slamming the door behind him. Then he leant out of the window to give me a paternal pat on the shoulder and, very delicately, to drop the real reason for the visit.

'Chief Inspector Laidlaw sends his best regards,' he said and winked.

The Land Rover swung round me in a wide arc and left the yard, tooting cheerily as it passed the gates.

I forgot to wave.

Whatever Chief Inspector Laidlaw might have sent, I doubt that his best regard was anything to do with it. Last time I saw him he promised that if we ever met again, he'd have me behind bars before I could blink and would see to it personally that my lawyer was not only bent but incompetent.

Laidlaw's not fond of women at the best of times, especially not those with investigative pretensions, and he loathes medics with a terrifying passion. It would, I felt, have been a great pity if Inspector MacDonald turned out to be cast from the same mould as his Glaswegian colleague.

Basic, dreary management took up the rest of the day. All the minutiae that follow death in a bureaucratic society.

The solicitors were effusive in their condolences and confirmed in passing that I was still the sole executor of the will. The girl in the *Herald* office took the death notice for publication later in the week with succinct efficiency. Friends and distant relatives took the news badly, solidly or dispassionately depending on temperament and the closeness of the relationship.

After the relatives came the riders. I trawled through the appointments book and found a long, detailed list in Bridget's angular scrawl of everyone who had booked a ride in the next fortnight with home and business contact numbers. There wasn't one of them who didn't love Bridget like a sibling and want to spend the best part of an hour conducting their own personal obituary for my benefit. Horse people are like that.

I thought I had been through all this for the last time when Mother died. Once in a while, I thought I might have to do it for Lee and occasionally that she might have to do it for me. I had never expected to do it for Bride. I didn't promise Caroline that I'd do it either, but, of the pair of us, I have the most practice. All through the intertwining threads of our lives, it's been me who's dealt with the formalities.

It was a very long afternoon.

Caroline came and went throughout the day, regaining stability in the routines of horse care and with it a sense of continuity. She finally flopped into a chair as I was getting ready to go and see Lee.

'Want to come?' I asked 'The Man does a wonderful haggis.'

'Me? Go and see Lee Adams?' She raised her brows to an improbable height. 'No thanks, Kells. She's not my type and you know it.' She helped herself to a pizza from the freezer and began to stoke up the Rayburn. 'And even if she was, I'm not up to socialising yet.'

'Let me put this another way,' I said, taking my jacket off and hanging it back on the door hook. 'I don't think you should stay in the house on your own. It isn't safe.'

'Crap,' she said cheerfully. 'It's a hell of a sight safer here than Byres Road on a Friday night. Anyway, I've got Tan. He's a brilliant guard dog.'

The collie grinned happily at the sound of his name and stood up with his forefeet on the counter to inspect the pizza. He looked about as dangerous as the average muppet.

I picked up the phone, shaking my head. 'It's not a joke, C. If you don't want to come into town, I'll call Lee and get her to come out here.'

Caroline took the receiver out of my hand and put it back on the hook.

'No way.' She smiled gently and handed me back my jacket. 'I'm a grown woman, Kellen. I can cope for a whole hour, even two, on my own, so you can stop being patronising. Go see your crazy girlfriend. I'll make the spare bed up for you if I've crashed out by the time you get back.'

Patronising? Me? I'm a therapist, for God's sake. This woman knows all the fast routes to my sensibilities.

I picked the car keys off the table. 'OK. Leave the back-door key under the water bucket. I'll probably be late.'

I left the car in a side street and found the back stairs to the Man, avoiding the queue for the cinema and the pair exchanging goods for cash in the service entrance of the restaurant next door. In the old days, the girls worked off their jocks in the recesses of the doorways. Now all the good sites are taken up by the guys trading crack and the girls work the multistorey car park over the supermarket at the top of the road. It keeps the residents on their toes.

The Man in the Moon on Byres Road has seen generations of students through their undergraduate years and, for those who stay on in Glasgow, the familiar mix of city-trend and oak-beam-trad provides a steady support against the terrors of the real world.

In the late 1970s and early 1980s, the Man rode the crest of a trend, attracting the cream of the cultural élite, spicing them with a sprinkling of the city's more innovative politicians and adding that extra flavour of spaced-out student that is unique to Byres Road. For a while it was somewhere special and, in its own way, it made a genuine contribution to the 'Glasgow's Miles Better' campaign and added flavour to the European City of Culture.

Now, with all the media hype out of the way, the cognoscenti have melted off to somewhere new and the Man has settled, with the rest of the city, into the muddled anonymity of recession, serving the same mixture of students and overpaid West End professionals that it always did.

And it still serves the best vegetarian haggis anywhere in the world.

Lee was there ahead of me, at one of the small rough-pine tables on the balcony overlooking the main bar. As a choice of seating it is noisy and exposed, but it gives a clear view of both doors and the floor area and it's almost impossible to eavesdrop unless the candles are bugged, which I doubt.

Adams ages with more grace than the rest of us. If I looked hard I would say her face showed a slight hardening of the edges; a sharpening of the cheekbones perhaps to show that life was beginning to take its toll. Her fine, black hair was shorter than it used to be when we were students, better shaped to frame the gamine features, and, in the top light from the wall lamp, a sparkle of silver threads visibly through the black. Thirty-five is not a bad age to begin going grey and, given her lifestyle, it's long overdue.

Lee Adams is not crazy, whatever Caroline Leader might think.

She's different admittedly, but then she has good reason to be. She is a medic and a pathologist and no one gets through to their finals, still less their FRCPath exams, without seriously disrupting their perspective on the sanctity of life and the injustice of death. We all rewrite the rule book, one way or another; Lee is just a little less compromising than most, that's all.

Having said that, Lee was undoubtedly unique before she ever went into medical school. She had the kind of upbringing that made it inevitable.

She was born Elizabeth Katheryn Adams, shortly after midnight one hogmanay in the Inverness General Hospital, the product of an island lass and an unnamed father. Her mother did a runner on the first train south after the holiday, leaving the infant Lee in the care of assorted grandmothers and ageing great-aunts, who took her back home to the islands and devoted themselves to her upbringing.

The Scottish Hebrides are inhabited by a divided population. At any one time, half the community lives in thrall to a peculiarly fascist brand of Presbyterian fundamentalism, while the other half practises a form of rural superstition that has survived since before the christians ever landed. Both halves speak Gaelic as the first language and neither is unduly fond of southerners.

From the sound of things, Lee's mentors were not of the christian persuasion and her early education was fairly unique, bearing only a passing resemblance to the national curriculum in any of its multiple incarnations. Then, as she grew up and it became apparent that she needed more formal schooling, the grandmothers sent her south to live with Mhaire Culloch in Glasgow.

In a world of mad old women, Mhaire is maddest of them all. Four years in her company would change anyone's view of the world, whatever their background. Lee couldn't have come out of it normal, even if she'd wanted to.

Mad Mhaire's central tenet of life says that rules are there to be broken. She breaks them with gleeful impunity and she taught Lee to do the same. But she also sent her to one of the best schools in the city; one where she had the many and varied rough edges polished rather than battered into shape and where, most importantly, they made sure that the lass got good enough 'O' grades and Highers to get her into medical school, which was where she wanted to go.

I met Lee the evening before the start of full term in the corridor of the Queen Margaret Hall of Residence. She was standing alone, waiting for the lift, a slight, dark figure with wild eyes and a wilder smile. Her voice was low and there were odd accents on the vowels that made me think she was Norwegian and a novelty to be explored.

My father helped to carry her bags into the lift and, by the time we reached the third floor, we knew that we had been allocated adjacent rooms, that we were both there to study medicine, that her school in Glasgow had once beaten my school in Helensburgh at hockey and that she had been rock-climbing in the same mountain range where I had done my Duke of Edinburgh silver medal. They were the kind of facts that seemed important at the time.

In the limbo between the old life left behind and the new one starting, social barriers tend to drop and friendships form overnight, built out of trivial coincidences. We sat together at dinner that night because by then a known face, even tenuously known, was better than yet another new one and by the end of the evening, we found that we had damn all else in common but that we enjoyed each other's company all the same. The next morning, we walked into the university together and the pattern was set. During the course of the first term, we developed tactics for sharing lecture notes and when the practical classes started, it was natural to pair up for those as well.

There must have been a point in early prehistory when it was possible to go through a medical training as a solitary individual, but as time has piled practical module on seminar on tutorial, it has become almost mandatory to take a team approach. The Adams/Stewart partnership worked better than most because we started early and we learned to delegate and, by the end, because we learned to think for each other. In the beginning, though, we came from quite opposite ends of a very broad spectrum.

In the early days, I was conventional in my nonconformity. A not-quite-head-girl, oozing street cred from every pore and heir to a set of wildly radical political views; the direct inverse of everything my parents believed in. I flaunted my green-socialist-feminism from the safety of my middle-class, Presbyterian background and thought I was being original. I hinted darkly at deviant sexuality without ever having set a toe over the line and watched my parents wither. In the hallowed halls of my single-sex, fee-paying school, I was labelled a rebel and I believed it.

In Lee, I met the real thing. Lee took risks because they were there to be taken. She had nothing to lose, no family values to overturn and nobody else's visions to fulfil. Instead, she had a rock-solid sense of identity, a restless, questing brain and a merciless sense of satire.

The student ego is a fragile beast and easily wounded. In our first year of medical school, I watched Lee stalk, cat-like, amongst the malleable, fledgeling identities of our colleagues, and there were very few who didn't catch the back end of a pensive, island stare and hate her for it. She never said anything out loud – the expensive private school had taught her the rudimentary principles of tact – but she never learned to turn her gaze in time. The general mass of the year dealt with her by pretending she didn't exist and she, in her turn, continued to observe and, apparently, to judge.

On the whole, I was immune. Not because I didn't catch her

looking at me as if I'd finally lost my marbles on regular occasions, but because I knew her well enough to ignore the looks, to tell her to bugger off when the comments cut too close to the bone and to argue my corner if I had to. We developed a mutual respect that slid, over the three years spent together on the third floor of Queen Margaret Hall, into a solid friendship.

At the end of our third year, a flat became vacant on the far end of Otago Street. The paint was peeling off the walls, there were cockroaches breeding in the kitchen and on a Saturday night the rugby songs floated down from the men's Union at the top of the hill, but it was no worse than any other student accommodation and it was within walking distance of the teaching hospital, which made it a prize worth having. I went to look at it one Friday afternoon when I should have been at a microbiology practical class and paid the deposit on the spot. By the end of the summer vacation, we had moved in, cleared the insect population and repainted every vertical surface in politically acceptable shades of lavender.

Lee turned out to know a lot of folk I had never met before. In the space of the next two years, she introduced me to a range of people I would never have met otherwise, except possibly on a stretcher in casualty, or drying out in the drink can.

On a regular basis, we were host to the Buddhist evenings and the Druidic evenings and the astrologer's meetings and once in a while, when the planning went awry, to all three at once, which made life fairly amusing.

In between we had the endless stream of visitors from the islands and Mhaire's drop-out friends who dropped in for a cup of coffee and a chat about the day's racing form. I learned to listen, to keep my mouth shut and to overcome my inherent Presbyterian fear of gambling for long enough to recognise a good tip when we heard one and to let her risk the housekeeping on something with decently long odds. We didn't always win but we came out on top overall by the end of the course.

47

Through it all was the single driving force of medical school – the long-distance obstacle course where the only way to escape is to fail. Whatever else we did, we were not going to risk that. We read books, we went to lectures and we attended tutorials. We put on our white coats, went into the wards and talked to patients. We put on our green cotton pyjamas, went into theatre and stared in mute admiration while the surgeons performed daily miracles of human carpentry and plumbing. We spent hours in the library staring at textbooks and we sat the exams – a long, endless stream of exams.

And we passed. Miraculous though it always seemed, we passed everything, first time, and were allowed to move on up the ladder to greater and better things. At graduation, we held a five-day party in the flat – one day for each year of the course – and the day afterwards we moved in, together, to our junior house jobs at the Western.

Internships are hell on earth, all of them. Perfectly sane adult human beings have nightmares about their houseman's year the way the rest of the population have recurrent dreams of exams. Amnesty International regularly cites sleep deprivation amongst the tortures for which governments are censured. In spite of that, most of the hospitals of the Western world are staffed by junior doctors who stave off sleep for twelve months with a frantic cocktail of caffeine, adrenalin and nicotine.

Neither of us smoke and Lee doesn't touch caffeine, tannin or alcohol, which put us at a significant disadvantage when it came to coping with the late-night sense-of-humour failures. If the partnership had been slightly less solid, or if her sense of the ridiculous had been slightly more mellow, we would both have gone under at one of the many black spots. Undoubtedly, I would have sunk without trace when Mother died if Lee hadn't been around.

Right at the lowest point of the surgery rotation, when we

had been on call for a week and had had no sleep for ever, my mother was admitted as an emergency with a ruptured aortic aneurysm. The consultants revealed a rare spark of humanity and gave me leave to go and sit with her as soon as they'd finished the basic work-up. I held her hand for an hour or two and made her stories of home, talking her back into the glorious ice caves of her past.

It was an odd kind of peace-making, but she listened and nodded and, when they came to take her to theatre, she reached out for my hand as she passed. Lee joined me for a while and I paced around, like ordinary family, until they sent out an anaesthetist with the news that the lesion was too big, the haemorrhage too great and the hopes of survival too low to speak of.

Lee covered my on-call for the funeral and the brief 'compassionate leave', which was all taken up with lawyers and distant, frigid relatives who wanted to know what they were getting from the estate and how soon. At the end of it all, I went back to the ward for a rest, bereft of my last living parent and in possession of a three-storey Helensburgh town house that I never wanted and didn't know what to do with.

The surgical rotation finished shortly after that and we moved to medicine. With medicine, came Malcolm and life after Malcolm was quite, quite different.

Malcolm was the kind of man who took medicine seriously and who, unusually, had managed to retain a sense of caring for his patients and his interns beyond the first few rungs of the clinical ladder. He was quiet – soft-spoken, with a slight fading of the consonants that sounded almost effeminate until one got to know him better. He was tall and slim and would have been fit if he had ever had time for exercise. He had the classic Donnelly hair: just one shade this side of black, thick and wavy and forever falling forward over one eye, so that he had developed a characteristic toss of the head to throw it out of the way when he was too rushed to have a spare hand.

49

The female patients loved him whether he liked it or not. The younger ones lusted and the older ones promised him their daughters, immune to the fact that the lad barely had time for a passing cup of coffee, never mind a passing liaison in the laundry cupboard. The nurses just fell at his feet at convenient opportunities and then sulked pointedly when he apparently failed to notice.

Somehow, at some time, the grapevine had spread the fact that Lee and I were not especially enamoured of men. I suspect it also spread the rumour that we were lovers, which happened not to be true, but at any rate it spared us the priapic attentions of the junior medical staff and, I suppose, may have made Malcolm feel safer in our company. At any rate, he took us in hand from the first day we hit his medicine ward and made it his life's work for the next six months to teach us all the things they never dared show us before the exams.

He turned life as an intern into something that bordered on an adventure and saw to it that we both came out at the end of the year fit to lead the worlds of surgery and psychiatric medicine respectively.

It never happened, naturally. We weren't the right kind of people to become world famous in either field. Lee got herself thrown out of surgery for asking the wrong questions of the wrong people at the wrong time and I had already left psychiatry under my own steam a year or so before that. Still, by then Malcolm was part of the family and Lee had grown to be one of the few stable points in my otherwise less-than-stable life.

Which is, no doubt, why she was sitting there waiting for me, leaning back on her chair with her feet up on the table and one arm slung over the balcony, holding a half-glass of mineral water at a crazy angle over the heads of the crowd below.

I pushed through the mass by the bar and dropped limply into the chair opposite.

'Lee, hi.'

'Hi. You all right?'

'Alive.'

'Hungry?' she asked.

'Starving.' I slung my jacket over the balcony 'I forgot to eat. It's been one of those days.'

'You'd forget to eat for weeks if you had to cook it yourself,' she said and, raising a hand, she called forth a minor miracle in the form of a waiter with a long, dark ponytail and a gold stud in one ear who appeared beside the table flourishing a brace of haggis, another bottle of mineral water to join the two on the table and a carafe of red wine. The usual. We never eat anything else when we go to the Man.

We ate together in silence for a while, letting things settle. Lee, for reasons of her own, kept a wary eye on the shifting mass of bodies by the bar and gave the occasional glance downstairs to the crowd round the door.

The wine was very good for a house red. I poured myself a second glass and pushed my plate to the side, feeling better than I had done for a long time.

This time Lee was watching me, not the others.

'I did the post,' she said.

'Bridget's?'

'Mmm.'

'And?'

'And you're not going to like it.' Her jacket hung over the balcony at her side. She fished a sheet of paper out of a pocket and slid it across the table towards me. 'Have a look.'

It was a preliminary post-mortem report form, sketchier than a final report to a coroner but complete enough to submit to the police officer in charge of the case.

I ran my eye down the page. Most of the organ systems were labelled NAD – no abnormality diagnosed. Only the cardiac section showed up anything different and then only the changes associated with terminal cardiac arrest. As reports go, it was one of the least meaningful I have ever seen. Dr David Kemp, he of the fast car and the snakeskin bedside manner, would have been absolutely delighted. I wasn't.

The ponytailed waiter appeared out of nowhere and we stared at each other in silence as he cleared the plates. The report sat on the table, soaking up a ring of wine from my glass. A claret wash flowed across the meaningless cardiac findings. Incongruous.

'So?' I asked, when we were alone again. 'Why did she die, Adams?'

'Good question.' Lee made a steeple of her fingers and tapped it against her pursed lips thoughtfully. 'Look at this.' She flipped a beer mat on to the report sheet and used it to underline the point where the stomach contents had been carefully recorded in order of digestion. It was hardly an appetising list: coffee, toast, eggs (cooked), beans (tinned; brand unknown), cheese (cooked), TMP (400 mg).

An average farmhouse meal thrown down in passing. Could have been breakfast, lunch, dinner or a filler in between.

The beer mat sat under the final word: TMP (400 mg).

'Temazepam?' I asked.

'Temazepam,' she confirmed.

'Shit.'

Temazepam. New-generation Valium. Mother's ruin. Daughter's ruin. Nowadays, business executive's ruin as well. And jelly babies for the crack-heads when the skunkweed gets too hot. A gateway to dreamland. But not usually lethal.

'Is 400 milligrams enough to kill her?' I asked.

'It might be.' She shrugged sparingly. 'It's more than enough to put her to sleep for a bit.' She looked at me across the table, her chin resting now on the looped arc of her fingers. 'How was their relationship, Kellen?'

'Bridget and Caroline's? Glowing, I expect. I don't know. The Christmas cards weren't exactly informative. Why?'

'There were twenty odd capsules in there, Kells. You don't take that much of anything by mistake.'

'Are you saying this was deliberate?'

'Well, I sure as hell don't think it was an accident.' She pursed her lips. 'More to the point, your friendly police inspector isn't going to think so either. I've got some bloods running through at the moment but unless there's something out of the ordinary, the interim report will go through tomorrow morning and it'll have "suicide" right at the top of the list of differentials.'

We stared at each other across the table.

'You don't believe that,' I said flatly.

'No.' She shook her head. 'I knew Bridget too. But it's still the most obvious diagnosis. As the pathologist, I have to put it on the report.'

'So where's the note?' I asked. 'Or the tablet bottle?'

She shrugged. 'That's up to the police.' Her eyes drifted over the crowd on the floor below and then came back to mine. Her lips compressed into a fine, white line. 'They'll be all over the place soon enough, Kellen,' she said. 'Laidlaw's going to have a field day with this. Jelly babies are public enemy number one on his drug list these days.'

'Oh, great. That's all we need.'

I looked away, staring down at the milling bodies drinking pale, foreign lager in the main bar below. A bird's-eye view of Glasgow's professional classes. Not the kind of folk to take temazepam, except to ring the changes once in a while when the crack and the skunkweed are running low. Jelly babies are the small change in the rich world of gold dust and diamond dew. Not exactly a major police problem. Not for a man of Laidlaw's calibre.

I said as much to Lee. She followed my gaze down to the designer haircuts on the floor below, eyeing the crowd round

the door. 'It's a problem when they raid the pharmacies for it,'
she said. 'Himself is not keen on folk breaking into places on
his patch. It's bad for the record.'

'I thought you could get it on prescription?'

'You can, up to a point. But the GPs know the street value as
well as anybody and when every man, woman and child on an
entire estate comes to you pleading chronic insomnia, it gets a
little silly. They draw the line once in a while and then the
chemists get nailed.'

'And that upsets the lads in uniform,' I said. I could imagine.
Laidlaw takes robbery on his patch as a personal assault.

'It does indeed.' Lee nodded abstractly, still staring into the
crowd below the balcony. 'And besides, if he can nick half a
dozen poor bastards before breakfast for abusing sedatives, he
can polish up his "drug prevention" halo without having to get
his fingers jumped on by the mob. Simple.'

'When was Laidlaw ever scared of the mob?'

'When they have well-paid friends in high places who warn
him off, largely.' She raised an eyebrow in mock resignation.
'The world of cops and robbers isn't quite as black and white as
it used to be when Cash Andrews owned everyone. We have
about thirteen different sets of organised militia now. One single
police force can't cope with it all.'

'How sad.'

'Absolutely . . .' Her voice trailed off and her attention shifted
suddenly on to a movement in the crowd below. 'Hell . . . 'Scuse
me. Got to go for a pee.' One shoulder lifted in an apologetic
half-shrug that said she didn't expect me to believe the lie.
'Don't go away. I'll be back in a minute.'

She still moves like a dancer. I watched her go, threading her
way neatly through the crowd in the general direction of the
ladies' toilet which, as luck would have it, is on the ground floor
next to the entrance.

I'm long past trying to take care of Lee Adams. Her problems don't become mine unless she asks. So I turned my back to the milling crowd that had closed behind her, picked up my glass of wine and thought my way through the psycho-pathology of a suicide. Most have a history of depression. Most try more than once. Most leave something for those left behind. Those who want to succeed do it sensibly where no one will find them and leave short, functional notes. Those who don't want to succeed do it publicly and leave long, vindictive literary landmines targeted on their nearest and not-so-dearest.

For Bridget Donnelly to have done either would have required a character transformation so complete as to render her unrecognisable to anyone around her.

Nothing may be impossible, but some things are seriously improbable.

I was staring into the wine glass with my brain spinning in unlikely circles when Lee reappeared, shouldering delicately through the crowd.

'Shall we go?' she asked, tapping me lightly on the shoulder.

A rhetorical question. She was on her feet with my jacket in her hand before I could answer, leaving me to follow her down the stairs and out to the lane at the back of the Man.

We dodged across the traffic on Byres Road, scaring the life out of a drunk on a bicycle.

'Where's your car?' she asked as we reached the safety of the pavements.

'Downside Road. Half-way up the hill.'

'Mind if we use it?'

'Feel free.'

The car sat in a pool of shadow between two lampposts. We slowed to a lope and I dug in my pocket for the keys, opening her door first so that she could pull the choke and drop the handbrake while I piled in the driver's side and stuck my foot on the gas. We were moving before she'd had time to close her door. One of Mhaire's outlaw friends taught us that one. We used to practise it after parties for the hell of it. I'd forgotten it was this much fun.

'Who are we running from?' I asked when my breathing had settled. I was driving a complex loop round the university and back along Great Western Road towards Byres Road.

'I'm not sure.' She wound down the window and reached out to angle the wing mirror so that she could keep an eye on the road behind. 'The bad guys, I think. The ones Laidlaw doesn't mess with. I was supposed to be meeting a lad called Danny Baird, but he didn't show.'

'And the bad guys showed instead?'

'I think they might have done. I don't know. They don't wear shades and Doc Martens any more. Makes them difficult to spot.'

'Do they drive a dark green Audi?' I asked. There was one on the road behind us, weaving in and out of the traffic, not quite far enough back to be safe.

'Possibly.' She kept her eyes glued to the mirror. 'How fast does this thing go?'

'Not fast enough.'

'Thought not.' The smile was tighter than it might have been. 'Why don't you take a right at the lights and run up the east side of the Botanics?'

'Right.'

I pulled over into the right-hand lane and took a right. We watched as the other car rolled on westwards down Great Western Road. Lee grimaced briefly and I heard her breath hiss through closed nostrils. She used to be cooler than that.

I made a U-turn at the top of the road and drove back to the lights at the Byres Road junction.

'Do you want a lift home?' I asked.

'No.' She shook her head. 'I thought I'd go into work for a bit.'

'Oh, give me a break, woman. It's almost eleven o'clock.' I thought she'd grown out of this. 'Repeat after me: "My name is Dr Elizabeth Adams and I am a workaholic" . . .'

'Hardly.' She had her eyes on the mirror again and when she spoke her voice was distant. 'What do you suppose would have happened if Bridget hadn't taken so much Temazepam?'

'She wouldn't have died.'

'Maybe. Or possibly she would have died anyway but there would have been damn all to see on PM. Like Malcolm.' Her eyes came off the mirror and she looked directly at me.

'Did you do Malcolm's PM?' I asked carefully.

'No.' She shook her head. 'Prof did that. A final gesture for an old friend and colleague. He does it once in a while to prove he can still use a scalpel.'

'So if there was anything there he would have found it.'

'Maybe.' She shrugged, unconvinced. 'But I only found the temazepam in Bridget because I went looking for it and even then there was almost nothing left. Two or three more hours and the gelatine would have gone in the gastric acid. Malcolm's body wasn't found for almost twenty-four hours after he died. He could have been doped up to the eyeballs and there wouldn't be anything to see in the stomach.'

'You could find it on plasma samples.'

'You could, but it's not on the routine test list. You'd only find it if you had a reason to look.'

'Did they keep any plasma sample from Malcolm?'

'I don't know. I never looked at the form. There didn't seem any reason to at the time.'

There are times when Lee's logic has a certain inexorable quality.

'Can we take a look now?

'We can indeed.' Her grin was positively wicked. 'How would you like to come back to work, Dr Stewart?'

Work. The Department of Clinical and Experimental Pathology. One small component of the Strathclyde Area Health Authority Hospital Trust. That well-known semi-private charity dedicated to the welfare of its patients. Something like that.

As an aesthetic amenity the place never had much appeal at the best of times. On a damply depressive September evening, it was like walking through a cemetery with an active recruitment policy. From the moment Lee let us in through the back entrance, I hung on her heels, bumping into her back every time she paused to open a door, until we reached the top floor, where, gratifyingly, some unnamed hero was working late and had left on all the lights.

Dr Elizabeth Adams has her office down at the far end of the corridor. Room 103: an upright coffin at one end of a row of other upright coffins. There's a small plastic name tag screwed to the door, in case she ever forgets who she really is.

Inside, there is just enough space for a filing cabinet, a chair and a desk big enough to hold a virtually obsolete Apple Mac. There's a window, which is something. In normal working hours you would have a good view out over Kelvin Grove and the Art Gallery – given a clear day and a decent pair of binoculars.

One wall is covered in posters with intricate diagrams of molecular pathology. The other sports an oversized Ansell Adams print of a frosted leaf in Yosemite National Park. The desk is forever tidy, with a box for everything and everything in its box. Even the Post-its line up in serial rows, keeping ordered messages from Lee to Lee in her indecipherable shorthand. It's exactly like the room we shared for nights on call in the houseman's quarters of the Clinical Department. Her half was always distressingly tidy.

Lee sat down at the desk and flicked on the computer. It chuntered quietly through the start-up routine and checked itself for viruses. All clear. She clicked the mouse button, typed her password and in a remarkably short space of time, we had full access to the hospital network – the final resting place of all hospital information ever recorded, at least in Pathology.

'Malcolm's middle initial was "D", right?'

'Right.'

She typed again and there was a pause while the hidden mainframe made up its mind, then threw up a window on the screen.

NO INFORMATION AVAILABLE

We looked at each other.

'You're sure it was "D"?'

'Sure. D for Daniel, as in the lion's den. You sure you typed it in right?'

'I'll try again.'

She did, several times, with different spellings of each name. Each time, the mainframe, with the patience of one well used to such temerity, gave us the same answer.

NO INFORMATION AVAILABLE

'It's lying,' I said, as we ran out of ideas.

'It can't,' said Lee and she should know.

'They must have done an autopsy,' I said. 'He was a medic, for God's sake.'

'They did do one. Definitely. I've seen it.'

'Maybe they forget to archive it?'

'They couldn't. It's done automatically.'

'Is there a hard copy?'

'There should be.' Lee began closing down files. 'Better than that, there's a full rack of back-up tapes in the basement somewhere.' She switched off the machine and stood up. 'You don't have to come if you don't want to?' Her voice had a kind of wary caution that made no sense of the sentence.

I paused, half-way to the door. Bridget, what's left of her, is also somewhere in the basement. I don't ever want to see anyone I've known in life after they've been the subject of a Lee Adams post-mortem. Especially not Bridget.

I sat down again.

'Would you mind if I stayed here?'

'Not at all.' She dug in a drawer and pulled out the latest copy of the *BMJ*. 'Here.' The rag flopped on the desk beside me. 'It'll give you something to else think about.'

It was a kind idea, if not entirely effective. I think Lee forgets how completely uninspiring medicine is to those not intimately involved.

I took me less than a minute to filter through the articles and only slightly longer than that to read the single interesting one – yet another epidemiological study of cervical cancer. The results were ambiguous as ever.

The 'Situations Vacant' at the back was slightly more exciting, if only as a reminder of how wonderful it is not to be stuck on the endless trek up the vertical slopes of the career pyramid. If I hadn't stepped out, I'd be one of the many going for the few free consultancies by now. Or stuck for ever at senior registrar, pretending that I preferred it like that. Either way, I'd be battling with the insanities of trust status and evaluating life expectancy versus cost at every step. Not my idea of a fun way to spend my most productive years.

I gave up on the *Journal* and picked up a pharmacology text-book from the shelf instead. It's a long time since I read anything useful about temazepam. They hadn't invented it when I was learning pharmacology – at least, it wasn't in sufficiently regular use for me to learn much about it. I flicked through the pages and browsed through the clinical data and overdose warnings. Interesting stuff. Far more useful than the *BMJ*. By the time Lee returned, my pharmacology was back up to finals exam standard, at least in the field of the benzodiazepine anxiolytics.

Lee emerged from the basement with a pair of floppy disks and some news of her own.

'He's still here. Did you know?'

'Who is?'

'Malcolm.'

I shook my head. 'He can't be. There was a funeral. They buried him.'

'No, they didn't. They had a memorial service. You don't need a body for that. Look.' She sat down at the terminal and slid one of the disks into the drive. The machine chewed on it for a second or two and then opened the single file: a post-mortem report of one Dr Malcolm D. Donnelly, deceased. It was meticulous in its detail. Far longer even than Lee's PMs, and she's not exactly lax in her approach. The kind of thing you'd expect from a man who made his name as a clinical pathologist before he sailed on to the brighter waters of toxicological research.

'Take a look at that.' Lee ran her finger across the bottom of the screen. The 'cremation/burial' section had been deleted and replaced by 'Anatomy Dept'.

I read it twice and then again to make sure. Medics very, very rarely turn over their earthly remains to the probing attentions of the student masses, however glowingly the concept is presented to the general public. The mere thought makes my palms itch.

'Malcolm wouldn't do that.' My voice rose a register. I coughed and brought it down again. 'I mean, *why*, for God's sake?'

'Who knows?' She leant under the desk and switched on a desk printer. 'Maybe he wanted to hang around for a while longer.'

'Don't be morbid, Adams.'

'Sorry.' She grinned to show that she wasn't. 'But it does mean that if we want to, we can have a look at what's left. At the very least, there'd be blood and organ samples in store. If we're very lucky, he might still be lying in a freezer somewhere and we could do another post-mortem.'

Nobody is that stupid.

'If you had just murdered someone, would you be careless enough to leave the body lying around for any passing pathologist to take a look at?'

She kept her eyes on the screen and hit a couple of keys. 'I might. It could be less trouble than trying to override a will. Folk get struck off for things like that. The lawyers get really upset. You can get away with murder if you know what you're doing, but it's the paperwork that catches you out in the end.'

The laser printer whined into action and a squeaky-clean copy of a squeaky-clean post-mortem slid out into the tray. *It's the paperwork that catches you out in the end.* I thought of Malcolm and what it might have taken to get him to leave his body for the vultures of science.

'We need to find the body and have a closer look,' I said, trying to keep my imagination in check. Anatomy ranks quite a long way below Pathology on my list of fun places to visit.

Lee saw me and smiled indulgence. 'Tomorrow, huh?' she offered. 'One more day won't make any odds.'

'True.' I let out a breath. 'But we could check the date on the will tonight. It might be useful to know if the sudden urge for anatomical preservation was a last-minute change of mind.'

'Could do.'

'All the paperwork's at the farm,' I said, ignoring a graphic image of what Caroline would say if I turned up on the doorstep with Lee Adams in tow. 'Would you like to come home?'

'Why not?'

It had gone midnight when we juddered down the track to the yard. An old VW Golf sat in one of the passing places half-way down the lane, the windows steamed to invisibility with the activities from inside. It rocked gently as we passed.

The house was in darkness. I found the spare key in its hiding place under the upturned water bucket in the corner of the yard and opened the back door as quietly as I could, signalling silence to Lee. Caroline used to be a fairly light sleeper when we were children and there was no reason to believe she had changed.

A throat-catching stench of dog shit hit me as I entered the kitchen. Beside me, Lee took a deep breath and swore. I put one hand over my nose, fumbling in the dark for the light switch with the other.

The faint whine of an embarrassed dog emanated from the far side of the room.

'Tan, you crazy hound, couldn't you wait?'

I found the light and stepped into carnage.

'Mother of God . . . *Tan!*'

He was still alive – just – lying in a pool of mixed blood and faeces, his small intestines spilling out fanwise across the floor from the gaping wound in his abdominal wall. There was cord binding his muzzle and more anchoring his front paws to one of the heavy, fireside chairs. He lifted his head to look at me and whined again. I retched hard and bile hit the back of my throat.

Lee got to him first. She knelt in the filth, cradling his head on her lap, talking dog-talk, holding the pain at bay. One hand unwound the cord from his nose. The whining stopped.

'Have you got a gun?' The words slid in between one piece of nonsense talk and the next and she didn't look up. It was a moment or two before I realised she was talking to me. She read the hesitation wrong.

'You can't put him back together, Kellen. Not like this.' This time she did look up and her eyes were black, unreadable pits.

'I know.' I shook my head. 'Malcolm's shotgun's in the loft.'

'Hell. That's too far.' Her eyes closed and she took a short breath in. 'Right.'

63

Her voice carried on, almost unbroken, spinning mindless canine fairy stories while one hand stroked his head, across and across, caressing, soothing, fingers seeking urgently for the atlanto-occipital notch down at the base of his skull. Her fingers locked on the back of his neck and she tightened the grip on his muzzle.

Her voice changed. 'Okay, kid. Time to go.'

The dog raised his head a fraction, sighting imaginary rabbits, and I watched his tail rise and fall twice in a tentative wag. The tendons stood out briefly on Lee's forearms and there was an ugly snap, like green wood breaking. The tail fell limply to the floor.

Lee laid her hand on his chest, behind the elbow, and kept it there for a moment, feeling for the heartbeat. Then she stood up abruptly. Fluid and filth smeared down from her knees to her feet. Her eyes slid across mine, unseeing. 'We'd better find Caroline,' she said.

I was already half-way to the door, my mind played havoc, tying the woman in the dog's place At the foot of the stairs we paused.

Lee raised one eyebrow. 'Split?' she whispered.

No chance. One dead is enough. There's safety in numbers.

I shook my head once and then led the way, silently, up the stairs to search the top floor.

We went through the entire house in less than five minutes.

No one. Particularly no Caroline

That left the barn and the outbuildings: three sheds, the wood store and the garage.

The barn door hung an inch or two open. It had been closed when we drove in, we both knew that. I caught Lee's eye and jerked my head round at the left side, sketching a window in the air between us. She nodded once and vanished, a shadow in other shadows. I made for one side of the open door, taking time, trying to avoid the gravel, keeping out of the patches of moonlight.

A tawny owl chick called twice to its mother. Except it was too late in the year for owlets and there are only barn owls round the farm.

Lee in place.

I eased open the barn door and slid inside, hugging the deep shadows at the edges of the stalls. Somewhere up to my left, a pony huffed a small snort of surprise.

'There, something up there. Far end. Past the horses.' Lee's voice. Ghost-like in my ear. We began edging up the row of boxes.

Two sounds, opposite directions. A scuffle in the chicken shed at the end of the barn and outside a car revved up in the lane.

'Split?'

'Go!'

Lee went for the shed. I turned and sprinted for the door, hurling myself through, out into the yard, over the gate and up the lane. Red tail-lights burned round a corner, leaving empty space and diesel fumes where the Golf had been parked.

Not a hope.

I cursed viciously and spat, tasting the metallic tang of blood in the back of my throat from the run.

A high-pitched whistle called me back to the barn, fast. Lee was there with Caroline, the latter lying on the floor of the chicken shed, bound hand and foot with the same white whip-cord that had held the dog. A wide gash on one ankle bled profusely. Otherwise she was alive, conscious and, as far as I could see, in one piece. I have never in all my life been so glad to see a single human being alive and well.

'Caroline. Christ, woman. Are you all right?'

Lee cut the wrist cords and helped her sit up. She looked up at me blank-eyed and shaped her lips round one word. 'Tan?'

I took her hand and met her eyes, trying to think of what to say.

'Dead,' said Lee, cutting the last loop of cord. 'I did it.'

I held on to Caroline's hand and, just for a moment, saw her teeter on the edge of emotional free-fall. Then she caught herself and the blank stare came back.

She nodded, her eyes fixed on nowhere. 'Thank you.'

I'm not sure she even knew she was talking to Lee.

We helped her back to the house and in through the front door to the living room. It was cold and smelt of disuse but there was no blood on the floor and the memories it carried were old and beyond harm. It was the best we could do.

Caroline sat in silence on the edge of the sofa, letting me dress the cut on her ankle and massage the circulation back into her hands and feet. She submitted with good grace to Lee's detailed medical check, drank coffee and answered our questions in a steady, controlled monotone, building layer after layer of shell around the nightmare. By the time we left, she could have passed in the street as normal. She's always been good at building walls. It's something to do with the need for control.

I let Lee guide the questions. She probed gently, keeping the language clinical, distant, carefully guiding past the nightmares to the facts. Good technique.

'How many?'

'Just one.'

'Male?'

'Yes.'

'What time?'

'I don't know. An hour ago . . . maybe a bit more. I went upstairs to make up the spare bed for Kellen and he was waiting . . .'

'What did he look like?'

'I don't know. I never saw him. He kept behind me. I just heard his voice.'

'Scots?'

'Yes. But not a strong accent. Like Malcolm's but deeper and . . . harder.'

'What did he want?'

'The bantams. Two of them got out a couple of weeks ago and we never got round to looking for them. He said they belonged to a friend if his and he wanted them back.'

'Did he get them?'

'No. I don't know . . . I don't know where they are. Really. I have absolutely no idea . . .'

Her voice cracked. Anger over the fear. Thin ice. I shook my head at Lee and she backed off. We could put the rest together ourselves. It wasn't difficult.

Lee rocked back on her heels and looked up at the ceiling, pensive.

'Take her somewhere safe,' she said finally. 'I'll stay and clear up here.'

There aren't too many options. 'I'll take her back to the flat,' I said, praying hard for a peaceful night. 'Give me a ring when you're done. I'll come and pick you up.'

'Okay.' She jerked her head towards the door. 'Don't hang around.'

The roads were too quiet and the weather too clear to take up much of my mind with the driving. I drove along on autopilot, trying not to think of the scene in the kitchen and failing. Caroline sat beside me breathing evenly, her eyes and her mind in neutral, until I drew up in a space at the corner of Beaumont Gate.

'Is Lyn still here?' she asked. Her voice was as colourless as her eyes.

'No. We split.'

'Oh.'

There was a diplomatic pause while I pulled her bags from the back seat and we made our way up the street towards number 57.

She put a hand on my arm as I juggled the bags into one hand and hunted through my pockets for the key. 'Are you living alone now?'

'Not exactly.'

'Anyone I should know?'

'I doubt it. She's a computer journalist. Specialises in electronic media. Her name's Janine Caradice.'

She thought for a moment. 'American?'

'Canadian.'

Wait for it.

'Rae Larssen's ex?'

Thanks.

'I wouldn't say that to her face if I was you. It was a long time ago.'

'Oh.' A flash of amusement warmed her eyes. 'Sorry.'

'Sure.'

I opened the street door and keyed a number into the alarm pad on the wall. We took a bag each and walked up the two flights together in a reasonably amicable silence.

It was half-past two in the morning by the time I turned the key in the lock and let us both into the flat. Janine, not surprisingly, was asleep. On balance, I had no real desire to introduce Caroline to my lover at that time of night, so by two forty-five the pair of us were crashed out, semi-clothed, on the sofa bed in the living room, with the phone and an alarm clock for company.

The front-door buzzer woke me. With a reflex left over from hospital days, I was on my feet by the speaker before my brain had cut in to ask what the hell was going on.

'Yes?'

'Hi. It's me.'

Lee. I hit the buttons, heard the outer door open and shut a floor below and listened for the ripple of rubber-soled feet on the stairs. I met her at the door and guided her quietly past the sleeping Caroline to the kitchen.

'Tea?' I found a box of peppermint teabags in the back of a cupboard. Revolting stuff, but it's about the only thing in the house that isn't laden with stimulants.

'Thanks.'

'Everything cleared up?' I asked.

'Yes.' Lee nodded, peaceably. 'I buried Tan. I thought perhaps we ought to keep this in the family until we've decided what we're doing.'

Quite. This is where the Adams/Stewart partnership comes into its own. She knows the problems and we both take the same route through to the same kind of answers. There were two things that really bothered me on the way home with Caroline and the first of them was what to do about Tan.

I floated a compost teabag in a mug and passed it over.

'There's a Stewart MacDonald in charge of the local law,' I said. 'He's a step or three up from your average rural plod. And he likes dogs. He met Tan the other night. I'll have to tell him something.'

Lee twirled the bag in the mug and a wash of peppermint vapour mixed with the coffee in a familiar, nauseating, early-morning cocktail. 'Can you keep it low key?' she asked.

'Tan? Sure. I'll have to. If they find out how he died, they're not going to follow the suicide line on Bridget for long.'

Lee blew gently across the top of her mug. 'Do you want them to?' she asked.

'No. Of course not.' There's no way I want the rest of the world to believe that Bridget was that kind of loser. 'But I'd rather that than Laidlaw. The second they call it a murder hunt, he'll be in there with both left feet, waving arrest warrants to the four winds and daring everybody to make his day.'

'Or he'll just sit tight and wait for us to make it for him.'

'Thanks, Dr Adams. You just made my morning.'

She raised her mug in a wry toast. 'Don't mention it, Dr Stewart.'

And that, of course, is the second problem. The catch in the Catch-22. The angled twist of the double bind.

If it was only murder, we could cope. Or at least, I'd give us decent odds. Even against the kind who gut dogs for the fun of it.

If it was only Laidlaw, we could run rings round him. We've done it before and stayed this side of the bars.

It's the combination of the two that makes life so bloody difficult. If you go looking for trouble, at some point you step over the legal limits. And wouldn't that just make his day?

'MacDonald's pretty good,' I said. 'I doubt if he'd want to hand it over. But I think we ought to have a contingency plan. Just in case . . .'

'You always do.' Lee leaned back in her chair and smiled. The kind of smile that grows out of a long night on the wards when the charts are all unwritten, there's a backlog of treatments enough to last through to the afternoon and the consultant is due to hold rounds at some unspecified time in the next twenty-four hours. 'Suppose we worry about that when we come to it, huh?' she offered. 'You never know. If we ignore him long enough, he might go away.'

'And the pigs might fly to the moon.'

'That too.' She was smiling still and there was no real point in arguing.

The best-laid contingency plans fail every time.

Lee finished her tea, stood up and rinsed her mug unhurriedly in the sink. 'If I go into work now,' she said, 'I could get Bridget's post-mortem report finished and out. If they have something in print with suicide written on it, they're less likely to start thinking of other things.'

'Thanks.' I poured myself a fresh coffee. 'I'll call in at the library later on, have a look through Malcolm's old papers. If there's anything useful, I'll call you.'

'What are you going to tell them about Tan?'

'Just that he's dead. They don't need anything else.'

'What about herself?' She angled her head towards the living room, where Caroline lay asleep on the sofa bed.

'I'll have a word with her. She can let sleeping dogs lie if she has to.'

'Very funny.'

Lee followed me through the living room to the front door. 'She thinks I'm a bad influence on you,' she said, nodding back over my shoulder to the sofa bed.

'No.' I held open the door. 'She knows it's the other way round.'

Breakfast was . . . different.

I heard Janine's alarm clock before she did and took her a conciliatory cup of tea. Her big-boned frame lay curled up under one corner of the duvet, the rest of it spilling, as ever, down on to the floor at my side. I don't steal the bedclothes, she throws them at me. I just don't throw them back.

Wan September sunlight filtered in slantwise through the gap in the curtains, lighting up flamelets in the massed copper sheet of her hair as it spread across the pillow, stretching flat light over a face blurred into childhood with sleep. Even after two years, she still does odd things to my heart rate.

I put the tea down at a safe distance and drew the corner of the duvet carefully away. One long arm stretched out sleepily towards my side of the bed, searching. I caught it and squirmed in close, tucking her hand round my waist. My free hand explored the rest of her, starting low and stroking lazily upwards to finish somewhere near her neck.

The grip on my waist tightened. I drew small circles along the line of her collar bones with my fingertip and watched her wake, slowly. Memory sketched in the lines on her face and she grew back to middle age. A stressed-out-professional-woman kind of middle age.

'Hi.' I picked up her other hand and kissed it. 'How's things?'

'I don't know.' The hand stayed in mine, unmoved and unmoving. 'You tell me.'

Great. I live with a sabre-toothed porcupine.

'Bridget's dead.' I said.

'I know. You said on the message machine.'

So I did.

Janine slid out of bed and pulled her dressing gown off the door, wrapped it round like an outsize bearskin and lay back down on the edge of the bed. It's a wonderful garment of chastity, that dressing gown. Completely inaccessible and totally concealing. Even her hands are invisible.

'There's tea on the table.' I offered.

'I know. I saw it.' She frowned up at the ceiling, ignoring the offering.

There was a pause and then she asked, 'Are you waiting for me to say I'm sorry?'

'I don't know. Are you?'

She snorted. Like a horse but with less humour. Her eyes rolled to the ceiling and back. 'Just for one moment there, I thought I'd finally stepped out of the shadow of St Bridget,' she said, 'and, no, I wasn't sorry at all.' Her smile turned wry at the edges. 'Then I remembered that being dead never stopped anyone from attaining sainthood.'

'So?'

'So, yes – ' she nodded – 'I am sorry. At least – ' she tipped her head towards the living room – 'I'm sorry for her. That *is* Caroline through there, right?'

'Right.'

'*The* Caroline?'

'Yes.'

'Why is she here?'

'She needed help.'

'Wasn't there anyone else?'

'I don't know. I didn't ask.'

'No.' She shook her head. 'You wouldn't.'

There was another pause. The tea on the table-top became steadily colder and the room steadily warmer as the sun moved further across the window.

'How long is she staying?' asked my lover, eventually.

'Not long. A day or two, I should think. A week at the most.'

'Your timing stinks, Stewart.'

'I know.' Story of my life. 'Do you mind?'

'Of course.' She finally turned her head towards me and smiled. An old smile, sad and warm and weary all at once. The kind of smile reserved for lovers past their prime. 'But I'm sure I can be reasonable if you ask me nicely enough,' she said.

The dressing gown rippled. A hand emerged from the depths and her fingers looped through mine. Familiar and friendly and still electric in spite of everything.

'How nicely?' I asked.

'This'll do.' Her thumb drew a tingling path across my palm.

I leant over and kissed her forehead. 'Are you sure you have time?'

'No.' Her other hand slid out and explored the buttons on my shirt. 'Any other stupid questions?'

'No.'

Neither of us touched the tea.

Caroline knocked on the door a while later to ask if it was all right to use the shower and suddenly I was in bed with a professional woman late for work.

Terrifying. It is possible to shower, dress, eat, dress again because the first lot doesn't look right, blow-dry your hair, find the car keys and get out of the door in ten minutes flat, all without tripping over the visitor in the living room, but it takes a lot of practice. Particularly the last bit.

The visitor in question picked up the dressing gown from the doorway, wrapped it around herself in a defensive cocoon and retired to the safety of the kitchen.

'Is it always like this?' she asked, as the whirlwind departed, five minutes over time.

'Nope.' I was half-way through a leisurely cup of coffee, still lost in the post-orgasmic glow. 'That's life in the fast lane. You should see the bad days.'

'No thanks. I gave it up for Lent.' Caroline looked pointedly at her watch. 'It's after eight. Do you want me to come and help you feed the ponies?'

I did not. Given the events of the past forty-eight hours, there was no way I was taking Caroline Leader back to the farm until I was sure that it was a great deal safer than it seemed. Caroline herself, thankfully, didn't seem inclined to press the point. She wrote me out a list of all the ponies indexed by name and with their feed rations appended. I, in turn, gave her slightly less ordered instructions on how to operate the security mechanisms to the flat and introduced her to Janine's computer technology.

By the time I left, she had found her way on to the Net and was browsing happily through the local fringe theatre sites on the Web with the ease of old familiarity. Everyone but me has become a techno-freak these days.

CHAPTER THREE

Great Western Road was choked with early-morning commuter traffic crawling through the heavy drizzle from one set of traffic lights to the next. Flocks of students wrapped up in layers of semi-waterproof clothing wove their mountain bikes in and out of the lines of cars and slowed progress to something near a standstill. Under normal circumstances, I would have cut through the side roads and bypassed Anniesland Cross altogether, but I needed time to think. The hypnotic tic of the windscreen wipers obliterated the outside world, turning the car into a thought-cocoon where I could juggle the facts until they made some kind of sense.

Fact: three deaths – Malcolm, Bridget, Tan. In that order. Of the three, only the dog died violently. Very violently. A break in the pattern. Or part of a different pattern. Either way, it was a professional job and they don't come cheap.

Fact: Caroline was left alive when she, too, could have been dead. Why? It wouldn't have taken long to turn her into exactly the same state as Tan and paid killers like adding to their body count. So he was paid enough to leave her alone. A warning, possibly, but without any obvious target.

Fact: Malcolm brought chickens to the farm and died. Bridget ate a last meal of eggs before she overdosed. The dog-killer with

75

the knife and the old VW Golf was on a chicken hunt. All round, birds are bad news.

None of it made sense. Like building a jigsaw when all the pieces are different colours and you've lost the lid of the box. All I had was a handful of hens and a row of dead bodies. It didn't make much of a picture.

I drove on, grinding the gears and riding the clutch up the hill towards Bearsden. I never liked jigsaws.

The traffic and the rain both eased on the outskirts of Milngavie and I had a clear, dry road to the farm. A blue police Land Rover waited in the yard, empty, with both doors open.

Inspector Stewart MacDonald was in the barn. His jacket hung on a hook near the door and he was working his way up the horse line in his shirt sleeves, filling hay nets.

His henchwoman sat on a bale near the door, watching him with practised indifference. She rolled her eyes to the heavens as I walked in, giving me the 'I couldn't stop him' shrug: palms out, eyebrows arched. Plucked eyebrows at that.

I leant over the door and waited while MacDonald made a fuss over Midnight and the pony, in turn, tried to undo his shirt. A love affair in the making.

'You're late, lass,' he said. 'They were starving.'

'Really? That makes up for the three feeds extra the other night then.' I took the empty hay nets from the barrow and hung them on a hook by the tack racks. 'I was going to turn them out anyway. The big paddock's a good twenty acres and it's not been mown yet. They should be happy enough on that for a week or two.' I found the key to the drug cupboard and began dragging out boxes. 'You can help me worm them first if you like.'

The Inspector took a handful of plastic syringes and walked with me to the end of the line. I put a head collar on the new Connemara filly and held her nose while he slipped the wormer smoothly into the corner of her mouth and squirted the dose on to the back of her tongue. She made a face, mouthing, and threatened to spit the lot on the floor. I gave her a mint to take away the taste and watched until she had swallowed everything before we moved on up the line.

We worked in companionable silence. Grab, squirt, swallow. Move on. An easy, steady rhythm. MacDonald caught on from the beginning. He could have been doing it all his life.

Half-way down the second line he nodded his head fractionally in the direction of the farmhouse and asked, 'Your friend's no here today?'

A loaded question if ever I heard one.

'No. I took her home. She needed a break.'

'Uhuh?' He had his face turned to Balder's neck, pulling knots out of his mane. The question hovered between us, waiting for an answer.

I watched the gelding try to spread wormer-flavoured horse spit all over the man's hair in a gesture of basic equine affection. MacDonald carried on levelling off the uneven ends of the mane, talking irrelevant nonsense in his baritone burr. The ponies trusted him. Pity I'm not a horse.

'The dog died last night,' I said. 'Caroline's . . . She doesn't want to stay here for the moment.'

'Oh?' His eyes asked more than his voice. 'What was up with him? He looked right enough when I saw him . . .'

'I don't know.' I shrugged. 'Sounded like a gastric torsion but I wasn't here when it happened.'

'You wouldn't think . . .' He drifted off. 'Aye. Maybe. It's a shame though. He was a grand dog.'

'He was.'

We left it at that.

The final box was at the furthest end of the barn from his green-eyed, arch-browed minion. It was inhabited by a small bay gelding with a voracious appetite and a predisposition to laminitis. I ran my hands over his feet and tried to remember if he'd ever had a bout as late on in the year as September. I thought not, but I couldn't be sure. Inspector MacDonald stood at the front and fiddled with the buckle on the head collar.

'Yon lassie there,' he said conversationally, 'WPC Philips. She's here on secondment from Central. She'll be going back to the town at the end of the month.'

'Really?'

I had two spare mints. We took one each, taking time to unwrap them from the folds of paper and silver foil. The pony made a grab for both and missed.

'Has she enjoyed her stay?' I asked.

'Aye, well, I think maybe "enjoy" might be overstating things a touch.' He adjusted the head collar to his satisfaction and clipped on a lead rope. 'But she's just bursting to tell Chief Inspector Laidlaw all about the weird things we rural types get up to when we're left to our own devices.'

He opened the door and led the bay out, raising his voice to carry. 'You'll be wanting a hand to turn out the ponies, aye?'

'Sounds good to me.'

Under different circumstances, I could get to like this man.

We led out eight at a time, two pairs each, jumping skittishly on the end of the lead ropes, and let them go into the big field at the back of the barn.

A burn straight off the Campsies ran down one edge, providing endless clean water, and the beech wood at the back with its coppery leaves falling into the field gave them shelter from the worst of the weather.

They sprang away from the gate and charged out, tails up and feet flying like foals in their first spring. The first lot had barely settled by the time we let out the second eight and then the whole herd went round and round, carving a race track in the turf at the edge.

The cloud had cleared while we were inside and the day was turning into a perfect West Coast September: clear and brisk, with a sharp nip to the air as an early reminder of impending winter. Under any other circumstances, it would have been entirely idyllic.

I leant against the fence watching Midnight spin and dance with Balder and slid, unthinking, into a backwards drift of memories.

Sun, cold air, the musky smell of horse sweat and the taste of it on skin. Her skin. It gets everywhere, horse sweat. A voice, her voice, laughing. Her body arching, head thrown back, hair dark against the pale grass under the trees, toes dangling in the river. Both of us playing at otters in the pool on the other side of the wood. Drying out on the grass afterwards, beech-leaf shadows dappling skin, blending the curves of breast and thigh with the darker grass of the *sidhe* mound.

And I knew, now, where Tan was buried.

'Are you not going to check the fence, lass? There haven't been horses in here for years.' Inspector MacDonald. The ever-practical Inspector MacDonald. Back to the real world.

'I suppose I should. Thank you.' I unhooked the gate and let myself into the field. 'And you, I suppose, should go and rescue your young molette. Unless you know where she was last time we went back to the barn?'

The bale by the door had been conspicuously empty as we led the last lot of ponies out. Neither of us had said anything, but the idea of a police snooper wandering around the farm made me nervous. Especially one with plucked eyebrows.

'Aye. We'd better go and find her, right enough. Can't have her getting lost in the muck heap first thing in the morning. Just one more thing . . .' He reached for the inside pocket of the jacket he wasn't wearing and then snapped his fingers in mock irritation. 'Oh, blast. It's back in the barn.'

The man's a terrible actor.

'Oh?'

'I got a fax of the post-mortem report on Ms Donnelly on my desk this morning.'

'Really?' Well done, Lee. 'Did it say anything interesting?'

'Aye, well, I think perhaps we won't be needing to take the fingerprints after all. But we will be needing a word with . . . What the hell . . .?'

Whatever he was about to say next was drowned by a high-pitched shriek and a frantic squawking from the barn. I vaulted the gate and sprinted up the yard after MacDonald, reaching the door at his shoulder. It burst open as we arrived, to disgorge a very dishevelled WPC Philips clutching her inspector's jacket to her chest. The jacket writhed, momentarily with a life of its own, and then a bright-eyed head popped out of one armpit and squawked loudly.

'It's a hen,' she said, her eyes shining. 'It's hurt its wing, poor wee soul. There's another in the hay shed but I couldn't catch it. It'll need the three of us.'

I doubt very much if the good citizens of Strathclyde know how their hard-earned taxes are spent. Most of the time it's as well they don't, but the odd choice morsel would warm the cockles of their hearts. The story of how the Inspector, his Constable and the Therapist chased a chicken round a barn for half a morning, for instance, would go down well in the bars and back rooms of the metropolis, if only as evidence of the insanity of country living. We caught it in the end, of course. Three adult humans against one unfit bantam hen is no competition, but you might not have thought so had you seen us half-way through.

Carrying crates that had held other chickens in other days stood stacked in one of the sheds. WPC Philips and Inspector MacDonald, who had metamorphosed into Elspeth and Stewart during the chase, held a chicken each while I selected the two boxes with the most intact lids and escape-proof walls. We carried them back in triumph to the kitchen for a well-earned coffee.

A very faint tang of blood overlaid the ingrained smells of wet dog and peat smoke as a reminder of the night before. Other than that, the kitchen floor was cleaner than I had ever seen it. Lee had worked off a lot of aggression with a scouring mop. A lot more than the mess should have needed. I nipped upstairs on the pretext of going to the loo and checked the bedrooms.

The whole place looked like a hotel in limbo, waiting for the next set of guests.

Tidying things up is as good a way of searching as pulling them apart. I wondered if she had found anything useful.

Downstairs, Elspeth was having serious trouble with the Rayburn. Inspector MacDonald, who could have made it behave itself in seconds, was suffering a blatant attack of chauvinism along the lines that inspectors don't make coffee for the underlings. He must have picked that one up from Laidlaw, it had a familiar ring to it.

I left the lass blowing ineffectually at the air vents and put on the electric kettle. Practical training might have been good for her soul but I needed my caffeine boost to kick my brain back into action. When I poured out the coffee, she left in a huff and went to talk to the hens on the porch. Odd girl.

The Inspector had draped his jacket over a chair. I raided the inside pocket as I handed him his coffee. He watched me do it and said nothing.

The post-mortem report was a finished, freshly typed version of the one I had seen the night before. The single addition was a concluding paragraph which suggested that the subject was almost certainly unconscious at the time of death, that there was a highly significant dose of temazepam in the stomach contents, reflected in an assay of plasma samples, and that this dose was likely to have been self-administered either for recreational purposes or with the intention of ending the subject's life. The cause of death was therefore considered to be either accidental or self-inflicted. The pathologist was unable to offer an opinion as to which. The signature at the base was that of one Professor P. G. Gemmell, MD, PhD, FRCPath. For all I know, it could have been genuine.

MacDonald slurped at his coffee, his eyes on my face. 'Did you know her well?' he asked. His voice lost the gravel, softened for the time being by a kind of paternal concern.

'Bridget? Yes. We're joint owners of this place.' I moved my head to indicate the farm and surrounding area.

'Uhuh?' It wasn't really a question. He knew that already. 'Would she have done it, d'you think?'

'I don't know. It's four years since I last saw her.' I shrugged. 'I'd be extraordinarily surprised if she did.'

'Mmm.' He wasn't really listening. Too busy watching the cats dissecting something small and feathered outside the window. 'What about Dr Adams?' he asked, mildly curious. 'Do you still keep in touch with her?'

'I'm sorry?'

'I was trying to call the Pathology Department to talk to the Professor about the results. He's away for the day but the lassie on the phone said I could talk to a Dr Adams instead. I remembered she used to be a friend of yours. I didn't realise she was in pathology.'

Ouch.

'She was in surgery when the Chief Inspector knew her.'

'And she's working with Professor Gemmell now.' He nodded as if it confirmed everything. 'He was a colleague of the brother's, is that right?'

'He was his PhD supervisor. They went on working together after, right up till Malcolm died.'

'He's a great friend of the Chief Inspector. Did you know?'

Nothing would surprise me.

'I suppose if you run the Forensic Department, you get to know the police fairly well.'

'Aye. You do.'

A diplomatic pause.

This man is seriously on the ball. Why is he stuck out here in the middle of nowhere?

We drank our coffee in silence for a while and I watched him think. Like watching a fox move in on a pheasant. Slowly, very slowly. But always forwards.

'I'll maybe go and talk to her GP first,' he said eventually. 'We can have a look at the prescription records and see if she got the stuff from there in the first place. Time enough to bother the pathologists after that.'

He gathered his jacket and stood up, depositing a cat on to the floor.

'Could you bring your friend back here for a chat?' he asked 'Say perhaps tomorrow lunch-time? Twelve o'clock?'

'Sure.' I took his empty mug from his hand. 'Do you mind if I tell her the post-mortem findings first? It might make it easier for her.'

'No problem.' He shook his head, smiling vaguely. 'No problem at all.'

I left him to collect his hen-loving assistant and see himself out. Sadly, neither of them accepted my offer to take the chickens as they went. Unsporting of them. I'm sure the local station would be improved by the presence of a bantam or two. And no one would ever dream of trying to lift the little dears from there.

Caroline was out when I got home and there was no indication of when she was due home again. I carried the chickens up the stairs, doing my best not to alert the neighbours, and put

83

the crates in the living room as a temporary measure while I made a sandwich and thought about what to do with them.

First-floor, two-bedroom, West End flats are not designed as substitute hen farms. The mere thought of what Janine was going to say made my head spin. On the other hand, it's my flat, I pay for it and I keep the mortgage going, and there really was nowhere else to put them.

In the end, I knocked up a makeshift chicken coop in a corner of the spare room, wrote a hasty note to Caroline telling her where I'd gone and when I hoped to be back, and then headed off for the library. Probably I should have thought more about the incompatibility of chicken shit and computers but it didn't occur to me at the time.

John Harries, chief librarian of the university library, is a dinosaur of the kind that justifies the theory of evolution: slow and ponderous, with a brain entirely resembling a filing cabinet and a charisma to match. It makes him the last of his kind, utterly incapable of reproduction. On the other hand, he has a brilliant memory and the kind of stunning naïveté that denies ever having made contact with the real world. As a combination, it has its uses.

He greeted me like a long-lost friend, which was true in part – it was years since I had last used the library – and waved me through the chicane of electronic security systems. Twenty minutes later I was safely ensconced in a booth with a microfiche reader digging out references.

In the days when the world and John Harries were young, cramming text in small type on sheets of blue plastic was state-of-the-art information processing. In the current era of on-line, worldwide data retrieval at the flick of a switch, it is slow, clumsy and inspires terrific headaches for minimal reward. But it is also untraceable and costs nothing.

By mid-way through the afternoon, I had a list of everything

Dr Malcolm Donnelly had ever published, from his days as an undergraduate right through to a posthumous paper published, together with several pages of heartfelt obituary from colleagues and co-workers, in the most recent issue of *Immunology*.

Once upon a time, Malcolm was a paediatric physician, a very good one. Good enough to be spotted by the academic moguls during his time as a registrar and enticed away from the wards to the scholastic haven of the pathology research laboratory. Once there, he sailed through a PhD in cytology, moving from there into immunology and eventually into genetics. From then on his career kept him in the forefront of medical science, with papers published at frighteningly regular intervals in all the major international journals as indices of progress and achievement. He spiralled up the ladders of medical achievement as far as he could possibly go, winning accolades and gathering kudos on the way. When I last spoke to him, just before I moved out of the farm, he was sitting on a senior lectureship and waiting for his professor to keel over so that he could take his place as head of department. In the meantime, he was working flat out to bring in grant money to keep himself and his multiple research projects afloat.

I gave up trying to understand Malcolm Donnelly's work while we were still on the wards. He had a brain like a surgical laser and a capacity for lateral thinking that kept him on the leading edge of half a dozen fields at once. Whatever he was doing, Malcolm was a man driven by the need to be at the forefront of science. To be acknowledged as the best at whatever it was he chose to do. To create things he could point to in his old age and say, 'Here I made a difference to the world.'

Except that somewhere along the line something had happened and there was not going to be an old age. All that was left of the man and his career was a three-page list of reference papers.

Somewhere, in one of them, there had to be a clue as to why.

Two floors up from the microfiche readers, back copies of all the world's medical journals are stacked in order of name and date. I picked up a coffee from the vending machine on the inter-floor landing and began the laborious process of finding and copying papers. Professor Norrie Lear still had his name on the credit list for the photocopier, which was fairly surprising given that he died eighteen months before I graduated, but his posthumous generosity saved me a substantial sum in photocopy fees all the way through my final year and beyond. There are reasons why the Health Service is broke and I am one of them.

Shortly after eight, with my head spinning and lines of text floating in waves past my eyes, I treated myself to coffee in the canteen and used the pay-phone to call home.

Caroline was still out and I listened to my own recorded voice informing me that I would attend to my message as soon as I got home. Some hope. All of my friends know that this is a fantasy, even when life is stable. I keyed in a four-digit code and listened to the single message, which was from Lee, telling me that she would be at the Man in the Moon at half-past eight if I wanted to meet her there. Even over the phone her voice had the kind of tone that suggested it would be in my best interests to go. The joys of modern high-speed communication.

I was late, of course, but not excessively so. Lee was there ahead of me, sitting at the usual place on the balcony, mashing a fork idly through the remains of her haggis and neeps, her concentration focused on a shorthand pad that stood on the table in front of her, propped up against the ubiquitous glass of mineral water. She was dressed entirely in black. Very odd. I thought she'd grown out of that years ago.

I collected half a bitter from the bar and sat down.

'You look like a spare part from a Pride march, Adams, you know that.'

She closed the notepad and glanced up, amused. 'Thanks. I

knew you'd appreciate it.' She flicked her fork at the food, still smiling. 'Hungry?'

'Are you finished?'

'It's all yours.' Her plate slid across the table towards me. 'Did you find anything useful in the library?'

'I hope so.' I pulled the sheaf of photocopies from my bag and dumped them on the table. 'I didn't have time to copy everything. This is the first and the last five years. If there's nothing in these, I can go back and find the rest.'

She shook her head. 'If there's anything to see, it'll be recent.'

'All we have to do is find it.'

'Right.'

We spread the papers out on the table and worked through them together while I ate.

The early papers were deeply familiar. The Donnelly trademark of good data, concisely presented and clinically relevant shone through them all. He combined the clinical instincts of the physician with the abstract understanding of the scientist and applied them to unravelling the mysteries of human genetic disease.

Then, gradually, there was a shift in emphasis away from the dissection of disease over to the grey area of quasi-academic, industry-funded, non-clinical lab work. First there was an increase in the list of acknowledgements at the end of each paper, showing the commercial sources of some, at least, of his funding. Later, the list of co-authors began to change, away from the medics on the wards and over to the back-room, white-coat, anti-clinical brigade.

Finally, a little under two years previously, he completed the shift from medical geneticist to genetic engineer with a change of address. Dr Malcolm Donnelly abandoned the safe, tenured hallways of the university and set up his lab in the pristine new medical science park built on the rubble of an East End redevelopment scheme. Why?

'Money,' said Lee, underlining the name of the firm in question, which called itself, with a stunning absence of originality, Medi-Gen.

'No.' I shook my head. 'Malcolm wasn't interested in money. All he wanted out of life was the chance to do good research.'

'I know. But you can't do good research without sensible funding and you won't find that in the universities these days. Can you imagine what the cutbacks did to a man like Malcolm? He couldn't sit on his backside and watch the world he had built crumble round his ears for lack of finance, when the boys at the drug companies have shiny new toys for the asking and the people to make them go. He might not have wanted it for himself, but you can't run a research programme without hard cash and there are not that many places to find it. Someone offered him a decent lab with good money and he went. Simple.'

'Mmm. Maybe.' It didn't sound like the man I thought I knew, but there was an easy way to find out. I pulled a biro from my pocket and wrote down the address of the laboratory on a separate piece of paper. 'I'll go in the morning and talk to the people he was working with when he died. We need to get more of a feel for what he was doing and what his priorities were.'

I began to make a list of the people I wanted to talk to: lab technicians, co-workers, the project director, other postdoctoral staff, friends. Some of the people he worked with must have been friends as well as colleagues, I just had no idea any more which ones they were.

Lee leaned forward, reading my writing upside-down. 'On the other hand,' she suggested, 'we could go now. It might be easier in the long run.'

I glanced at my watch. It had gone ten o'clock. 'No, it's too late. There'll be nobody there at this time of night.'

'I know.'

The penny dropped rather later than it should have done. I stopped writing and looked up. Lee was watching me, sitting very still, waiting. She had that predatory look. And she was dressed in black.

There are times when I think Caroline might be right. I put the pen down carefully and shook my head slowly. 'You're crazy, Adams.'

'True.' She nodded and twitched a shrug. 'But all things are relative. I don't, for instance, gut dogs as a hobby.'

'Neither,' I said pointedly, 'do the people who work for Medi-Gen. Professional killers do not spend their daytime hours working in a medical genetics lab.'

'No,' she agreed, 'but the one who pays the cash and gives the orders might well do.' She reached under the pile of papers and pulled out her notepad. 'Whoever killed Malcolm knew their way around the place.' She flipped open the pad. 'Look at this.'

On the top page was a map of the medical park: an outline of the perimeter wall and a rough diagram showing the layout of the buildings inside. On the page beneath was a detailed floor plan of an L-shaped, single-storey building. Offices and laboratories had been sketched in with minimal attention to detail. The doors and windows, on the other hand, had been drawn to scale and beside each one, sketched in red biro, was an alarm. A multicoloured wiring diagram had been scribbled to the right of the main sketch.

Lee turned the pad round for me to read and laid her thumb on one of the long, windowless rooms at the back of the building.

'This is Malcolm's lab. A technician found his body here at eight a.m. on Monday the fifteenth of August. Time of death estimated as Friday night or early Saturday morning. Either he was murdered in here or they killed him somewhere else and moved his body in afterwards. Whichever it was, they had to get past three alarms and a locked gate to do it.'

'Which means they had inside help?'

'I think so.'

'Or they had access to the same information as you?' I tapped at the map with the pen. 'If you can buy this, what's to stop half of Glasgow getting hold of it first?'

She shook her head 'It's not for sale.'

'Really? So how did you get it? Services rendered?'

There was a long gap and this time neither of us was pissing about. In the past, I never questioned her sources or their integrity. But things change and loyalties change and trust doesn't always come easily.

'I was owed a favour,' she said eventually. 'This is good and nobody else has a copy. I trust it. You don't have to come with me if you don't.'

Quite. People keep reminding me of my personal rights. I don't have to stay. I don't have to do anything. And if I do, it doesn't have to be something at this level of insanity. I could walk in the front gate tomorrow morning as a legitimate citizen, ask reasonable questions of reasonable people and reasonably expect to be given an answer. But then, if Lee is right, someone will pick up a phone, amend an order and Caroline will join the growing list of the dead. Or Lee. Or Janine. Or me.

The logic was perfectly pedestrian. I didn't have to like it. I just had to make a decision.

I stared at my fingernails and tossed mental coins.

Lee reached into her bag, drew out a bundle of black clothing. Black sweatshirt. Black leggings. Black trainers. Black gloves. Just like hers. She laid them on the table, on top of the pile of papers. A faint patch of white showed at the shoulder of the sweatshirt as if an old paint stain had been washed and washed again until it had almost gone. A triangular tear at one elbow had been stitched with surgical precision.

A wash of adrenalin hit the back of my neck and flowed, cold and unwelcome, down my spine.

'You really don't have to come,' she said carefully. 'I know what you said last time. But I brought you these in case you decided to change your mind.'

The half-pint of bitter sat on the table in front of me, untouched. I was, without question, totally, perfectly sober.

'You're going tonight?' I asked.

'Yes.'

'Now?'

'Yes.'

I picked up the sweatshirt and shook it out, eyeing it critically. 'Do you think it'll still fit?'

'I would think so,' she said mildly. 'You haven't changed much.'

'Only on the inside.'

'Not even there.' She picked up her bag and jacket from the chair. 'Especially not there. Come on. You can change in the back of the car on the way.'

Lee's car, strangely enough, is black. Every single one of her cars has been black, right from the beginning of the second year, when she blew an entire term's grant on a dying Renault 4 with no brakes and a dodgy clutch and spent the best part of a week on the respray. I don't think it has ever occurred to her that she might have one of a different colour. The reasoning has something to do with the desire to be inconspicuous. In real life a Saab 900i turbo is entirely visible whatever the colour, particularly to the average passing joy-rider, who can estimate the horsepower of any car at 500 paces on the basis of its silhouette alone. To reduce the risk, this particular model is fitted with an inordinate array of defence accessories, including a short-wave radio permanently tuned to the police waveband. I sat in the back, changing out of my day clothes into the sweatshirt and leggings, and listened to live dialogue from a raid on an illicit video copier.

We pulled up in an unpleasantly conspicuous side street about a block along from the rotting hulk of the Great Eastern Hotel: home in the old days to tramps and beggars and now, in the liberated nineties, to the teenage fall-out from the crack wars. In the dark and the rain it looked like a bad memory from Victorian London. There but for fortune.

I watched as a handful of differently conscious figures began to accumulate in the doorways. All of them could see the car and most of them looked aware enough to work out its street value.

Nodding a head in their general direction, I asked, 'How much do we pay them to keep their paws off?'

'Nothing.' Lee bent and stuffed the folder of Malcolm's papers under the passenger seat. 'They won't touch it.'

'Really?' I pulled on the gloves she had given me and thought twice about opening the rear door. 'What does it do? Forty thousand volts to the genitals?'

'Nice idea, but sadly, no.' She opened the door and held it for me to get out. 'But I bet you a tenner it will still be here when we get back.'

'Fine.' If she's lost the car, another ten pounds isn't going to make any significant difference.

Lee handed me a spare rucksack from the boot. I took a moment to adjust the straps before following her along the road away from the car.

'Is there an easy way in?' I asked, as we jogged steadily eastwards towards the medical park.

'More or less. Want to look?'

'Might be an idea.'

We paused in the orange glow of a streetlight and she produced the notepad from her rucksack. The ink ran slightly in the drizzle, blurring the outlines.

'Can you still abseil?' she asked.

'Of course.' Well, I could the last time I tried. It's not that difficult.

'Good. The external walls are alarmed with remote bells in the police station. If we touch the wrong place, the whole lot goes off. MacRae's in charge of the local law. We don't want to attract his attention.'

'Absolutely not.'

MacRae is Laidlaw's second in command. A pit bull terrier in human form, without a lead or a wire muzzle. Everywhere else it's illegal to take one on the streets. Here they put it in uniform, give it a gun and point it at the bad guys. That's us.

I examined the map. If we couldn't touch the wall, there was only one other way in. 'We're going in from the top, right?'

'Right.' She grinned cheerfully. 'It's dead easy. Whoever designed the place needs their head examining. Look.' She ran her finger along the route: up a fire escape on an adjacent derelict tenement block, across a roof, fix a rope to the safety bar on the top and abseil down half the length of the rope. First person swings across to the roof of the closest building inside the perimeter wire. Second person slides down the taut rope. Both take a second abseil to the ground. Easy.

Only one big flaw.

'How do we get out, Adams?' I asked.

'Disable the alarms and walk,' she said, wiping the rain from her eyes and giving me a look that took me back years. ' "Simple is safe".'

Simple is safe. It was our motto in the surgical wards. The real surgeons hate simple answers to simple problems, but in the perpetual battlefield of hospital medicine it kept a lot of innocent civilians alive.

More than that, it had become our rallying call in the face of the enemy. Adams and Stewart versus the rest of the world. The cold mass in my abdomen began to give way to a humming anticipation. The still, small voice of reason finally abandoned the unequal struggle to make itself heard.

'Okay, Dr Adams, let's go.'

We ran the rest of the way, keeping to the dark shadows away from the streetlights, jumping puddles and empty lager cans. It stopped raining as soon as we were out of sight of the Great Eastern.

The medical park was a high-tech oasis in the middle of a derelict urban wasteland. The perimeter wall looked imposing enough to the average bystander; solid brick about eight feet high with double-stranded wire on bent angle-iron at the top. A solid double gate prevented uninvited entry from the road.

Near the back wall, a tenement block more resilient than its neighbours rose three full storeys above the height of the Medi-Gen complex. Lee signalled me into a doorway at its base and we pulled on caps and gloves and tucked pen lights into holders stitched on the sleeves of the sweatshirts. Each rucksack carried a lightweight sit harness of the type sold for competition climbing and a thirty-metre length of narrow black rope with pale tape markings at metre intervals.

'Time?' I asked.

We checked our watches. Ten forty-five. Pub closing time at eleven. Just over fifteen minutes of relative peace and then the place would be crawling with folk looking for somewhere warm to sleep for the night. In the meantime it was quiet. And very dark.

We fitted the harnesses, slung the ropes across the top of the rucksacks and ran up the fire escape to the roof. From there, it was a quick crawl to the edge and a decent view of the buildings below.

Inside the wall, halogen lights shone at intervals in doorways and in the corridors between buildings, creating puddles of white in the darkness. The buildings were all of modern, architecturally correct design. Single-storey labs and offices in nice red and yellow brickwork with intriguingly reflective glass windows. Every roof was flat and most had skylights. Very inviting.

They were arranged in an ordered pattern, radiating out from a central, circular reception suite. Only one building – our target – sat apart from the rest, close to the outer wall, on the opposite side from the main entrance but with its own smaller gate giving direct access. Two sets of automatic barriers provided protection against uninvited guests.

I wondered how they managed to keep the journalists away from such a patently dodgy set-up and decided they must have a brilliant PR department. The thought of Malcolm Donnelly working there made my skin crawl.

We hit the first problem on the roof – no safety bar and so no obvious point to anchor the abseil. Minutes ran by as we rigged up a hanging belay off the edge of the building, using a loop cut from the second rope running back to a fixed block on the other side of the roof.

We both clipped on to the rope. Lee lay on her stomach and peered over the edge.

'Ten-foot gap. D'you want to belay or swing?'

'I'll swing.' I needed the practice.

'Fine.' She handed me a descender for the abseil and then lowered herself off the edge to a static point four feet below.

My palms began to sweat inside the gloves. I pulled them off with my teeth and wiped both hands on the sleeves of the sweatshirt. A patch of thin cloud moved slightly and a three-quarter moon heightened the shadows and lit Lee's face as she looked up and gave the rope two tugs for go.

I slid my hands back into the gloves and turned to face inwards, clipping the rope into my harness. Nerve. It's all a question of nerve. I looked up at the moon and thought of Tan and then of Bridget. Odd they should come in that order. The soles of my trainers gripped the bricks at the edge of the wall and I lowered over the side.

Four feet. I stopped and Lee switched the ropes so the fulcrum of the swing focused at her harness point – a lever to keep me away from the edge of the building and allow me to build up a pendulum.

'Go.' A voice in my ear.

I let the pressure off the rope and ran backwards down the wall in sliding six foot steps. It's fun once you remember how. At thirty-five feet I stopped and began to step sideways along the wall, drawing back as far as I could to give myself momentum on the swing. Kicking out, I pushed off from the side and swung out over the perimeter fence towards the flat roof below.

Too high, much too high. My feet clawed air a good ten feet above the landing point. I needed more length and less of a drop. I spun in the air, bringing my feet round to break the impact with the side of the tenement as I swung back.

Second go, eight feet lower. Further back along the wall and more of a kick.

Almost.

I cursed, silently but with feeling, as I grazed along the wall on the return swing. I am, without question, too old for this.

Third try lucky. I swung out over the target and released the rope, dropping down the last few feet to land clumsily on the roof top. It was not an elegant entry.

A balustrade of pale stone projected up an inch or two above the roof top. I sat down with my feet braced against it and fixed the free end of the rope into my harness loop before pulling it taut.

Two tugs for go.

Lee slid down feet first to land smoothly beside me.

'Well done.' She patted me gently on the back.

Very funny.

'Sure.' I left her to free up the first rope and began setting up the belay for the second abseil. This time the handle of the skylight provided a sensible anchor point and we were down to ground level in seconds.

The main door to the lab was round the corner. I left Lee coiling the rope and went to have a look. A single halogen light lit up the doorway, throwing harsh black shadows into the corners. Shadows that moved.

I froze in place, reaching out for Lee as she slid past. Putting my finger to her lips I jerked a nod at the furthest mass of shadow. She followed my gaze. Four blood-orange points glowed at us from the darkness and there was the very faintest of panting sounds.

Dogs.

'Shit.' She let the word through between her teeth on the outbreath.

Quite.

Dobermanns, two of them, standing about five feet apart. As we watched, they edged out into the circle of light, mouths open, tongues lolling gently, waiting. The noise of their panting was damply harsh in the quiet. The air smelled faintly of old meat and saliva.

A cloud slid briefly over the face of the moon again and when it cleared, they were another two feet closer. Still silent. Still waiting.

Ordinary dogs don't wait. Ordinary dogs take out people who drop into their nocturnal domain and they are not generally quiet about it. It takes a lot of work to train a dog to kill and then to persuade it to be silent and selective in the process; to get it to wait for the right move or word to trigger the attack. Or the right absence of a word.

I took one step forward and held up my hand. Both dogs exploded from a standing start to a full gallop, coming in an arrow formation with its apex on my jugular.

There wasn't time to think again. There was only time to

take one deep breath and take my voice as deep as it would go and say 'Diolch' in my best fake Welsh accent.

They stopped, both of them. To get two dogs to go from full gallop to a standstill on a single word takes a quite remarkable amount of work. There is only one man in the whole of Scotland who trains dogs that well. His name is Dafydd Thomas and he lives half a mile from the farm which Bridget and I bought together eight years ago. Seven and a half years ago, he helped me train up a new collie pup by the name of Tan.

'You're out of your tiny mind, Stewart. You know that?' Lee stepped up quietly, level with my shoulder. 'What the hell did you say?'

'Diolch. It means "thank you". It's Welsh.'

'Is that an intelligent thing to say to a dog that's going for your throat?'

'It is if it's one of Dafydd's Dobermanns. It's the only thing that'll stop them. He trains them to inverse commands.'

'In Welsh?'

'Yes.'

'Wonderful,' she said drily. 'I knew there was a good reason I brought you along.' She looked over their heads to the door. 'Do they roll over and die on command or do we stand here all night and wait for the handler to come back in the morning?'

The two dogs lay motionless on the ground, watching. I snapped a finger and told them politely to bugger off. In Welsh. They whined and grinned and trotted forwards to sit hopefully at my feet. I wasn't carrying doggy chocs, which was an unfortunate oversight, but they seemed happy enough with a pat on the head and a lot of overdone Anglo-Celtic insults.

Lee stepped past them carefully and went over to look at the door. It's more her style. When I finally joined her, she was holding her pen torch between her teeth, working at the lock.

'Okay?' she asked, as I took the torch from her mouth and focused it on her fingertips.

'Okay.' I nodded. 'They'll be all right as long as I come out first.'

'You're welcome.' She nodded absently, frowning at the lock.

'Did nobody give you the keys?' I asked.

'Nope.'

'Thoughtless of them.'

'Nearly as thoughtless as forgetting to tell me about the dogs.'

'Maybe you didn't owe someone a big enough favour.'

'Maybe not.'

The lock clicked and the door opened. We paused, waiting for the alarm, and when nothing happened slid inside, closing the door behind us.

Lee's map showed a fairly accurate floor plan. A cross marked the lab that used to be Malcolm's. Main corridor, down to the far end, third on the left. The inner door opened with less resistance than the first, letting us into a medium-sized office much like Lee's place in Pathology but bigger and more salubrious, although without, of course, quite the same view of the Kelvin Grove.

A Macintosh workstation with a double A4 screen occupied the main desk. A laser printer, a modem and a phone sat on a smaller desk beside it.

I opened the disk box at the side of the computer and began to read the labels.

'What do you suppose happened to Malcolm's disks?' I asked.

Lee was on the far side of the room, notebook in hand, working on another door. 'Does Caroline not have them?'

'Not that I know of.'

'Better find them then.' The door opened. She shone the fine torch-beam inside. 'Right. This is the lab. You check for the disks. I'll go through here.'

None of the disks was labelled in Malcolm's writing. I searched through the desk and surrounding cupboards looking for more. There were a couple of spare packs in a wall cupboard but the seals were unbroken.

The rest of the office yielded nothing. No papers in progress, no letters, no rubbish in the bin, no pens on the desk. The coffee rings on the desk top were old, which was odd. Even computer freaks drink coffee.

The filing cabinet was locked. I fiddled with it briefly but cracking locks was never one of my strong points.

I turned back to the disks in the tray. One or two had printed labels with out-of-date program titles: Statview, Word 3.0, File-maker Pro 1.0. Nothing out of the ordinary for the average overpaid research scientist. Most of the rest had a single three-letter label with no indication of the contents of the files: MIC. FRG. HAM. HEN.

Hen. I reached round to the back of the machine and found the power switch by feel. The machine bleeped quietly to itself and hummed to life. I fed in the disk, drumming my fingers quietly on the desk while it went through the start-up routine, and opened a file at random.

Bingo. A hatching log of temperatures and humidities for sixty eggs. Sixty eggs mean sixty chickens and chickens are part of the jigsaw.

I contemplated taking the entire disk tray home, but the whole idea was not to let anyone know we had been. Super-tidy, anally retentive computer freaks notice disks that go missing by the boxload, even if they don't drink coffee. They might notice less, of course, if the missing disks are unused.

There were twenty blank double-sided, high-density disks in the cupboard above my head and eighteen worth taking in the tray on the desk. I sat down on the ergonomic office chair and began the tedious job of copying.

Floppy disk into drive, copy to hard disk, new disk in, copy from hard disk. Next disk. Eighteen disks packed full of hard data and research papers. One of them had to say something useful. All I had to do was find out which one.

Eighteen high-density disks, two minutes' copy time each, thirty-six minutes.

Six disks down the line, the novelty value began to wear off in a big way. I checked my watch: eleven thirty. We were pushing too many limits to be safe. I stared at the screen, willing it to go faster. The screen stared back and the disk drive chuntered at the same, monotonous, steady pace. I stared harder at the screen and began reading the files on the hard disk. Files with names like 'MDD letters'. Malcolm Daniel Donnelly. Letter file. Jackpot.

And a new problem. The hard disk held several hundred megabytes of memory and a lot of it was used. It would take dozens of floppies and several hours to copy it and there was nowhere near enough time to read it all and decide which files were useful and which could be left.

A pencil torch flickered in the door away to my left. 'Kellen! Come and see this.'

I shoved a new disk into the external drive. 'Bugger off. I'm busy.'

Lee appeared like an errant poltergeist at my elbow. 'What have you got?'

'A locked filing cabinet. Can you open it?'

"Spect so.' She fiddled with the lock. It made a satisfying chunk and a drawer slid open. 'Ask and it shall be given.' A smile in the darkness. Arrogant brat. She began to rifle through the drawers. 'What else have you got?'

'Goldmine.' I showed her the HEN disk. 'Hen equals chicken equals bantam.'

'Oh. That's nice,' she said. 'Want to see where they come from?'

Utterly arrogant brat.

A lab is a lab the world over. White, aseptic and boring, unless you enjoy watching mould grow on bits of glass or water drip down a pipette. Personally, I'd rather live my life for real, but some folk enjoy it.

This lab was like all the others – except that one of the benches was not a real bench. It looked fairly real to the average bystander – white lab-cote top with figures scrawled on in biro, cupboards ranged underneath and a clutter of lab stools around it. Undoubtedly, if I was the average health and safety officer walking past I would have said something useful about the state of the paintwork but very little else. But Lee got there first and shoved her palms under the top lifting it slightly and sliding it smoothly backwards to reveal a carefully constructed cavity that took up the entire area of the bench. Inside that was a silvered steel cabinet with water pipes running in from one end and an array of dials and lights on the top.

I stared at it in fascination 'What is this?'

'It looks like an incubator to me,' she said, stating the obvious. 'Unless there's something else I haven't found, there's only eggs inside and none of them are close to hatching.'

'Is this what we're after?'

'There's nothing else worth looking at.'

'Have you taken any eggs?'

'Of course.' She hefted her rucksack. 'From the middle of the stack. It'll be a while before they notice they're gone.' She reached over and pulled the false bench top back into place. 'The rest of the lab is clear.' She looked up at the clock on the wall. Eleven forty-five. 'Closing time was almost an hour ago. The streets should be fairly quiet by now. Shall we go?'

'Good idea.'

We walked back to the computer, which waited patiently for the next instruction.

I swapped the disks and copied the files, thinking hard. 'You didn't find any spare disks?' I asked.

'No.' Lee was working her way through the filing cabinet. 'But there are other offices. They probably all have Macs. I could find you some. How many do you need?'

'About three dozen. But there isn't time even if you find some spares.' I left the machine to do its work and switched on the modem, checking that the telephone wire at the back was plugged into the wall socket. 'Can you hack into one of these?'

'Nope. Never tried. Can you?'

'No. But I know a woman who can.' I pulled the last disk from the drive, opened the communications software that activated the modem and gave access to the hard disk, and then dimmed the screen to black. From a distance, it looked as if the machine was switched off. Risky, but I couldn't think of any other way.

The telephone number and extension code were printed on the phone. I found a pen and scribbled both on to the back of my hand, checking it twice before nodding to Lee. 'Okay, partner. Let's get the hell out of here.'

Two Dobermanns blinked at us sleepily as we slipped out through the main door. The male gave a low, husky cough and wrinkled an upper lip in greeting. They escorted us to the perimeter gates after Lee had found the control box for the pressure alarms and thrown the switch. She locked the main gates behind us and I pushed an arm through to pat the big dog on the head. He wriggled his rump and nudged at my hand with his nose. Friends for life.

We ran carefully up the fire escape of the old tenement and dismantled the rope belay from the top without intruding on anyone's reality. If there were people in there, they were all asleep.

The car was where we had left it. Intact.

'You owe me a tenner,' said Lee, throwing the rucksacks in the back.

'In that case, you can let me drive,' I said and nearly touched the door handle. 'Once you've disabled the traps.'

'No traps, partner.' She smiled and unlocked the door for me. 'I just switched the plates to Laidlaw's numbers. His car's the same as this one. Even the crack-heads wouldn't mess with him.'

I looked at the yellow plates glowing dimly in the sodium glare of the street light: L999 SCC.

SCC. Strathclyde Central Constabulary.

'The arrogant bastard.'

'Quite.' Lee fished a plastic bag from under the front seats and handed me a screwdriver. 'Here. There's a single screw, top and bottom. You take those off. I'll put the new ones on.'

It took us less than five minutes to complete the change. The replacement plates were grubby, anonymous and entirely unmemorable.

Simple is safe.

I drove slowly back through the deserted streets to the flat.

CHAPTER FOUR

I woke the next morning, alone in the bed, with the duvet wrapped round me like a silkworm's cocoon. Janine was long gone. Her clothes, which had been piled neatly on the chair when I got into bed, had disappeared and I could hear the noise of the washing machine spinning away in the background. A mug of stone-cold coffee with a skin on it like school custard sat in mute accusation on the bedside table and the sun glared through the gap in the curtains.

I sat up and stretched experimentally. My body felt as if I had been run over by a joy-rider in a road roller. Muscles I hadn't used in years panicked and seized solid as I rolled carefully out of bed. Over-stretched joints jagged with incipient arthritis and the palms of my hands ached hotly with sub-clinical rope burn.

You would think I would know better by my age.

I collected my dressing gown from the back of the door and made my way through the living room, past the debris of two take-away meals, to the shower. Probes of hot water sought out a selection of cuts and grazes collected during the night and filled them with acid before soothing them out into a dull throb. A gash on my forearm bled freely and I spent several minutes trying to wash my hair left-handed before giving up and sploshing across the bathroom floor to find a waterproof dressing.

Ten minutes later, with dry hair, clean clothes, a fresh plaster and a body that moved more or less as nature intended, I felt fit to face the rest of the world.

The rest of the world was not greatly in evidence. I found Janine, eventually, in the bedroom, folding her work clothes with obsessive precision and arranging them with care in the largest of her three suitcases.

'Where's Caroline?' I asked.

'Gone to the farm. The horses needed feeding and we weren't sure if you were going to surface this side of tomorrow. She took the hens with her.' My lover paused in her folding and looked me in the eye. 'Before they wrecked anything else.'

Ominous.

'I left them in a pen,' I said.

'So I noticed.' Her eyebrows arced beyond her hairline. 'I think you forgot to put a lid on it.'

Ah.

'Have they done a lot of damage?'

'Depends on your point of view.' She turned round to pull a silk suit from the wardrobe behind her. 'They trashed most of the floppies and the keyboards are completely glued up with chicken shit.' She smiled thinly, like a lioness on point. 'I suppose, under the circumstances, we should consider ourselves lucky.'

I suppose we should. I suppose also that I should ask about insurance. Or offer to pay. Or both.

Later perhaps. When she's feeling less aggrieved. Or when she has finished packing. If she's still here.

I sat on the bed, hugging my knees up to my chin, and watched my lover empty the contents of her bedside drawer into a small box with an odd sinking sensation somewhere below my diaphragm.

'What's going on, Jan?'

She closed the box with exaggerated care, sealing it carefully with two loops of Sellotape before she looked up. 'Rae's looking for someone else to share the flat,' she said carefully.

'I'm sorry?'

'Rae's looking for someone . . .'

'Yes. I heard. Are you going?'

'Yes.'

'Could you tell me why?'

'Because one of us has to do something and since it's obviously not going to be you, then it has to be me.'

Really? You don't come up with lines like that off the top of your head. 'You can come up with something better than that, surely?'

'All right.' She put the box down and sat on the floor beside it. 'When you went to the States,' she said, 'you gave me your word that we would talk when you got back. You're back. I haven't noticed any burning urgency even to share a cup of coffee.'

'Yes, I know. I'm sorry . . . There hasn't been time . . .'

'How long have you been home, Kellen?'

I counted up on my fingers. 'A fortnight?'

'Ten days,' she corrected. 'And ten nights. How many of those have you spent here?'

'I was here last night.'

'You got in after three o'clock this morning, Kellen. It's not what I'd call a normal night in. And I didn't hear you say anything.'

'I thought you were asleep.'

'Sure you did.' She picked up the box and left the room. I followed her out on to the landing, where she added it to a pile that started with her other two suitcases. I didn't think I'd been in the shower that long.

'Look – ' I stood with my back to the door, blocking the way

107

back inside. 'You're not serious. You can't honestly believe that going back to Rae is going to solve anything.'

'It'll do for just now.' She rearranged the pile of boxes. 'Unless you wanted to talk?'

'Now?'

'If you talk, I'll stay.'

Bloody hell. I don't believe this is happening.

I looked at my watch. Eleven twenty-five.

'Look. Can I have two hours? The police want to interview Caroline at the farm. I've got to talk to her first. Really. I'll come back as soon as they've left.'

'Fine.' She put a hand on my shoulder and moved me carefully out of the way. 'I'll be at Rae's,' she said, stepping past me into the living room. 'When you think you know what you want, you can call me. I'm sure you still know the number.'

And that was it.

The traffic on the Great Western Road was abysmal. I tried every back route I could, cut all the corners that were there to be cut and jumped most of the ten sets of lights along the way. It was a particularly cathartic journey but not especially useful. I was still late.

I drove flat out down the last half-mile of the lane and spun round the final bend, only to see the gate hanging open and a familiar blue Land Rover parked tidily beside Bridget's Rover.

The temptation to turn the car round and head for home was overwhelming. Or even to turn it round, head for the airport and get on a plane back to Oregon. But a lingering sense of promises made and a rather more pressing sense of innate loyalty got me through the gate and out of the car before my nerve broke. The cost of early conditioning.

I coasted the car to a relatively quiet halt beside the pond and took one of the less noisy routes across the yard. It wasn't exactly intentional but there seemed no need to advertise my presence unduly.

The back door, like the gate, hung open. Inside, Inspector MacDonald stood with his back to the breakfast counter, looking like a man on the verge. Caroline was standing opposite him, with her back to the fire, quite clearly the one who was driving him there. All I could see of Elspeth Philips was the back of her head, low in the fireside chair, well out of the way. Down on the floor, Ashwood crouched with his ears flat to his head and his eyes slitted to nothing. A cat with a problem.

The conversation was nearing its natural end. Caroline glared at MacDonald from the fireplace. 'What *exactly* are you asking, Inspector?'

She learned that tone from her mother. It was one of her best.

I watched the Inspector take in a single deep breath.

Go for it, man.

'Ms Leader, is there any reason at all why Ms Donnelly might have killed herself? Or tried to make it look as if she had?'

There was a long, long silence. The cat twitched its ears and left. The fire crackled with unpleasant ferocity. A tap dripped on to the stainless-steel sink at irregular intervals.

I waited and forgot to breathe.

'No,' said Caroline Leader eventually and with absolute finality. 'It's not possible.'

Even the police have to believe something as solid as that.

That was probably a good cue for an entry but there seemed no real need to intervene. I took myself outside to talk to the horses and waited for those inside to sort themselves out. It didn't take long.

MacDonald came out first, running a weary hand through his hair. There was a short gap and then he was followed by Elspeth Philips and Caroline walking side by side, black hair and blonde: a pair of non-identical twins. The WPC was dressed in a different kind of uniform: jeans and a loose-fitting shirt, both in regulation blue – the soft, unconstrained approach, carefully tailored to provide solace and support for the newly bereaved. I'm sure it made all the difference at the time.

Caroline herself looked over-bright. Sharp-edged teeth in a sharp-edged smile and a difficult tilt to her head. A woman genuinely pushed to the edge and holding on too tight.

In all the rest, I forget at times that she has lost her lover too. She doesn't need this.

I let MacDonald reach the safety of his cab before I left the horses and wandered over.

'How did it go?'

'Dr Stewart.' The nod was fairly amiable under the circumstances. 'Your friend is a very forceful woman.'

'I know. I'm sorry. I meant to talk to her first.'

'It's all right. Somebody had to do it.'

'Did she say anything useful?'

'Not that I noticed, no. I think perhaps we need to talk to her another time when she's feeling less ... excitable.' He sounded faintly amused. A man of iron constitution.

'Do you think it'll help?'

'No. But we'll need a couple more facts for the inquest. Nothing big. I'll call round some other time.' He held the door open for his colleague, who managed a remarkably human smile as she jumped up into the cab. Very resilient, the two of them.

I joined Caroline at the fence as the Land Rover vanished up the lane. The horses had separated into small cliques and were spread out across the paddock grazing, gossiping or sleeping, according to temperament. Midnight and Balder wandered over to the gate to frisk us for nibbles, but the rest barely noticed our existence. Caroline hid herself behind Balder and began pulling the knots from his mane.

'Nice to be needed, huh?' I said. It wasn't addressed to anyone in particular. I scratched Midnight idly behind the ears.

'We could bring them back into the barn,' suggested Caroline, invisible behind Balder's massive head.

'I think they're safer out here.' I knelt down to check the state of the defences. 'As long as we can find a new chain for the gate. This one's too easy to break. We're going to have to tighten up the security in the next day or two if we're going to stay here for long.'

There was a slightly blank pause and I felt her go still. Balder snickered quietly and turned his head to lip at her hair.

'Are you expecting more trouble?' The question came more lightly than it might have done.

'I've no idea,' I said. 'But there's no point in taking chances.'

Caroline slid back to lean on the horse's withers so that she could see me properly. She was dressed in washed-out jeans and the old lumberjack shirt with too much blue in it for the pale of her face. Her fine blonde hair stuck out at odd angles where it had defeated the morning's token comb-through. She was draped like a rag doll across her horse, with both fists full of pulled horse hair, and her eyes were so screwed up against the light that it was impossible even to see what colour they were. But she has a degree in organic chemistry and four years in the country hasn't stopped her mind from working the way it used to.

'What's happening, Kellen?' she asked, and there wasn't a lot of compromise in the question.

I leant across and touched her lightly on the shoulder. 'Let's go somewhere else.'

We tried the orchard. Even in September, with the apples rotting to moulded cider on the grass and inebriated wasps holding orgies on every branch, it's still a good place for sorting things out. I slid down with my back to a pear tree, leaving Malcolm's rope swing for Caroline.

She hitched herself on to the lower loop and swayed for a while in silence.

'Why didn't you tell me?' she asked eventually.

'I didn't get here in time.'

'Oh.'

More silence.

'She didn't do it.'

'I know.'

'How?'

Good question.

'Do you want the easy answer?'

'No.' The rope swing stopped. 'I want the truth.'

So I gave her the truth. Or at least as much of it as was sane without compromising Lee. I told her everything I knew about Lee's post-mortem and about Malcolm's decision to donate his body to anatomy and about the odd recurrence of hens in an otherwise ill-fitting picture. I told her about the evening in the pathology block and the cleared records and what I thought of what Malcolm had done. I told her about temazepam and what it was for and what it could and couldn't do, and how much Bridget was supposed to have taken without leaving any empties. By the time I finished, she knew almost as much as I did and if the gaps were visible, she didn't say. She asked the obvious questions and thought her way through the obvious logical paths and, at the end, she came to the same blank wall as the rest of us.

'What do you want to do?' I asked, when we had sat together in silence for a while.

'Get on with living,' she said flatly, 'that's what it's all about, isn't it? The Stewart life plan. Live. Learn. Keep living.'

'Something like that.' I'm not over-keen on having my own home-spun philosophy thrown back at me. 'Do you still want me here?'

'Mmm.' A classic Leader non-answer. She swung for a while, staring silently into the middle distance, weighing things up.

Then she stood up and flipped the back-door key from her pocket.

'Coffee?' she asked, as if there was nothing else that mattered in the world.

The kitchen was as pin-neat as Lee had left it, barring the three empty coffee mugs in the sink. There was a pervading smell of damp cat covering what might have been left of the blood and peat smoke.

Caroline worked on the Rayburn and I tackled the fire. Half an hour later we were sitting in the big chairs on opposite sides of the fire, nursing mugs of fresh coffee.

'So?' I asked again. 'You've had time to think. Do you want me to stay?'

'Is it safe for either of us to stay?'

'I think it's probably as safe as anywhere. We need to sort out the locks and do something about the gate to the paddock.'

'And find somewhere safer to put the chickens?'

Quite.

'I think it would help if we had someone else here,' I suggested.

'Janine?'

'Hardly.'

Caroline lowered her mug to her lap and cocked her head on one side, appraising again. She walked to the window, picked the portable phone off the bench and held it out to me. 'You want Lee Adams here too. Right?'

Right.

Lee was out of the office and not answering her bleep, neither of which was altogether surprising on a routine Saturday. On a Saturday after a distinctly non-routine Friday night, it was tedious, largely because I had no home number and therefore no way of finding where she was, how she was or what she was doing with the disks and the eggs we had retrieved from Malcolm's lab.

The answer-phone in her office was polite but useless. The duty secretary at the Pathology desk had a lilting, sing-song voice that sounded as if her brain was firmly locked in the Mills and Boon alternative universe, but she did repeat my message back word perfect and promised to deliver it the moment Dr Adams set foot anywhere inside the hospital complex.

I tried to think positive thoughts about the wider sisterhood, failed and hung up, feeling frustrated.

Caroline watched from her chair by the fire, her features relaxing into something close to amusement. One eyebrow angled upwards and in the flickering light she looked exactly like my mother, hearing the words and listening to the meaning underneath. Only Mother didn't always hear the meaning that was meant.

'Do you need her that badly?' she asked.

'Not particularly. But she has all the available evidence and I think we're losing time.'

'We could fix the locks,' suggested Caroline. 'It'll take a while. She might be in by the time we're finished.'

Fitting new mortise locks on the front and back doors took us into the late afternoon. Bridget was the kind of person who kept a spare set in a numbered cabinet – just in case. The tools were all in the back of the shed, clean and oiled from the last time she built a fence or fixed a loose box.

It was relaxing work. Caroline unscrewed the old locks and measured up the new ones. I sharpened the chisels, more for the feel of smooth metal on the whetstone than because they weren't sharp, and cut the grooves for the metal insets.

Each lock came with comprehensive fitting instructions but we added a couple of variations I had learned from Lee in the hope of dissuading the average passing house-breaker.

In all honesty, they were more for psychological protection than anything else. Nothing short of a minefield would keep out the real professionals for long but there seemed no harm in encouraging a siege mentality for a while.

The cats came through, one by one, in the coffee breaks, picking their way delicately over the piles of curled wood shavings and discarded screws to check that the cat flap on the back door was still there and still worked.

In the last hour before the light left, I dug around in the wood store and found enough spare timber to make the chicken shed at the end of the barn virtually impregnable. They could set fire to it, given enough petrol, but no one was likely to be able to break into it again.

When I was happy with the results, I released the two bantams from their incarceration in the back of my car and returned them to their original home with enough food and water to keep them happy till the millennium.

It felt almost like the old days.

The smell of goulash wafted past me as I kicked my boots off outside the back door and carried me back the final few steps into the past. I walked into the kitchen with my mind full and my mouth open, ready to tell Bride that the horses were in and the chickens were fed and that what we really needed was to build another line of boxes at the back of the barn. But Tan never moved from the fireside and when the steam cleared from the space round the Rayburn, the figure was blonde, not dark and the smile was that of a friend and not of a lover.

'Hi. Chickens all right?' Caroline backed out of the haze and came round the end of the breakfast bar with a couple of glasses and a bottle. 'I found some wine. I thought we could . . .' The smile died on her face. 'What's up?'

'Nothing.'

'It doesn't look like nothing.'

'It's nothing important. Don't worry.'

I uncorked the wine and poured two glasses without spilling

anything which was a reasonable achievement under the circumstances.

'Here.' I handed her a glass. 'What are we drinking to?'

She thought for a moment with her eyes on mine. She doesn't read far below the surface, but she has known me for years and she isn't stupid.

'A safe future?' she offered.

I hope so.

'All right.' I brought my glass up to touch hers. 'A safe future.'

A pan lid rattled on the Rayburn and the frown deepened slightly. 'Does burnt goulash count as safe?'

'Of course.' I managed a smile. 'As long as it's not one of mine.'

Her smile matched mine. 'Even I wouldn't ask you to take that kind of risk.'

The tension cleared over the next half-hour as we set the table and dinner, when it came, was relaxed and sleepy, the way it is after a day's hard work. We fell back gradually into the patterns of years ago, drawing back old memories and reforging old links.

As the fire settled down into a heap of glowing peat ash, we moved on into more recent times, filling in the gaps from the past four years.

By the time we reached the coffee, we were more or less up to date with each other's present circumstances. I knew more of the recent details of the business than had ever come through the monthly statements from the accountant laying out my share of the profits. Caroline knew what little there was to know about the Counselling Centre and about the regular trips to larger centres in Oregon, where the annual training courses were held. We still fought shy of the people in our lives – still too many unhealed wounds there – but we shared new ideas and our new ways of looking at the world and slowly talked ourselves back into the way things had been when we knew each other as friends.

We cleared the table together and I turned on the taps to wash up. Same fair distribution of labour as ever. I hate cooking; everyone else in my life hates cleaning. I worked out the balance a long time ago. As long as everyone knows where we're at, it works out well.

Caroline came and sat on the stool at the end of the breakfast bar and watched me work my way through her dirty pans. There's something about not facing each other across a table that makes things easier to deal with. And filthy saucepans give the fingers something else to do.

There was a file in a pot on the breakfast counter. She began to shorten a set of very short nails. 'Did Janine get a chance to talk to you this morning?' she asked.

'Not really. I didn't have time.' The pan responded to a wire pad and a lot of scrubbing.

'Has she gone to Rae's?'

'Apparently so.' I dumped the pan on the rack and started on the lid.

'Will she come back?'

'I don't know.'

'Do you want her to?'

'Pass.' I gave up the pretence and turned round so that I could see her. 'I was supposed to be thinking about it in Oregon. It's one of the reasons I went away.'

'And?'

How should I know?

'There's a kind of peace in being single,' I said. 'I think it might be easier to go back to that for a while.'

Caroline dropped the nailfile back in the pot, her gaze oddly focused. 'Did it hurt that much, losing Lyn?' she asked carefully.

'No. It hurt that much losing Bridget.' I dried my hands on a tea-towel and threw it in a crumpled heap on top of the Rayburn.

117

'We all make mistakes. Just that mine tend to be more permanent than most.' I manufactured a smile from nowhere. I don't imagine it was very convincing. 'Can we drop this? Please.'

My successor-in-love put an elbow on the counter and propped her chin on her hand, watching me try to brush off the past. She looked across at me, shaking her head slowly from side to side.

'How long did it last,' she asked quietly, 'you and Lyn?'

'Six months.' I shook my head, counting. 'Less. We split about two days after I heard you were with Bridget.'

'You should have called.'

'She told me not to.'

'And you believed her?' That drew a real smile. 'Are you really that stupid?'

Yes.

Caroline turned sideways to stare out of the small leaded window over the sink. One narrow hand threaded a strand of blonde hair into the gap behind her ear.

The silence between us waited for an acknowledgement.

'You should have called,' she said and left it at that.

We put the rest of the dishes away together, Caroline showed me the places where things were not exactly as they used to be and then brought a book down from the bedroom. I brought Malcolm's notes through from the study and we settled down, each in our own world, while the questions lay unanswered and the dust of the past settled back, as it should, almost to where it had been before.

Late on, the high-pitched, tinny sound of a small engine, not quite tuned, clattered through the still evening air and there was a tentative crunch on the gravel outside.

'Lee?'

'Should be.' I pushed a mass of cats sideways on the Rayburn and put the kettle back on to boil.

Caroline walked to the window and peered carefully through one side of the curtains.

'If it's Ms Psycho,' she said, 'she's gone seriously downmarket. That's a 2CV. And it's white.'

Lee wouldn't drive a 2CV if it was the last car left on earth.

'You sure? We don't know anyone who drives one of those.' I left the kettle on the hot plate and killed the lights above the mantelpiece, leaving the orange glow of the fire as the only light in the room.

'Yes, we do,' said Caroline, letting the curtain drop. 'It's your friendly policeman.'

Inspector MacDonald waited patiently outside the back door while we found the right keys to the right locks and remembered which directions to turn them in.

When we finally pulled the door open, he was huddled down on the mat with a green oiled jacket pulled round his shoulders against the wind, talking to the ground.

'Inspector?'

I knelt down to eye height and saw a scrawny black she-cat coiling itself round his fisherman's boots, purring like a cross-cut saw.

He stood up and the cat pushed past me into the house, leaving him on the doorstep, shifting slightly from one foot to the other.

'Evening, ladies,' He nodded to us both. 'A lovely evening for the time of year.'

Oh. Right.

He wasn't even in uniform. Back in his fisherman's outfit, looking like a rustic version of the man from Milk Tray. I wondered for a moment whether he had completely misunderstood the relationship patterns and whether Caroline would be better at putting things straight.

The kettle began to sing to itself on the Rayburn and I was about to invite him in for coffee when he turned back towards the car, put his fingers to his lips and whistled – a low, looping note, like a questing owl.

Or the call to heel of a sheepdog.

It appeared as a shadow at his heel. A scruffy, half-grown pup: white, blotched with pale red patches, like an anaemic, piebald fox with a brindled mask and a black tip to the scragged tail and big, bat-wing ears that focused like sonar cups.

And eyes. Mesmeric, spine-tingling eyes. One glowed amber and burned like a searchlight in the fire-glow from the kitchen. Impossible to hide from.

The other was the pale, pale blue of the sky after rain and as reflective as glass. Impossible to see what lay underneath.

Less than a hundred years ago, they would have drowned this dog at birth for her eyes alone and, looking at her standing there in the darkness on my back porch, generations of racial memories tugged at the forefront of my mind, reminding me why. Eyes like that see straight through your soul and out the other side. It's not a comfortable feeling.

The Inspector twitched a finger and the dog sat, moving her haunches without moving her eyes.

'You'll be needing another dog if you're planning on staying,' he said, as a matter of fact and not of debate. 'My brother's bitch had pups half a year back and this one was left. I was going to take her on, but then I thought that maybe you would be needing her more.'

Not this one. I prefer to keep the contents of my mind to myself.

I shook my head. 'We're staying. But we couldn't . . .'

'Of course we could. Why not?' Caroline knelt beside me on the step and the dog stretched out its nose to nudge her hand, like any normal pup. 'It's a really kind offer. She's gorgeous.'

Hardly.

'No.'

'It's a bitch,' he said, unnecessarily.

Strangely, gender is not the issue.

'No. I'm sorry. It's too soon.'

The dog put its chin on her knee and Caroline ran her hand over its head, pulling gently at the oversized ears.

'Don't listen to her,' she told it. 'I'll take care of you.'

'How?' I resorted to basic brutality. 'We've lost one dog already this week. What makes you think we can look after this one any better?'

'I wouldn't worry about that. She can look after herself.' MacDonald smiled enigmatically and failed to elaborate.

The dog lay flat at another hand command and the man played his trump card.

'She's called Tîr,' he said. And then, in case I didn't make the link, 'From Tîr na'n Og.'

Caroline made the link. She looked up, smiling, her eyes clear, and explained it for me. 'That's it then. Tîr na'n Og. The Land of Youth. It's what Bridget used to call the old grave mound with the cairn in the beech wood. It was Tan's favourite place. We have to take her, Kellen. It's perfect.'

Really.

I looked at the dog and the dog looked back and I don't think either of us was particularly happy with the way things were moving. But we weren't about to turn and swim against the tide either.

Besides, not all that long ago, they would have drowned me too. If I was lucky.

'Right. Thank you.' I nodded defeat to the Inspector, who accepted with due grace. 'As long as the cats are happy.'

I turned on my heel and led the way back into the kitchen, just as the kettle finally blew its top.

The cats were cool. The cats were so cool they let me rescue the screaming kettle and make three coffees around them and they stayed, riveted to the top of the Rayburn, in various postures of extreme relaxation, all of which happened to be in full sight of the uninvited incomer.

The dog migrated by instinct to Tan's place by the fire and lay there in dignified silence with both eyes closed, waiting.

The Inspector followed me over to the small kitchen space behind the breakfast bar and leant against the sink with his back to the window, watching me measure out the coffee grounds and spill the milk.

'I had a look at the lass's medical records,' he said, when I had finally produced a drinkable dose of caffeine.

'And?'

'She had a cervical smear test every three years. Anti-tetanus once in a while. Nothing else.'

'No one prescribed any temazepam?'

'If they did, they didn't write it down.' He held the mug cupped in both hands and blew across the top. 'Checked the other one too,' he said carefully, 'nothing there either. Clean, the two of them.'

Neither of us looked at Caroline and the woman herself, if she was listening, was very discreet about it.

'So where did she get them?'

'That's the question, Dr Stewart.' I couldn't see his face but his voice held only the mildest curiosity. 'Where did she get them? Why did she take them? And then where did she put the container afterwards?'

Who knows?

'You could always ask Caroline.'

'Aye. But you heard what she said the other day. She doesn't believe the lassie did it.'

'And you?'

'I'll believe what's there to believe until I see something different.'

We both watched Ashwood yawn widely and unroll down the side of the Rayburn.

MacDonald finished his coffee. He turned to swill out the mug in the sink behind him. Under cover of the running water he said, 'There was a break-in last night at the place her brother used to work.'

The cat lay down with his nose a hand's length from the dog and then he too closed his eyes.

'Really?' I kept my eyes on the dog. 'Did they get anything useful?'

'Nothing reported missing. Chief Inspector Laidlaw's not best pleased, though.'

'I can imagine.'

He switched off the tap and the final few drops splashed noisily on the stainless steel in the sudden silence.

I stood with my back against the warmth of the Rayburn and said nothing because there was nothing to say.

The Inspector eyed me for a long, silent moment, then smiled, a little sadly, and looked away.

We lapsed back into silence, watching the non-event happening by the fireside.

Dog and cat opened their eyes and locked in ocular combat.

It was an even match. Ashwood is not the kind of cat that would have survived long in the witch-hunts either.

Tension grew, like static electricity, until the atmosphere tingled, then collapsed away as if suddenly earthed, and the remainder of the cat pack slid down from the safety of the high ground, one at a time, to assemble round the fire for the routine introductions.

Caroline broke the verbal deadlock.

'Looks like the cats are happy,' she said, with the accent on cats.

'Looks like the pup has a new home.' I began to clear up the space around the Rayburn. Pointless exercise, but it kept my hands busy.

'Aye.' MacDonald sounded flat, and suddenly very tired. He wanted something more. In many ways, he deserved something more. But I had nothing I could safely give.

He gave a small huff of irritation and stood up, pulling out a wad of paper from his hip pocket.

'This is the pedigree for the pup,' he said, holding it out to me. 'Her parents are both good working dogs and she's training up fine. And this – ' he produced a tattered page, covered in scribbles, from an official police notebook – 'is her feeding plan.' It went on the breakfast bar. 'She's on four feeds a day still. I've brought a bag of the puppy meal to keep you going till Monday. After that, McFarlane in the village has all the things you need and he'll keep you good lamb bones when she's older as long as you take her in to see him once in a while. He owns the sire.'

He eased himself away from the sink and headed for the door, brushing through the cats and bending down to give his dog a quick pat on the way past. In the doorway he paused and looked back.

'And mind, when she has pups, I want first pick of the litter.'

'You've got it.'

Bitch puppies never go last from any litter. Especially not ones with working champions all the way down both sides of the pedigree, whatever their eyes are like.

CHAPTER FIVE

Old farmhouses are prone to cold and damp and this one is no exception. The spare bedroom is hidden under the eaves at the back of the house, as far away from the spreading warmth of the Rayburn and the chimney stack as you can get, and neither the slanting windows in the roof nor the big one in the side wall has ever fitted particularly well. On a sunny morning, it is a beautiful place to sit and look out over the fields, but as a place to sleep it has serious drawbacks.

In my day, we let visitors have the big bed in the double room and Bride and I slept on a mattress in front of the fire, feeling like kids on an adventure holiday and acting about the same. I can't remember a time when we needed to open up the spare room. From the reek of damp wood and the feel as I opened the door, that hadn't changed much after I left either. Unless they never had any visitors, which is always possible. Whatever the case, in its present state, the room was close to being uninhabitable.

As soon as the Inspector was safely out of the drive, we left the animals to introduce themselves in peace and went upstairs to begin changing it back from a junk room into a bedroom, so we could each have somewhere to sleep.

125

The saving grace was the fireplace on the inside wall. The grate was blocked over but the chimney was clear and it was still more or less possible to light a fire after we had spent the best part of an hour moving cardboard boxes full of Caroline's old college files and most of her childhood memorabilia up to the attic. To be fair, not all of the junk was hers. One or two of the boxes had a 'K' scribbled on the side; the ones I had meant to come back for one day and never quite remembered.

With the fire going and the doors and windows open, the room came to life. I found a set of flame yellow sheets and a primrose printed duvet cover in the airing cupboard and began to make up the bed.

It was a somewhat academic process. If Lee failed to appear at least one of us was going to have to stay awake all night and the odds were that one would be me. I thought so at any rate. Caroline was less convinced, but then she believed in the power of the mortise locks.

She followed me as I carried the bedding through to the room and watched as I wrestled with the pillowcases.

'When was the last time you had a decent night's sleep, Kellen?' she asked, tucking in the bottom sheet. 'You can't stay awake for ever.'

I spat out a mouthful of cased pillow, tossed it on to the bed and handed her one end of the duvet cover.

'No problem. I can watch the dog learning how to be a cat. Wouldn't miss it for worlds.' We fitted the duvet into the cover and threw that too on to the bed. 'One of us has to stay up, just in case our friend with the knife comes back. It may as well be me.'

Caroline sat on the end of the bed and folded her legs into a respectable half-lotus. Very impressive.

'I want to do my share, Kellen.' She sounded serious.

My dear, you have no idea.

'When was the last time you stayed awake past midnight?' I asked, forgetting the obvious.

'Two nights ago.' Her lips were a fine, pressed line. 'You were there, remember?'

Touché.

'All right.' I gave the mattress a quick test bounce. It sagged dangerously in the middle. 'I'll do the early shift, then come up and wake you. It's easier to stay awake if you've already had some sleep.'

'Is that a promise?'

'It's a promise.'

'Right. I'll turn in.' She slid off the bed and went to poke at the fire. A banner of flame curved upwards, lighting some of the old soot in the chimney, and for a moment the wall seemed to burn, taking the old air in the room with it.

Good things for laying ghosts, fires.

Caroline used the poker to turn the knob on the grate and the blaze died down to a steady glow.

She turned round, her face ruddy in the heat. 'Kellen?'

'Mmm?'

'I'm sorry about Janine.'

Me too. These things happen.

'Thanks.'

I stayed and kept watch on the fire for a long time after she had gone.

Lee arrived a while after midnight.

I sat with a coffee by the fire watching, as I had said, while the cats taught Tîr how to use the cat flap and then took her out hunting in the night. Periodically, she came back, as if retracing her steps to memorise the route. Or possibly she just wanted to check that I was still awake. Difficult to tell.

On the second or third time, the clatter of the flap was underscored by a creak in the floorboards behind me. The dog

127

flopped to the floor by the fire as ever, but the pale blue eye followed a shape that moved across the back wall.

It was barely worth turning round.

'You could always knock.'

'Then I wouldn't know how bad your security was.'

'Really.'

'Don't worry, I didn't touch your new locks.'

'You're too kind.'

'The windows need a bit of attention though.' Her voice was light and acerbic as ever, but there was a weary undertone. She moved round into view. 'Sorry I'm late. Things to do.'

'Tea?'

'Thanks.'

She kept my seat warm while I hunted through the pantry for something she could drink. There was a box of camomile teabags at the back of a shelf by the fridge.

I waved one at her across the room. 'This okay?'

'Fine. Thanks.' She didn't look up from the dog. 'What's this?'

'My new familiar.'

'Oh?'

'Donated to the cause by Inspector Stewart MacDonald of the local constabulary.'

'Why would he do that?'

'Good question. He called her Tîr. I suspect he feels she belongs here. Or he wants me to think so.'

'Mmm.' She shifted down to sit on the floor and introduced herself carefully. The dog moved slightly to give her room and then moved again as a pair of the younger cats piled in through the flap and demanded fire space.

The tea smelled strongly of used cat litter but apparently it was supposed to be that way. I found a cold beer in the back of the fridge and sat down on the floor at the other end of the hearth rug. Only one bit of recent news seemed relevant.

'Laidlaw knows someone broke into Malcolm's place.'

'Mmm.' She didn't sound like it was news.

'MacDonald thinks he knows who it was.'

'As long as he only thinks, there's no problem. He can't have proof. There isn't any.'

'No. But it may be worth you keeping out of the way when he's around.'

'Right.'

She played absently with the cats and kept her attention on the dog. Now and again, she looked as if she was going to say something, then she changed her mind and bit back the breath. I drank my beer and watched the pale reds and golds in the dog's coat glimmer in the firelight. Very peaceful.

At that time in the morning, there's no rush for anything.

Eventually, she made up her mind.

'How are you?'

'Stable.' It was true. Painful in places that used not to hurt. But stable all the same. 'Why?'

She looked me in the eye and there was a warning there that said I might not be as good as I thought.

'What's up, Adams?'

'Bridget's gone.'

Gone. Medical-speak. A way of referring to the recently deceased without mentioning the fact of death.

I know she's gone. I've seen the body.

I looked at Lee. 'What kind of gone?'

'Gone. No longer here. The body in her slot isn't her. It's somebody else and that somebody else was supposed to have been cremated this afternoon. They've done a body switch. They cremated Bridget instead.'

Denial is the first line of defence.

'They can't do that,' I said with blind conviction. 'It's not legal.'

'Neither is murder. It doesn't mean it doesn't happen.' She

129

stood up and walked over to the window to look out at the night. 'I'm sorry, Kellen. I should have seen it coming.'

'How do you know it's not her?' I've seen enough of Lee's forensic post-mortems in the past to know that I'd have difficulty recognising my own lover after the first half-hour. Human distinguishing marks can be distressingly superficial at times. 'You can't be sure.'

'I'm sure. I left some . . . markers when I did the first PM. The body that's left isn't her. I can prove it if I have to.'

'We could do a dental screen – find out who it is.'

'We could, but I know who it is. Sally Wentfield. Caucasian woman, similar height, similar build, similar age. Easy to switch. That's not the point.'

'What's the point?'

She shrugged, loosely, as if trying to rid herself of the guilt. 'It narrows the list of suspects down to less than a dozen. No one outside the department knew she was there bar you, me and Caroline.'

'And Stewart MacDonald.'

'True.' She nodded thoughtfully and pulled a piece of paper from an inside pocket, unfolding it on the table in front of us. 'Do you want to add him to the list?'

'I don't know.' I don't want to have to think about that.

I ran my eye down the list of departmental names. The only one that rang any bells was Professor Peter Gemmell. I folded the sheet under his name. 'Why did the Prof sign the post-mortem, Adams?'

'I asked him to.'

'I gathered that. Why?'

'Two reasons.' She ticked them off on her fingers. 'One, if there's going to be an inquest, I don't want to be the one to stand up in court and make statements, not if Laidlaw's around. The man is perfectly capable of adding two and two and getting

130

any number he wants. The Prof is far better at handling him than I'll ever be. They like each other. It's a useful asset.'

The mind boggles.

'And really?'

'Really?' She angled her mug and eyed the tea leaves with interest. 'It was as good a way as any of getting him involved. He signed the form so he had to at least look at the bits. It was enough to get him to prick up his ears and take notice. We went over her together earlier this morning.'

'Anything useful?'

'Maybe. You were right about temazepam. There wasn't enough in there to kill her.'

'So why did she die?'

'I don't know. The Prof's running a full toxicology profile on Bridget's plasma in case there was anything else in there. He'll do the same on Malcolm if we can find the samples. We should have some answers by the end of the week.'

For what it's worth.

'What are we going to do now?'

'I don't know.' She caught a half-grown kitten on its way towards the fire and balanced it on her knee. 'I suppose we could lock everyone from the department in a sealed room with our favourite Chief Inspector and wait until they crack. Shouldn't take too long.'

'Or we could try to make a more rational list. It doesn't have to be someone in the department, just someone who knows their way round. It's not that difficult to get in. All you need is a white coat and a stethoscope. Or a known face. I could walk in there tomorrow and no one would bat an eyelid.'

Me and half of Glasgow.

'Possibly.'

The cat levered its way on to her shoulder and tried to make a nest in her hair. She prised it loose and dropped it back on to the floor on the side furthest from the fire. 'The list names

131

everyone who's been through the department in the last five years. If you can think of any others, stick them on the end.'

There's only one. The kind of person who could walk into pathology and wander around unchallenged, even if he wasn't wearing a white coat. I found a pen on the breakfast bar and wrote 'Inspector Stewart MacDonald' at the bottom. Unlikely but not impossible.

I handed the list back. 'Guilty until proven innocent, right?'

'Right.'

It was too late to think coherently and we were both short of sleep. I took the list and put it deep in a folder on the desk in Bridget's office. Time enough later.

Lee stayed on for a while, finishing her tea, and we talked over ways to make the farmhouse more secure. She left eventually, to drive home and sleep in her own bed. It wasn't a good time to start sharing the spare room.

A promise is a promise. At four thirty, I woke Caroline and fed her tea and toast until she looked reasonably awake. Then I retired to the sagging mattress and spent the rest of the night in a series of uneasy, disjointed dreams full of fire and burning bodies and amber eyes that shone in the dark.

The smell of fresh coffee and a warning tingle down my spine that had nothing to do with the dip in the bed dragged me back to the here and now. A faint image of mist on water overlaid the afterthought of the nightmares, blotting them out.

'Sweet dreams?' A voice near my feet.

I opened my eyes slowly.

Lee, looking very much the better for a decent night's sleep, leant on the curved bedstead holding a mug of coffee in both hands. She blew gently over the top, sending a cloud of coffee-flavoured vapour floating across the space towards me. Sunlight angled in through the small, square window in the roof above my head, catching the dust in the air, making a pillar of sparkling light between us. Noise from the garden filtered in through the open side window and I could hear the local blackbird raising a racket that sounded rather more aggrieved than the average dawn chorus.

I sat up, pulling the duvet around my shoulders like a back-to-front cloak.

'What time is it?'

'Eleven-ish. Sunday.'

Lee moved round to put the coffee on the bedside table. I shifted my feet and she sat on the end of the bed, haloed by the iridescent column slanting down from the window. Very picturesque.

She smiled and shook her head, leaning backwards out of the light. 'Relax. Everything's peaceful. Your new dog is developing a nicely rounded identity crisis, courtesy of the cats. She's spent the morning learning to stalk birds in the vegetable patch. Young Caroline is tending to the livestock and after that we're going to reinvent the ancient craft of laying alarm wires. There's nothing else that needs doing urgently. We thought you might appreciate a long lie-in.'

I did.

I hugged the coffee mug to my chest like a long-lost friend and felt the caffeine burn through the late-lie fog in my brain, revealing a cluster of memories. Only one mattered. A dull, dragging, darkening memory that took the edge off the morning.

'Bridget's gone?' I asked. Just to make sure.

'Yes.'

Lee put a hand in her pocket and brought out a white-capped blood tube, holding it up between finger and thumb so that the sunlight glowed through it on to the bed. The contents had separated, plasma to the top, the cells a thick layer of sediment at the bottom. As I watched, she rocked it gently in the light. Amber fluid mixed with red sludge to make whole blood.

Life blood.

'I brought you this.' She held it out, pale and unalive on the palm of her hand. 'I thought you might want to say goodbye.'

'Hers?'

'Yes. It's all that's left.'

'You don't need it?'

'No.'

'Caroline?'

'She knows.'

'Right.' I took the tube and laid it in the patch of light at the end of the bed. 'I'll take the dog out for a walk before lunch.'

'Right.'

Tîr abandoned the blackbirds in the vegetable patch and came to heel for the shepherd's whistle. Generations of breed selection cut through the novelty of the new game and she transformed from leggy pup to fine-tuned sheepdog in the time it took her to cross the yard to the field gate.

The ponies provided an interesting challenge, resisting repeated attempts to gather and move them and generally ignoring a glare that would have had genuine sheep sprinting for the shedding pen. Only the young Connemara had not been through the same with Tan. She put her head down and snorted hard through flared nostrils as the pup edged forward, belly to the grass, in an attempt to exert canine authority. There was a moment's eyeball to eyeball confrontation and then both discovered they had better things to do in other parts of the field.

I left her to play and meandered across the grass from pony to horse to pony, checking legs for knocks and feet for signs of heat.

Balder and Midnight followed along, as ever. The rest had other things on their minds: grass and the itch between the shoulderblades and the faint promise of winter that hid behind the sun and warm air.

At the fence, I whistled the dog back and she hung obediently on my heel, following me across the fording stones at the narrow part of the river. The rain had raised the water level almost to the top of the stones and the two of us skipped across, hopping from one dry patch to the next, trying to avoid the slimed areas of wet lichen round the edges. Above us the beech trees in the wood clung on to handfuls of bronzed leaves, waiting for the autumn winds to twist them off the limbs and spin them down into the water below.

The beech wood is oval and spreads over a small, very old and not particularly natural hill. The Ordnance Survey maps for the area list it as a burial mound, which stretches a point a bit. The mound itself is a barrow twenty feet long with a stone cairn standing at one end that lies in a clearing on the southern face of the hill. The hill itself was thrown up in an earlier era, when the indigenous populations needed a raised fort to keep the invading Scots at bay.

Now, it's a hidden backwater in a hidden backwater. A peaceful oasis, walled off by the encircling trees against the noise and stress of the world outside.

I would have found it alone eventually, no doubt, but Bridget took me there as a way to relax late on a Sunday evening after one of those hopelessly chaotic weekends when we seriously believed we could run the farm, build a new set of stables, fix the car and still remember to be reasonable to each other while we were about it.

We'd been together almost two years by then, although we'd heard a fair bit about each other, through Malcolm, for another six months before that. With a characteristic sense of clinical duty, Malcolm Donnelly worked the rotas so that neither Lee nor I got near his sister while we were still on his rotation and needed our full concentration to look after his patients. On the last day of the six months, however, all embargoes were dropped and Malcolm invited Bridget over from Edinburgh for the end-of-rotation party. To be honest, I doubt if he could have kept her away by then. Malcolm may have kept us apart, but we knew more about each other than most folk know after six months in the same house. It's amazing what you talk about to fill in the late nights on the ward.

The party itself was, without question, one of the most spectacular events ever to hit the Western. It was the one and only time that the Helensburgh monstrosity I inherited from my mother proved itself useful. We invited the entire class, plus partners, siblings, nursing 'friends' and other adherents, and they all fitted in with room to spare. By the end of the evening, we had consultant surgeons who hadn't been seen mixing with the ranks for decades dancing alongside junior nurses and students and all three groups jostled, uncomplaining, with the pariahs of the system, the hospital porters. The miracle of it all was that, with the alcohol flowing like water and food enough to feed the entire Strathclyde Health Department, not one single person threw up inside the house or on the pavement outside. It's probably the only thing that stopped the neighbours from calling in the police.

I'm not sure exactly what time I went to bed and I don't remember a huge amount about the next twenty-four hours, except that Bride and I talked a lot more than I was used to on a first night and when Lee left a magnum of champagne outside the door for us at about two in the afternoon, I was afraid to drink any in case it somehow broke the spell. I do remember that she was everything that Malcolm had said she would be and that, for the first time in my life, I didn't feel that I could walk away safely the next morning and keep my sense of self intact.

There followed a hectic year of trans-Caledonian courtship. I learned the fastest ways to and from Edinburgh by every form of public transport and Bride learned her way round wards so that she could find me if I was still on call when she arrived. She introduced me to the Edinburgh scene while I backed away, with unbounded relief, from the tangled mess of the Glasgow student ghetto. She taught me the rudiments of the Scottish legal system, I taught her to ride and, with Lee's help, to climb.

The four of us, me and Bridget, Lee and Malcolm, plus Caroline, who had become one of the group by then, made a pilgrimage out to the islands. We went to visit Lee's clan of grandmothers, all of whom, without exception, fell for my new lover, proclaiming her 'one of them', whatever that was supposed to mean. It was crazily chaotic and absolutely exhausting, but it was fun.

By twelve months later, the novelty of travel and fortnightly meetings began to wear a bit thin. As luck would have it, that was around the time the house prices peaked and, with a lawyer for a lover, selling my albatross of an inheritance in Helensburgh was smooth, painless and very, very lucrative. Overnight I became better off than if I'd saved every penny from ten years of medical pay.

We took almost another year after that, deciding what to do with the money. Bridget had saved enough of her own to raise a mortgage so that it wasn't as unbalanced as it might have been and we knew that, between us, we had the capacity to do something totally different. Something that would last and that would keep us going, together, for the rest of our lives.

The farm came on the market in the summer and we fell on the first visit. The agent spent the best part of an hour trying to divert us away from the outhouses and stables so that we wouldn't see the state of the timbers, but there were five of us and only one of him and he didn't stand a hope in hell. By late afternoon, we had seen everything it was possible to see, poked fingers into the rotting woodwork, flaked off the peeling paint and lifted bricks out of mortar-free walls. But we still loved it and, after that, it was only a matter of haggling the price down to something vaguely manageable.

By autumn it was ours and by hogmanay Bridget had prised herself loose from the talons of the Edinburgh legal vultures and set up the beginnings of the business, making the transition from urban socialite to rural agrarian in a single, instinctive step. The island grandmothers were right, she was one of them. She just hadn't had the chance to find out.

The visit to the cairn took place on a foul, wet, windy Sunday evening. Most of the preceding two days had been spent staring at spreadsheets and financial forecasts in the fractional spaces between rides.

Never try to get anything done on a working horse farm in the summer. Especially not if your name is on the pinboard in the local tourist board offices. We had more foreign visitors wanting to ride 'real Highland ponies' in the first four hours of the morning than the Burrell Collection on a wet Saturday in June. By five o'clock on Sunday we were both frazzled, irritable and ready to blow a fuse at the slightest excuse. On top of that, I was having hourly cold sweats at the thought of returning to Monday morning ward round and the catalogue of chronic patients I'd left behind in the ward.

It was blowing a gale and threatening rain and the forecast was ghastly for the rest of the night. Bridget force-fed me a double-strength white coffee with extra sugar, pushed my oldest jacket into my hand and dragged me off across the fields before I could get my brain together to ask where the hell she thought we were going.

I suppose she must have known the cairn was there. It's not much more than a fifteen-minute walk from the back door, it's just that you have to know where you're going and be prepared to lose some skin or some fragments of jacket on the brambles on the way in. The path was even more overgrown then and I was in a filthy temper by the time we reached the final ring of beech and hawthorn bordering the clearing. But the trees buff-ered the wind and the rain hadn't started and the clouds thinned to let the odd strand of moonlight filter down into the clearing and it was one of the most spectacularly peaceful places I have ever been.

We sat together on the grave mound with our backs against the mossed stones of the cairn and decided that, whatever the spreadsheets said, it was time for me to get out of medicine and move to the farm for good.

It felt like wilfully stepping over the edge of a cliff.

I remember Bride sitting there in the half-toned moonlight, a kind of anxious concern overlaying her usual organised calm.

'Are you sure?' she asked.

'Yes.'

'Absolutely sure?'

'Absolutely sure.' My stomach had long ago ceased to adhere to normal gravitational forces and my small intestines were twisting in knots but I was one hundred per cent, completely and absolutely sure.

'Thank God for that.' She reached an arm round my shoulder and hugged me hard enough and for long enough for all my anatomy to settle back into place. By the time we rocked apart, the moon had moved down below the level of the trees and the rain was becoming a serious possibility. We stood up, feeling a little foolish, creaking the cramp out of our knees and the cold out of everywhere. I was about to head off between the trees looking for the path home when a tug on my sleeve pulled me back.

Bridget was standing by the cairn with both hands on the flat, moss-covered stone that lay at chest height across the top. 'Here – ' she nodded down towards the stone – 'help me shift this.'

There are times with Bride when it's better not to ask why.

'Sure.'

Together we twisted on one corner, sliding it sideways until there was a space big enough for one hand to slide in. We both stood there, looking down into the hollow centre of the cairn.

'Bride, I hate to appear . . .'

'You make a wish and throw it in.' She looked serious. She sounded serious. 'It helps make it real,' she said.

Stupidly, she was right. At the very least, it was something concrete to remember in the days and weeks afterwards when the entire world of medicine informed me exactly why, in its individual and collective opinion, I had lost every last one of my marbles. In the face of that, the memory of the dark and the rain and the weight of the roof stone as we slid it back afterwards was oddly tangible and secure.

We spent a lot of time at the cairn after that, in ones and twos. Lee spent hours there, hunting with the dog, and Malcolm used to make it his Sunday desert island, taking a picnic and a pile of books as an escape. Once, when Tan was about three years old, all five of us, me and Bride, Lee, Caroline and Malcolm, plus the pup spent an afternoon swimming in the wide part of the river just below the wood and then the evening in the clearing, eating the remains of the picnic and enjoying the last of the sun as it filtered through the trees.

That was the last time I was there. Other things got in the way for the winter and then in the spring everything began to fall apart and the cairn ceased to be a part of my life, along with the farm and the horses.

It felt odd coming back. Like going back up into the bedroom but more so. I pulled my jacket up round my ears and tried to keep my face clear of the clinging brambles.

The rain began as I made my way to the edge of the wood. A light saturating haze that seeped in past a turned-up collar and ran down past the neck of my shirt. At least the path through to the grave mound was less overgrown than it had been. As if more people passed more frequently in the last four years than the four before them.

Other than that, it's amazing how little the clearing has

changed, given the rate of progress in the world outside. The hawthorns forming the inner ring have never aged and never will. The grave mound still looms at the back of the clearing, the grass on the top darker as if the bodies of the dead underneath still feed it with something richer than the earth beneath the paler grass of the clearing.

The dog whined and trotted to the north end of the mound, heading for a tree at the back of the clearing. The pile of leaves at its base was too big, covered the ground too well. Together we cleared them away, me with my hands, the dog with her nose, casting them aside in flurries of ragged bronze to get to the grass beneath. I ran my fingers across it, feeling for the knife cuts and found them. A criss-crossing grid where the turf had been lifted and relaid. At the base of the tree lay a single, unmossed river stone. A marker on the grave of a dog.

Tan's grave.

The obvious place and the only place. Hidden and private and still easy to find.

The pup circled on the spot and lay down, eyes closed against possible orders.

I left her alone and walked over more slowly to stand with my back to the cairn, searching for memories of the dead that bring a reverence to the place. Tan as a pup, joyously delinquent. Scourge of butterflies, slugs and billowing leaves. Tan older, more stoic, learning that horses kick if you wind them up far enough. Tan and Malcolm, swimming at the bend in the river, both chasing the same stick in the current. Tan and Bridget. Bridget and Tan, lying asleep in late summer, hiding from clients and riders and horses and, once, from an absent lover with no sense of discretion, or even of tact.

I must have been mad. Completely and utterly mad.

The cairn still stands at the end of the grave mound: a conical beehive reaching up to my shoulder, with a crust of ancient moss and flat, spreading lichen so thick that the stones could crumble and the shape would stay. On the top is a wide, flat stone and on that the moss is thinner. The roof stone. The only bit of the whole thing that moves.

The inner surface of the wall stones is washed with the blood of the dead. It was the way they used to say goodbye. So much cleaner than digging a hole in the ground. She told me that a long time ago. I never asked how she knew.

I slipped my fingers into my pocket and pulled out the blood tube, turning it over and over as Lee had done to mix the straw gold of the plasma with the mahogany dark cells at the bottom.

If it's all that's left, it's better than nothing. More than there was of Malcolm.

The roof stone gave way, slowly and at the cost of skin and blood, as it always did. I suppose it was designed that way. The sun rode high over the clearing by then. High enough to angle down through the gaps in the cloud and let some light into the black cavity of the cairn. Down at the bottom, something glinted. Just once, but enough to be different. Mud and stones don't glint.

It's not a friendly place, the inside of a cairn. The walls are unworn and sharp-edged and I would believe without question that they are washed in blood. The insects skittering across them run faster than in daylight and with more evil intent.

Sliding in a hand felt like a trial by ordeal and I had no idea if I was innocent of the crimes laid against me. But I came back up at the other side with my prize and it was worth a knuckle of lost skin at least.

A watch. A man's watch. Gold with a fading black leather strap, and a second hand big enough to take pulses even in poor light. I reached in and lifted it out, turning it over as soon as it reached daylight to look for the inscription on the back.

It was there. Just where I remembered it: *MDD, MD. Take Care. B.*

Malcolm's watch. Put there, without question, by his sister. Because there was nothing else.

I reached in and slid it back over the projecting spur of stone where it belonged.

A shadow moved to my left, too hard and too fast to be anything but human. A hand fell on to my shoulder, catching me in place as I spun round.

A voice, like water over gravel said, 'Now then, you're not looking so happy with life.'

Inspector MacDonald. The ever practical, ever present Inspector MacDonald.

Bastard.

'What the hell are you doing here?' I'm not at my most tactful when scared out of my mind.

'The same as you, lass,' he said placidly, 'the same as you. I came to see where your young friend had put the old dog. It seemed the best place to look.'

I turned round to look at the man. He still wasn't in uniform. He wasn't even in the fisherman's jersey. He was dressed in an old wax jacket with its collar turned up to the rain and an inside pocket that bulged with a rabbit-sized bulge. His moleskin trousers had fresh mud caked around the knees and his boots had seen the best part of a lifetime's wear. On top of it all, there was something uncommonly like a ferret box hanging from his shoulder on a webbing strap. My dog sat at his feet, ears up, waiting for the chance to work.

Inspector MacDonald may have been here to look at the grave but he was making the most of an afternoon's rabbiting while he was at it.

The last time I heard, ferreting on land without the express permission of the owners is defined in legal terms as poaching, a felony which tends to be unpopular with the local law. I suppose that if the local law is the one doing the poaching then it must be all right.

143

He saw me looking at the box and one eye drooped in truncated wink.

'Do you mind?'

'Of course not.'

'I thought so.' He looked up at the greying sky, wiping the rain from his face. 'I was on my way home anyway,' he said. 'There'll be nothing more out in this. Would you like a hand to put the stone back over?'

Why not? I'm not about to do anything more useful now.

He did as he offered and then we walked together in silence back through the wood towards the fording stones and the paddock. 'It's a good place to end your days, that clearing,' said MacDonald as we followed the line of the fence back round to the gate.

'It is.'

'And a grand place to go when you need a break from the family wars.'

'Mmm.' Odd. I never thought of him as over-talkative before. I hitched my jacket collar higher against the wind and the rain and the unwanted conversation.

'You're all back in the farm, I see. Dr Adams as well.'

'Safety in numbers.' I said.

'Aye.' He nodded carefully. 'That's not a bad idea.'

We parted at the gate and the last I saw of him was his back as he strolled on up the lane, the ferret box concealed under his jacket against the weather.

Lee met me at the back door, her hair white with plaster dust and smears of filth wiped across her forehead where she had pushed the hair up out of her eyes.

'Good?'

'Reasonable.' I held out the hand with blood tube so that she could see it clearly. 'The dog knows her way around well enough,' I said.

'Oh. Good.'

'I saw Tan's grave.'

'I thought you might.'

'It's a good place.'

'Yes.'

We stood and looked at each other while all the things that might have been said were not, and then she stepped back to let me in.

'Kettle's on,' she said.

'Thanks.' I followed her in out of the rain.

Inside the kitchen, the electrical team had been in action for most of the afternoon. Dustsheets covered the kitchen surfaces, with a special rack set up to prevent the hot plates of the Rayburn from setting fire to the entire arrangement. Reels of cable, boxes of square-pin sockets and jars of wall clips were laid out in organised rows on the flat surfaces. The entire contents of the drinks cupboard over the fire had been consigned to a cardboard box on the floor of the pantry and the cupboard doors had been unscrewed from their hinges. An industrial-sized, hammer-action drill and a set of drill bits you could dig roads with lay in a neat row on the hearth.

I turned down the invitation to join in. Caroline, dressed in ancient overalls with her hair held up by a cable-tie, a set of tools in her hand and a list of things to do, was in her element. Better still, she and Lee were reforging a working partnership in the shared business of practical creation. The last thing either of them needed was anyone else stepping in to examine, comment or, gods forbid, offer to help.

Instead, I took a shower and then retreated to the small study-cum-conservatory at the side of the house, where I could work with the big french windows open and keep an eye on the dog, who had gone back to worrying blackbirds. Periodically, the teeth-aching scream of the drill rang through the whole house and eventually I stuffed a rolled-up wad of old sheets along the gap at the floor to keep out the worst of the noise and the dust.

Malcolm's papers, most of his old correspondence and Lee's suspect list were laid out on the floor in order of importance and I sat across the window, half in, half out of the room, listening to the birds in the garden and the chatter of voices in the kitchen, and tried to bring my mind back to the matter in hand.

It was very heavy going. Malcolm used to be a practical man. In his days as an academic, he was the champion of plain English, believing that if the work was strong, the world should know about it in straightforward terms. In the last four years of his life, his style had changed and the plain English had been replaced by increasingly convoluted science-speak designed expressly to hide the implications of what he was doing from anyone not conversant with the vocabulary of genetic technology.

Each time my brain reached overload, I went out to the kitchen to stretch my legs, clear my head and see how the team were getting on.

Late in the afternoon, I found Lee on her own, completely absorbed in the work, kneeling by the fire, holding a bunch of wires like spaghetti between her teeth and inserting them, one at a time, into a black console that exactly fitted the dimensions of the cupboard.

I watched, fascinated by the blinking amber lights.

'Where's Caroline?' I asked eventually.

Lee spat out the remaining wires and wiped her mouth on her sleeve. 'Up the lane, wiring in the detectors.'

'Is that safe?'

'I'll check it out later.' She stood up, stretching out her back. 'She's fine. She knows what she's doing.' She went back to the wiring, testing connections with a hand-held ammeter. 'How's the work going?'

146

'Slowly. Most of the stuff from the last couple of years is written in undiluted techno-jargon.'

'What was he trying to hide?'

'I think it's more "who from?" that matters. I'll let you know.'

She grunted through another mouthful of wires. I cleared the dustsheets from the stool by the breakfast bar and sat down.

'Lee?'

'Mmm?'

'Does the Prof do translocation work in his spare time?'

She paused for a moment, frowning into the guts of the box, then she spat the wires from between her teeth and swivelled on her heels to face me.

'I shouldn't think so. He hasn't got any spare time. He's up to his ears running the department. Why?'

'He and Malcolm are joint authors on a short communication in the *BMJ*. It's the only thing I've got that isn't in Malcolm's field.'

She put down the tools and sat back against the wall, the electronics momentarily forgotten. 'Doesn't sound very likely. Can I look?'

I brought the file through from the study and laid the relevant paper out on a clean bit of floor.

'Here. "Gemmell, P. G. and Donnelly, M. D." It was published about a year ago but the work was probably done before that.'

Wiping her hands on a rag, Lee picked the paper up carefully by the edges and read the title and then the abstract. It was a fairly basic paper on gene translocation in the Xenopus Toad. Not particularly related to the studies Malcolm had been working on, not in the least bit high-powered and certainly not written in Malcolm's usual style. It had the ring of someone feeling their way into writing and it would have benefited from a serious brush-up by an editor.

I watched in silence while Lee read and reread the title page, shaking her head.

At length, she put it back on the folder and looked up at me. 'Philippa,' she said.

'Come again?'

'Prof's daughter. She did her fifth-year project with Malcolm. He took her on as a favour to the boss.'

'Doesn't look like she was up to much.'

'You said it.'

'What's she doing now?'

'Pass.' Lee shrugged. 'Spawning the next generation of medical superstars as far as I know. She got married two weeks after graduation.'

She stopped, arrested in mid-thought.

'Kemp,' she said succinctly.

'I'm sorry?'

'Kemp. She married a guy called David Kemp.'

'The same David Kemp who does locums for the Bearsden practice?'

'Could have been. There can't be that many.'

'Find out will you?'

'Sure.'

I went back to the study and wrote 'Kemp?' at the top of my list, then sat back feeling more optimistic than I had done in a long time.

The light was beginning to fade and there was a fine mist rising from the fields out beyond the garden by the time I reached the end of the pile and put my notebook down. The coffee was cold, the fire had burned down and my brain felt like scrambled spinach.

Malcolm was undoubtedly good at his job, probably one of the best. He was developing a new technique that involved taking the gene for an existing protein, splitting it in half and splicing the DNA code for another protein into the middle so that two proteins would be made in the place of one.

Then all he had to do was put the engineered DNA into something that naturally produced protein – say, a bacterium – and watch it spit out an endless supply of something useful.

By two years into the new research programme, he had done it successfully with bacteria and had buckets of bugs producing albumin: a simple protein found in blood and egg whites. All very laudable in scientific terms, but hardly earth-shaking stuff. Certainly not worth dying for. His method may have been slick and an advance on existing technology, but dozens of genetic engineers spend every day doing much the same thing, only with fancier bugs and with far more commercial end products. None of them dies for it.

I threw a couple of peat bricks on to the fire and crouched in front of it, watching the flames crisp the dried-out fuzz at the edges, trying to work out what it was about genes and proteins that was enough to make a man forfeit his life.

Somewhere along the line, there were a lot of pieces of jigsaw still missing.

'Problems?'

Lee. Standing in the mist at the open french windows.

'Mmm.' I stayed where I was. 'I need to see the disks we got from Malcolm's lab.'

She came in and knelt beside me, holding her hands out to the fire. 'They're in my bag, under the bench in the kitchen,' she said. 'I had a look at them yesterday. All the interesting ones are booby-trapped.'

'What's that in English?'

'If you try to open them without the right password, they'll erase the contents automatically.'

'Shit.' I stared at the burning peat, avoiding the obvious train of thought.

Change the subject.

'How's the electrical engineering going?'

'Done. We need to change all the sockets over to square-pin plugs but it shouldn't take too long. There's a bit of replastering to do after that, but we'll have it finished by bedtime.'

She sat back on her heels and put both hands lightly on the back of my neck. 'Can you ask Janine to help with the disks?'

I threw another brick on the grate. It rolled to the back and messed up the balance of the fire.

'I don't think I'd get much out of her just now.'

'I know.' She pushed the balls of her thumbs into the taut muscles running up the side of my neck, easing them out. 'Caroline told me.'

'Caroline talks too much.'

'Possibly. But she still cares about you.' Lee took hold of my wrist and turned me away from the fire so that I had to look at her face. 'I'll go if you want,' she said, 'but I don't think I'd necessarily get any results.'

CHAPTER SIX

Rae Larssen lives in one of the more prosperous micro-suburbs wedged between the Botanic Gardens and Queen Margaret Avenue near the top end of Byres Road. I parked the car in the 'Residents Only' spaces marked out on the pavements and flicked a 'Doctor on Call' card left over from my respectable past on to the dashboard to keep the wheel clampers at bay for a while.

The street door hung conveniently open and I let myself in. The hallway and stairs were lined with late-1980s designer tiles: a random sea of line-drawn lavender triangles on a white glaze background swirled up the stairway towards the flat.

A lady of very individual tastes, our Rae. I don't visit often.

Upstairs, multicoloured light flooded through the stained-glass panels above the door, turning the pale marble landing into an Impressionist seascape.

Opium perfume clung in the air, catching the back of my throat as I stood waiting for an answer to the genteel burr of the doorbell.

A tall woman with Nordic features and ice-white hair opened the door. Her face was set in the same half-quizzical, half-friendly smile that greets the television cameras on the nightly Scottish news programme. It froze in place as she opened the door. A wash of warm-bread scent billowed out into the cold air of the hallway.

I fixed my own smile and looked past her into the flat, checking rooms and occupants: four doors, only one open and that leaking a hum of mixed women's voices in low conversation. A handbag lay on a hall seat. Definitely not Janine's and probably not Rae's; she is not the kind of woman to leave a handbag lying about in her own hallway.

Company.

'I'm sorry.' I took a step back. 'I'm interrupting. I'll call back later.'

Rae Larssen inspected me briefly, pale eyebrows flickering upwards. 'Kellen? Did Jan call you?'

'No.' I began to turn away. 'I needed to talk to her. It's all right. I'll call her at work tomorrow.'

The woman caught hold of my arm. Her face creased in the faintest of concerned frowns.

'I think you should come in,' she said. 'She'd never forgive me if I let you go.'

I wasn't sure about that but I let her lead me through into the clinical neatness of the flat. There was a perceptible pause. She was about to offer to take my jacket and I was about to refuse. We looked at each other for a moment, then she inclined her head towards the open doorway and this time there was a hint of amusement in the pebble grey eyes.

'She's in there with the others.'

Her voice was straight off the Orkney ferry. Pure Viking. Pure music. Not bad given that it's three generations since her family moved over the water and down the mainland to Cambuslang.

Her eyes flicked to a closed door to my left.

'You can use the spare room to talk if you need it.'

'Thanks.' I took a steadying breath and walked towards the murmur of voices, braced for the severing silence.

There were eight of them, talking in pairs. Janine was sitting on the floor, leaning back against the sofa, holding a tall wine glass in one hand and drawing imaginary shapes in the air for the woman at her side with the other. The epitome of the happy, relaxed party animal.

I knew all of the rest by sight, so most of them must have known me and I have no doubt that the grapevine had carried the news of my circumstances with its usual efficiency.

The conversations wavered and died as I walked in through the door. All except Janine, who carried on for a moment or two, laughing in the sudden silence, then stopped, abruptly, in mid-phrase. Her arm hung, unnoticed, in mid-air and her eyes blazed in the way only a redhead's eyes can.

'I'm sorry, I didn't know . . .' I began.

And then I saw who it was she was talking to.

She was still dressed all in blue but not in uniform this time, much softer, much more relaxed. Smooth, dark hair curled under at the ends, framing an open, friendly face and neatly sculpted eyebrows rose over a pair of green, green, feline eyes. Eyes that were suddenly very blank.

I took one very slow breath and let it out into the hush.

'WPC Elspeth Philips,' I said. 'What a tremendously interesting surprise.'

Behind me, a roomful of women held their collective breaths.

Rae Larssen, her perfect hostess instincts tuned to impending conflict, appeared at my side with a fluted glass and a bottle of white Burgundy.

'Wine, Kellen, now that you're here?'

'I don't think so,' said Janine softly. 'I don't think Dr Stewart was intending to stay.' She looked directly at me. 'Kellen?'

I shook my head. 'No.'

Rae stepped back, her eyes full of a smile that didn't quite intrude on to her face, and gestured towards the door. 'I'll hold dinner till you're ready, Jan.'

Ms Larssen's spare room is a study in Scandinavian asceticism. Beautifully appointed but spectacularly sparse. A pine bed sits in exact asymmetry on a white rug, which in turn lies to one side of a polished pine floor. I sat carefully on the perfectly flat, white linen coverlet, grateful that I had changed into something passably clean before I left the house.

Janine closed the door and then slid down to sit with her back against it – either protection against the curious intruder or a way of keeping me in the room. She cocked her head on one side and chewed her bottom lip.

'I thought you were going to call when you were ready to talk?'

'I am. I didn't come to talk.'

'You surely didn't come to crash the party?' Her voice acquired a freshly sharpened edge.

'No.' I stood up and moved back to the window. There's safety in distance. 'Is this working out?' I asked.

'I don't know,' said my ex-lover from the doorway. 'I've only been here twenty-four hours and I spent most of this afternoon at work trying to sort out tomorrow's leader from a mess of floppies.'

'How's it going?'

Her eyebrows rose as far up as they could go. 'Kellen, did you really come here at this time of night to talk about work?'

No.

The curtains hung half-closed, leaving a two-inch gap. I looked down at the streetlights and the dark, captive trees lined up inside the fenced compound of the Botanic Gardens and tried to assemble a logical train of thought. The disks hung heavy in my pocket. I lifted them out and laid them on the floor at my feet.

'How well do you know our friend in blue?' I asked.

'Elspeth? Not as well as you from the sound of things. I've only ever met her here. She's usually at Rae's parties.'

And I am not, because I don't like Rae's parties. Point taken. 'Did she tell you she was one of Laidlaw's blue-eyed kids?'

'I'm sorry?'

'She's in the force. A woman police constable of the Strathclyde Central Constabulary. Did you know?'

'Of course.'

'So what's she doing here?' I asked. 'Is she the token straight?'

There was a long gap then. Janine looked at me as if I had, perhaps, finally gone over the edge. Her lips compressed to a single line and her nostrils flared whiter at the edges. 'I don't think so, Kellen,' she said quietly, 'she only split up with Rae two months ago.'

Oh, hell. That explains too many things.

I really should have known.

The disks were still lying on the floor. I stood up, slipping them back into an inside pocket and slid back into my jacket. 'I'm sorry. I didn't know. I better go.'

Janine watched me, confused. 'What are you playing at, Kellen?'

'Nothing.' I leant down and gave her a hug, kissing the top of her head. 'It's not important. I'll see myself out. Talk to you later?'

'Sure.'

At least she had the sense not to ask when.

Elspeth Philips stood in the living-room doorway and watched me as I let myself out of the flat.

My car remained unmolested by the wandering wardens, so I left it parked where it was and, pulling my jacket tight against the blustering wind, walked round the corner to Bee's for a coffee and a chance to do some serious, uninterrupted thinking.

Bee's is a café with wine-bar pretensions two blocks down the Great Western Road from the Botanic Gardens. It's been a queer dive since long before I was a student, first by default, then, after

155

a sudden change to a less-than-sympathetic management, by sheer force of numbers and finally, after a local group buy-out, by design. The name changed in the process, settling into a tacky, unmemorable acronym which is painted in livid pink on the front boards.

For the local clientele it has stayed as Bee's; only the straight population use the official acronym and very few of them venture inside more than once. Being in the minority can be intimidating when you're not used to it.

The downstairs bistro was filled with the usual Sunday evening throng; boys on one side, women on the other and the ubiquitous fag hags hovering in the middle, trying not to look conspicuous.

Small cliques gathered in opposing corners. The university crowd, nervously experimenting with sexuality as a form of self-expression. The town dykes, paired into the butch and the very butch, here for a quiet coffee in a smoke-free zone before moving on somewhere with a late-night licence and louder music. The occasional professional couple, keeping to the shadows, conducting the beginnings and endings of affairs in strained, muted undertones.

And me, playing at being the average citizen-off-the-streets, with my lover three streets away chatting up a professional policewoman who very probably will never come out at work and would almost certainly not dare to cross the threshold of a known lesbian bar.

The cross-section of a cliché. Sad but true.

I looked around for a free seat in the crush and spotted one, eventually, at a table for two on the far wall, under the stairs. One problem. A small plume of blue smoke spiralled upwards from the seat at the opposite side. Smoking is absolutely forbidden in Bee's; there's only one person who ever gets away with lighting up and that's only because no one in their right mind would think of trying to stop her.

Mad Mhaire Culloch.

Lee's 'Auntie Mhaire' is a wee Irish crone, well into her eighties. She has white hair, stained yellow at the edges from her nicotine habit, no teeth, a voice on her like the three Furies with amplifiers and she is, in my professional opinion, barking.

But very bright with it.

If she had behaved as she does now when she was younger, they would have locked her up and thrown away the key. So she didn't. She played the bonny lass, got married at sixteen and had her seven children to keep her mad mother happy. Then she waited until the war was providing good reasons to go missing, left the lot and moved to Glasgow, where she slowly turned into the kind of person she had always been.

Now, in her prime, she runs a very healthy social security scam from her council flat on the South Side and makes a killing on the side reading palms and Tarot cards and star charts and generally telling people the things they need to know but might not want to hear. She is, unquestionably, the most terrifyingly accurate psychic I have ever met and she knows how to use it when it suits her.

Her position as island-appointed mentor to Lee means that she knows more about her than anyone else in the world and that, by extension, she knows more about me than I find comfortable. So when she was sitting at the only table with a spare seat on the first time I had been into Bee's since the hogmanay party, there was probably a good reason.

I picked a particularly sticky, sticky bun from the counter and carried it over to her table, holding it in front of me like an offering in the vague hope that the sight of so much congealed carbohydrate might keep her quiet until I got close enough for her not to shout.

No such luck.

'You've blood on your hands, woman.'

She screeched it across the room while I was still negotiating a path through the student contingent and half a roomful of heads turned.

I had showered twice in less than six hours and I knew that my hands were, to all intents and purposes, spotless.

I kept them in full view and hoped that everyone knew Mhaire well enough to know that she was mad and not quite well enough to know that, more often than not, she was right.

At the table, I moved the saucer that was serving as an ashtray and laid my offering in front of her.

She ignored it.

'You drink too much coffee.' At least her voice was down.

'I know.' I sat down. 'Who's blood did you see, Mhaire? Mine?'

'Yours. Aye, yours.' She rocked backwards in her chair once or twice and hummed tunelessly past the butt end of her roll-up. Bad news. Mhaire in humming mode is not easy to handle.

She grinned winsomely. 'Some is yours and some is hers and some is someone else's.' She sang it in a lilting, playground rhythm. For someone with no teeth, her 's's are remarkably sibilant.

The key with Mhaire is not to get sidetracked.

'Some is hers. Who's that? Bridget?'

'Ahhh.' A long, mournful sigh. 'Poor Bridget. Dead and dead and all for an egg. Poor Bridget. Poor, poor Bridget.'

She rocked forward abruptly and poked a finger at my sternum. 'It's no on your hands you keep that blood, woman. It's in your heart and it's all clotted up and cold and hard like a stone and you'll no end this while you keep it there.'

Her voice rose back up to a screech and the finger jabbed hard like a blunted knife. 'Learn to weep, woman, learn to weep.'

Brilliant. Other folk pay their therapists by the hour to hear the things they don't want to know. I get it for free from a batty old Irishwoman in a bar with half of the Glasgow queer community listening in as my very own personal encounter group.

'I'll weep when it's all over, Mhaire.' I kept my voice as low as I could. 'Who's blood is it then? Lee's?'

Her face twisted. 'Aye. Her. The black one. Her. Forgotten her Auntie Mhaire now she's gone up in the world. Never comes to visit. Never comes to see if I'm still alive in the cold and the rain with no money and no one to take care of me. You tell her to visit old Mhaire if she wants to know what to do when the blood runs on the stones.'

I imagine she can work out that kind of thing on her own by now.

'I'll do that, Mhaire.'

'Aye, well mind that you do. She's too clever by half, that one. Thinks she knows it all. She'll get her fingers stepped on one of these days if she goes about sticking them into other people's business.'

Don't get sidetracked.

'I'll tell her, Mhaire. You said someone else. Who's that? A man?'

'A man?' She made the word a treasure, rolling it round in her mouth and tasting the flavour of it. Then she took a hefty bite of the pastry. 'Aye. A man. Not good with the gentlemen are you, woman?'

Look who's talking.

'No, I'm not. What man's that, Mhaire? The one who killed Bridget?'

She thought about that one, squinting at a far horizon with screwed-up eyes.

This time when she answered, her voice had come back to ground level, as lucid as it ever gets.

'No. Not yet. There's others before him. He'll not die until it's all over and maybe not even then. He could live for ever, that one, if you let him.' Her head cocked to one side suddenly, as if struck by a fresh idea. 'Choices, my pretty one, choices. Do you know how to choose?'

I have no idea.

The finger drummed again, on my forehead this time.

'It's anger you carry in there, woman, not love, whatever you like to think. Anger. If you've not got a clear mind, you'll not be able to make clear choices. Remember that.'

Tell me something I don't know.

'I'll work on it.'

'Hah.' She lit the charred roll-up and waved it in circles before my eyes. 'Hah. And hah. And hah. Man, but you're the arrogant one. Here I am, the oracle, talking for you and you think you know it all.'

She rocked back again and rolled her eyes up in her head, showing the whites, and her voice sank deep into the sepulchre. I'm sure it impresses the clients on the South Side.

'Red and black. Black and red. The one is yours, the other's dead.'

Give me a break.

'I think we're a bit past that, aren't we, Mhaire?'

Her hand slammed on the table. Heads failed to turn.

'How can you think you know the answers when you've never listened to the questions, woman? There's more that's red than blood and more that's black than her who's dead and don't you forget it. You can't have them both. Red or black. Only one. Remember that.'

Time to go. Rhyming couplets are the widening end of a very tedious wedge.

I left her, giggling happily to herself through mouthfuls of pastry. As I reached the foot of the stairs and began to go up two at a time, I heard her voice shriek again behind me.

'Mind the fox, woman. Remember that while you're about it. Mind the fox.'

Back at the farmhouse, the guard lights failed to come on as I drew into the yard. The kitchen was in total darkness but there was a blaze of lights and the screaming dialogue of a television soap blared from the living room at the front.

Last thing I knew, the farm didn't have a television and I would put money that no one's paid the licence. As I walked up to the back door, I heard the telephone ring in the far room and then Caroline's voice answer it, except that the telephone sits under the window in clear view and Caroline was nowhere near it.

A scrape of gravel stopped me as I was about to knock on the back door and I felt the faintest touch of a finger just under my ear. I stood very still, cursing with reasonable invention. There seemed very little point in keeping quiet. If it was anyone other than Lee, I would have been bleeding to death on the doorstep.

A hand wrapped lovingly round my throat.

'Bang.' A voice breathed warm in my ear. 'You're dead.'

I extracted myself from her grip. 'Thanks, partner.'

'You're welcome.'

She stepped ahead of me and opened the door. Inside, the kitchen was pitch black. The fire had been doused with water leaving a strong, acrid smell of saturated peat ash. Lee walked round me, feeling her way to the cupboard over the fire and flicked a series of switches. The lights returned in the kitchen and the yard, the racket from the television stopped in mid-row and the answer-phone reset itself with a quiet ting.

Caroline was leaning, hands in pockets, against the wall at the far end of the room, with the dog lying quiet at her feet.

'Like it?' She looked peaceful. Satisfied with her work.

'Wonderful.' I looked around. 'All this and square-pin plugs too.'

I turned to Lee. 'Does it light the fire again?'

'Sour grapes,' said Lee cheerfully. 'Ignore her, she's just jealous she didn't get to play.'

Which only goes to show that I am transparent too.

We spun coins to decide a rota for the night watch. I landed

161

the middle shift, sandwiched between Lee and Caroline. It went some way to restoring my faith in the fates. More than anything else, I wanted to sleep and not to think.

Caroline began work on another minor culinary adventure, while Lee made up a bed for herself in the office. I was left to the fire. Fair division of labour and as good a way as any of keeping my hands occupied and my mind focused on something other than the events of the day.

Lee came to sit in the chair while I cleaned out the grate and laid some more kindling.

'How did you get on?'

'Grim.' I pulled out the disks and slid them across the hearth rug towards her.

'She wouldn't, or she couldn't?'

'Neither. I didn't ask.'

'I see.'

She kept the question out of her voice.

'Elspeth Philips was there. She's on Laidlaw's force, working with MacDonald. I think we don't need to hand either of them proof on a plate.'

'Would it be passed on?'

'I don't know. Possibly not, but I'm not about to find out the hard way.'

I changed the subject. 'Mad Mhaire was at Bee's. She sent you her love.'

She grimaced painfully. 'You mean she sent the great green curse of the wee Irish pixies for me not visiting her more than twice in the past month.'

'Something like that. And she hummed.'

'Hell. That's bad. I thought you were looking rough. Did she say anything intelligible?'

'That depends on how good your translation is these days. Apparently I have other blood on my hands that's not mine and not yours and there are more men dead than we know of. Also we have to be careful of foxes. Is that intelligible?'

'It might be if that was what she said.'

'Almost.'

'Tell me.'

I rocked back on my heels, closed my eyes and relayed most of the conversation verbatim. With Mhaire, there is no basic sense, the key is in the choice of words, and I have never known her well enough to decipher the time of day, never mind the deep, cryptic analyses of relationships and events.

But Lee can, sometimes. One of our basic differences is that Lee thinks Mhaire Culloch is ultimately sane and has our best interests at heart and I think she is an interfering old bat with not a good thought in her soul. The fact that she's more often right than wrong is hardly the point. However, Lee knew Mhaire long before she knew me and I'm not likely ever to be able to convince her that she's wrong. Persistent if misplaced loyalty is a cornerstone of the Adams psyche.

When I had finished the recitation, I opened my eyes. Lee was sitting forward in the chair, balancing her chin on her hand, her eyes on my face.

'Any ideas?' she asked.

'Lots. Like we could lock her up and throw away the key until she learns to talk real English. You?'

'Some.' She looked at me and her eyes were only half-amused. 'Loosely, I'd say it's going to get worse before it gets better, but then we know that already. With Mhaire, we'll only know how much of it's right in retrospect.'

'If there is a retrospect.'

'Ever the optimist, Dr Stewart.'

'You'd be sad if I changed, Dr Adams.'

'Surprised, anyway.'

I finished laying the fire and lit the edges of the paper, kneeling forward to blow into the air vents at the base. Kindling caught and flared and then the peat flickered smokily to life. I watched until I was sure it wasn't going to die out, then I stood up, leaving the disks where they lay on the floor.

'I'm going to bed. Wake me when it's my watch.'

'Not hungry?'

'No. Just tired.'

I undressed messily, draping my clothes, unfolded, over the chair by the bed, and crawled under the primrose printed duvet. Slipping a hand under the pillow, I wrapped my fingers round the vial of blood that had come back with me from the cairn.

It didn't stop the nightmares but it added an interesting edge.

Lee broke through the thundering fires, showering them with water so that the red-hot earth hissed and spat. 'The horses,' she said, 'we need to get them in.' And then, as I opened my eyes, 'Rise and shine, Stewart, there's a storm coming.'

There was indeed. I dressed in a hurry, throwing on the clothes discarded earlier that evening, and listened to the fabric of the house groan in muted anticipation of a hard north-westerly gale. The hills protect the farm on the east side, but the storms from the west come in straight off the Atlantic with precious little in the way to soften the impact.

I grabbed a jacket from the coat rack and followed Lee at a run out of the back door.

Outside, the smell of pre-storm ozone prickled in the air. The wind laid the reeds around the pond flat in sudden, buffeting blasts. Loose bucket handles flapped in odd corners of the yard with a discordant metallic clatter and, in the far wood, the beech trees shed leaves like confetti. Massed banks of clouds spewed up over the horizon and fragments torn from the leading edge raced across the face of an almost-full moon.

The dog danced and twisted at our heels, pouncing at the shadows rippling across the gravel. Her coat glowed pale in the moonlight and she became a ghost-fox, hunting for the souls of the dead through the cracks in the night.

Nights like this are alive with everything you ever imagined. Magic.

'Race you.' I grabbed the corners of my jacket, sheeting in so that it became a galleon sail in the wind. Then, turning broadside on to the blast, I let the gale haul me, feet skittering on the gravel, towards the field.

One after the other, we careened into the gate.

I clung on to the rails, winded by the impact and breathless with laughter. 'I won.'

'Cheat. You started first.'

'Only because you're so bloody slow, Adams . . . Oh, shit . . . the horses.'

The ponies, milling on the other side of the gate, shied as a group in a whirl of black manes and rolling white eyes. A couple of the youngsters propped and turned, and somewhere, in the darkness, a single set of unshod hooves hammered on the hard earth. The Connemara.

Without thinking, I put my fingers to my mouth and whistled. Tîr wriggled under the bottom rail of the fence and vanished, a pale blur whipping through the grass. The running hoof slammed to a standstill and there was a horse-snort of sheer astonishment. I whistled again and the footsteps walked, and then trotted, back to the group. Rain's filly glared at me with undisguised disgust.

Lee was impressed. 'Did you know she could do that?'

'No.' Life is full of small surprises. 'Good though, isn't it?' I whistled the dog to heel and clipped back the gate. 'Let's get them moving, the rain's on its way.'

It began as we walked the herd up the hill. A few heavy drops beat a slow drum roll on the roof of the barn, the rhythm gathering pace as we hauled back the big main doors and ran down the rows, opening boxes. By the time each horse was safely in bed, with hay and water to last the night, it was a solid, unrelenting downpour. Quite enough to soak all three of us on the run back to the house.

Lee stood watching the water run down the windows while I towelled the worst of the wet off the dog.

'Seen the moon?' She sounded thoughtful.

'Uhuh. It'll be full the night after next.'

'That's the equinox.'

'I know. These are the equinoctial gales. We'll be lucky if there aren't trees down by the morning.'

The dog wriggled free and flopped to the floor in front of the fire. The smell of wet canine percolated steamily through the room.

I went to join Lee by the window. We both stood for a while and watched the water run in rivulets off the glass, thinking.

'Will you go and see Mhaire?'

'No.' Her eyes looked out through the window, but her mind was somewhere else. 'Things will happen whether we know about them or not. On the whole, I'd rather stay in blissful ignorance for a while longer.' She turned round and the voice carried nothing more than gentle irony. 'You could always try, but if she's started on the rhyming couplets, you could be in for a bad time of it.'

'No thanks. Once a year is enough.'

She went to bed soon after that and I spent the rest of the graveyard shift reading Malcolm's papers through until I knew the contents inside out and back to front. It passed the time, but I can think of better ways to spend an evening.

At four, I woke Caroline and left her sitting in the chair by the fire with a copy of yesterday's *Herald* crossword. I crawled back into bed, too tired this time to dream of anything.

The rain was still sheeting down against the windows and running in torrents off the cracked guttering at the side of the roof when Lee woke me at seven.

'I'm off. I have to be in for the department rounds at eight. Caroline's still asleep. She wants to be woken at midday if she hasn't surfaced before then.'

I came round slowly, fighting up through layers of black cotton wool. 'Fine. Call me if there's anything special on Bridget's blood results.'

'Sure.'

I took a leisurely shower and dressed slowly, listening to the radio news with the forecast of rain and more rain, then took the dog out to the barn and spent the next couple of hours working off mindless frustration, trundling barrowloads of horse dung to the muck heap and forking out bales of straw to make the new beds.

Just before coffee time, I remembered to check the bantams. Food and water stocks were holding out nicely. The two hoppers in the middle of the floor were designed to keep a dozen or so hens well fed for a week and this pair had barely made an impact. They sat in the far corner and clucked at me nervously as I ducked in the door, refusing to move until I was almost within reach. When they finally scuttled off, complaining briskly, each neatly rounded dip in the straw revealed two small, brown eggs – replicas of the ones we had taken from Malcolm's lab. I scooped them into a pocket and left, locking all the multiple chains and bolts behind me.

Caroline, half-awake and wrapped up in a vast blue towelling dressing gown, was sitting at the breakfast counter with a piece of toast in one hand and the phone in the other when I walked, dripping, in through the back door.

'It's Lee,' she said, 'for you.'

Who else?

I laid the eggs carefully on the counter and took the handset. Small puddles of water began to form on the flagstones at my feet.

'Hi. What's up?'

'Things are moving. Can you meet me in town?' It was her professional medical voice: clipped and terse.

'Where?'

'The Man. Half an hour.'

I looked at my clothes and imagined walking into the Man carrying that much horse debris.

'I need to change. Can you make that forty-five minutes?'

'Fine. Upstairs bar. Usual place.' She hung up.

I left Caroline with all the alarm systems switched on and a series of numbers to call if she thought there was going to be trouble. Not the best security in the world but the best that common sense and a reasonable amount of invention could produce.

The drive in to Byres Road was wet. The dash down the hill from the multistorey car park to the Man was wetter still. I arrived, soaked to the knees from car spray and with water running off my hair down the inside of my collar.

The bar was as busy as ever. You would think that anyone with any conscience would be at work at half-past ten on a Monday morning, but the business breakfast people seemed to be working their way towards a liquid brunch and the lower lounge was packed out with postgraduate students busily generating a degree of enthusiasm for research after a hard weekend's drinking.

Lee was sitting at her usual table on the balcony over the main bar, reading the morning paper.

I picked up a fresh coffee and a glass of mineral water on the way past the bar and carried them over to the table.

'Hi. What's up?'

'All sorts of things.' She flipped the paper across the table towards me. 'Have you seen that?'

Janine had an article on the science pages. One I hadn't read before. One, by now, of the several I hadn't read before. This time, she was writing about computer protection and the sub-editor had pulled out a phrase to highlight in a box under the main picture.

No protection system in the world is unbreakable, the best you can hope for is to make it so boring for the average hacker that he (or she) gives up before the end.

Lee held her thumb under the by-line at the bottom of the page: "Jay Caradice". Is this herself?'

'Janine? Yes.'

'She writes as if she knows what she's talking about.'

'She does.'

'Could she hack into the computer at Malcolm's lab?'

'I'm sure she could, yes. Whether she would is entirely another question, and whether it would be sensible to ask her is something else again.'

'Why not?'

'She's got a habit of believing that rules are there to be kept. Hacking into other people's systems is against the law. If you read the rest of the article, it'll probably tell you what the penalties are.'

'I have. It does.' She folded the paper and slipped it into the bag at her feet. 'But I think some time soon, you're going to have to decide which side she's on. We're running out of options.'

'Why? What's happened?'

She looked down and drew a line between the damp rings on the table, thinking. When she looked up, her eyes were blank. 'All the blood samples I put into the lab have gone. And there's no record they ever existed, on the computer or in the day book.'

She stared at me over her glass while I tried to believe yet one more impossible thing before lunch and failed. The Pathology lab has one of the most up-to-date filing systems in the university. Facts do not go missing overnight.

'That's impossible.'

'No.' She sat back and stared out over the balcony. 'It just takes someone who knows their way around the inside of the Pathology labs.'

We know that already.

'Have you checked out who Philippa's married to yet?'

'Yes. It's the right David Kemp. And I was wrong about her spawning the next generation. Apparently she discovered the joys of science and stayed on as research assistant after she qualified. She's one third of the way to a PhD, with Malcolm as first supervisor.'

Wonderful.

'I suppose you haven't got a good reason, just off the top of your head, why the reptile would want to wipe out the last remaining scions of the Donnelly line?'

'Not off the top of my head, no.'

I thought not.

I'm too tired, or too old, to play games like this. I pinched the bridge of my nose and squinted past my thumb. 'Did you get anything useful from the bloods?'

'Some.' She reached into her bag and pulled out two sheets of computer printout. 'Take a look at these.'

The paper spun across the table towards me, sticking on the damp coffee rings.

It was a Pathology lab report: a full blood screen for a female patient, name of Sally Wentfield. Age: thirty-eight; medical diagnosis: chronic diabetes mellitus; possible cause of death: insulin overdose.

The abnormal figures were in bold type. The blood glucose was catastrophically low, easily consistent with the diagnosis of insulin OD.

The odd thing about the figures in front of me was that,

whereas the glucose had fallen through the floor, there was no insulin to speak of at all.

I looked at Lee. 'What's this?'

'It's a blood screen. Too many things were going missing so I put in a duplicate set of samples under a pseudonym. This is the result.'

'These are Bridget's blood results?'

She nodded. 'Yes. One of the few things consistent with her pathology picture was an insulin overdose. It was worth a try. The late Ms Wentfield did genuinely overdose, so she was a rather obvious choice.'

I remembered the name. 'Sally Wentfield's the body they switched for Bride?'

'Right.' She gave a humourless smile. 'One of life's smaller ironies, but not entirely relevant.'

'What makes you think she overdosed on insulin?'

She shrugged. 'A hunch. And the temazepam in the stomach. Insulin ODs usually have fits towards the end when the blood glucose gets too low. If you filled someone full of temazepam first, it would stop the seizures, so there'd be no signs of self-trauma on post-mortem. You'd get a very peaceful death. It's what I would do if I was trying to cover up.'

Brilliant. Absolutely bloody brilliant. Except that the results don't make sense.

'If it's an insulin overdose, Doctor, where's the insulin?'

'I don't know. That's where the hunch falls through. There's nothing in the blood and no obvious route of administration either.'

'Did she have needle marks?'

'No. We went over her with a magnifying glass on Friday. She was clean. Whatever it was, it wasn't injected.'

'Oral tablets?'

'Doesn't exist. There isn't an oral form of insulin. The HCl in the stomach denatures it. Besides, it'd be lethal if you put it

171

on the market. If you can OD by accident on the injectable stuff, imagine what you could do with tablets.'

She spoke absently, her eyes fixed on the lounge bar below. She saw me looking and nodded her head down towards the crowd.

'Does anyone down there look out of place to you?'

I scanned the room below. Twenty-something jeans and sweatshirts mixed with thirty-something business suits. Hair length varied at random. Drinking habits were more or less uniform.

On the second scan round, one stood out. Almost directly beneath us: a very, very quiet suit with cropped blond hair and an untouched pint. Male. Mid-twenties. Someone trying so hard to be invisible that, in itself, it made him conspicuous. That and the radiating sense of unfocused panic.

If he had been dressed differently and sitting in the library rather than the lounge bar of the Man, I would have put him down as a student with resit exams on the way.

Then he stretched out his hand for the pint and blew the cover completely. There, all the way round his wrist where it was exposed by the receding cuff, was the thin blue band of a tattoo.

A vague memory tugged at the back of my mind. A square blond outline framed in a doorway. 'I've seen him before somewhere. Recently.'

'Here. Last week when we had to leave a bit faster than intended. We were his diversion. His friends have unpleasant habits. Not the kind of people you want to meet unprepared.'

Or, indeed, at all. I looked at Lee. 'Friend of yours?'

'An . . . acquaintance. His mother's from the Island.'

Which probably makes him at least a second cousin.

'Has he come up with the goods?'

'More or less.' She pulled a tightly folded sheet of paper from an inner pocket. 'He gave me this before you arrived.'

The paper was a page torn from a notebook. On it was a

child-like drawing of a bird. The beak was over-large and had a shark's-tooth pattern along each edge. Underneath that was a price: £200/gram.

I smoothed the sheet flat and fixed it on the table between my cup and her glass. The hen's eye had been coloured in with a gilt pen, giving it a manic gleam as it stared up from the table. 'Am I supposed to understand this?'

'Not unless you're good at cryptic puzzles, no. Our Daniel can't write. He copped out of school before they got that far. He draws things instead.' She ran her finger round the gilt-eyed chicken. 'This is Hen's Teeth. It's the ultimate designer drug. Heroin buzz in a capsule. Crack by mouth. No needles, no fuss, no mess and, so far, no fatalities. The crack-heads love it. Laidlaw hates it. He's doing his nut trying to find out what it is and where it comes from.'

'Do you know?'

'Not yet.' She tapped the paper again. 'This is a step towards finding out. Young Daniel's offering access to the storehouse and he might be a lead back to the hen coop. I haven't had a chance to test any yet but I think it's probably an endorphin derivative. If they've got the formulation right, they could have something that would give you a heroin buzz without any of the legal complications.

'How so?'

'Easy.' Her smile was positively cheerful. 'It's not illegal to possess endorphins, Kellen. You can't legislate against something that every marathon runner generates by the bucketload every time they hit the road.'

'Hell.' No legislation. No arrests. No risk. Liquid gold. 'It's not surprising Laidlaw doesn't like it.'

'Not just Laidlaw. This'll play havoc with the current drugs controls.'

'Has this got anything to do with the matter in hand?'

'I think it might.' She traced a finger around the drawing.

'The hen has teeth. And Malcolm sent hens to Bridget. Then the woman herself dies on a last meal of egg.'

'That's a lot of synchronicity.'

'I thought that. Try something else. Malcolm was a genetic engineer and he was making new proteins. Supposing one of the things he made was illegal?'

'Like Hen's Teeth?'

'Right. It raises the stakes a little. Something like this would be worth dying for. Or, at least, worth killing for.'

'Malcolm wouldn't do that. He may have sold out to commerce but he wasn't bent.'

'Malcolm might not, but he had made the technology and someone else might have thought of a new use for it. This retails at £200 a gram. If you have hens that lay eggs full of the stuff, you might kill to keep it secret.'

You might well. And Malcolm, unless he had changed beyond all understanding, would never have stood around and watched someone else abusing science to that extent. He would have tried to stop them, one way or another.

The pattern was beginning to make sense. All we had to do was to test it and see if the facts fitted.

'We need to see what's in the eggs we picked up from Malcolm's lab and then compare it to the stuff from your friend downstairs.'

'We do. Which is a little sad because I don't have them any more. Someone turned my office over during the weekend. Nothing else was touched, but the eggs have gone.'

'Oh, bloody hell.'

'Quite.'

We stared at each other silently across the table.

Nothing is impossible, but some things are less probable than others. I would have thought that breaking into Lee's office was fairly low down the list of likely events. Obviously not.

Small spasms of paranoia vied with simple disbelief and an overwhelming urge to return to the normality of everyday life.

I pulled myself back together.

'You mean, all we have left from the other night is the disks?'

'I'm afraid so. That's why we need your tame journalist. The only other option is to go and look for Malcolm's body in Anatomy, and even if we find it, there's no guarantee it'll tell us anything.'

Worth a try, though.

'Have you got a password for the Anatomy records computer?'

'Sure.' She produced a blank file card from the bag at her feet and wrote out a series of numbers and letters in upper and lower case, then pushed it across the table towards me.

'Are you going to go now?' She looked at me sceptically.

'Of course.' I met her eye. 'I'll think about going to see Janine later on. If you could warn McNeill that I'm on my way, it might make getting in easier.'

'Will he recognise you?'

'I doubt it.'

'Fine. You can be my research student. You'll need a name.' She thought for a moment. 'How would you like to be Ms Mhaire Culloch for the day?'

The thought of stepping into the madwoman's shoes made my hair stand on end, but it had a certain symmetry. 'I'd hate it, but it'll do.'

'Poetic justice.' She grinned cheerfully and stood up, handing me the newspaper. 'Here. You can read this on the Underground. Have a look at the front page. It'll restore your faith in humanity.'

The lead item was an article, complete with full frontal pictures, of Chief Inspector Laidlaw addressing a conference in Edinburgh on improving police attitudes towards women as the victims of crime.

If my faith in humanity could have fallen any further, it would have disappeared through the floor.

CHAPTER SEVEN

Anatomy is the department they left behind when they moved the medical school to the West End in the late 1970s. The anatomists never really considered themselves to be part of the medical fraternity and saw no reason to disrupt the habits of several lifetimes when they were all happily fossilised in their insulated time-warp of a building. So when Physiology and Biochemistry and all the other pre-clinical departments moved into the shiny new labs in the hospital complex, the Anatomy Department sat tight as a single, immovable mass and suggested that if Mohamet wanted to know the secrets of the human frame, then Mohamet in the shape of 200-odd medical students a year, could put on his shoes and walk. Or, rather, hop on the Underground and pray for a fast train.

It took our class less than two weeks of shuttling backwards and forwards across town between lectures to realise that the timetable had not been designed taking basic geography into account. By the end of the first month, the class had split: some went to anatomy, some attended physiology and biochemistry and each group swapped notes. In the middle were the few entrepreneurs who attended no lectures at all and borrowed everyone's notes on the night before the exams. None of them made it through to the second year.

In our particular pairing, Lee, the budding surgeon, had picked anatomy, while I sat at the feet of the physiologists and dreamed dreams of internal medicine. At the time, it had seemed like an obvious choice. Fifteen years later on, as I fought my way out of the southern exit of the Buchanan Street Underground through the crowds of drenched commuters, I wished I had paid more attention to the route.

I found the place eventually, guided by half-remembered images of street corners and old advertising hordings, in a dead-end street two blocks away from George Square. A huge Victorian sandstone edifice, the pale red stone blackened to ebony with age and a century's worth of car exhaust emissions. In its day, it was the gold-standard of imperial values, designed to remind the good citizens of Glasgow that the Empire reached north of the border and the Scots had made their due contributions to the forward march of progress.

Now, the alley was filled with unemptied rubbish bins, and the stink of household garbage joined the background flavour of wet pavements. A sodden copy of the *Sunday Sport* was plastered to the step just outside the revolving door and a handful of loose pages had been trampled inside, jamming the base. I gave up trying to push the thing round and took a small side door round the corner instead. From the look of the trail of footprints leading across the marble floor into the hallway, everyone else that morning had done the same.

I was standing in the doorway, shaking the rain out of my hair, when I was accosted by Mr Archibald McNeill, the Anatomy caretaker. McNeill is a small, anxious mouse of a man with a permanent drip of serous fluid hanging suspended from the end of his nose – the product of a long and fruitless battle between his nasal passages and the allergenic effects of the formalin that pervades the atmosphere. He has been a permanent fixture of the department since long before I was a medic, but he tends only to remember the students who have been to more than two

177

lectures and, of those, only the ones who have finished the *Herald* crossword before they arrive for the first class at ten o'clock. That made me safe on both counts.

He left the safety of his cubbyhole and scuffled over as I did my best impression of a dog out of water.

'May I help you?' He cocked his head to one side and peered round the edge of his glasses.

'Mhaire Culloch. You should be expecting me.' I held out a hand.

He ignored it and scurried back to consult his notes.

'That would be Dr Adam's research assistant?'

I suppose it would.

'Yes. That's right.'

'You'll be needing the files first then. They're on the fourth floor. If you'll follow me?'

For a moment, I thought we might actually be going to use the lifts. But no one in Anatomy uses the lifts, not even Archie McNeill. Life is too short to spend large portions of it suspended in a disaster of Victorian engineering that takes twenty minutes to travel a distance that could be walked in five.

On the other hand, taking the lift means you don't have to walk past the specimens on the stair. Formalin-filled cases on black marble plinths sit in gaps along the wall at intervals up the wide, spiralling marble stairs. Each one has a small brass plaque stating the name, age and date of death plus a single word or phrase describing the clinical condition that brought it there. Things that have been engraved on my stomach wall since the first time I tried to walk past them.

Siamese twins, foetal stage. Two pre-infantile heads, joined at the neck, sharing one body. A single umbilical cord coursed up and round the left side of the neck to float, rigid, in the enfolding yellow formalin.

Anencephalous – neonate. A body and a face with a vague rictus grin, but no head behind it.

Ventricular septal defect. A hole in the heart. Or, in this case, a hole with a bit of heart muscle vaguely wrapped around it. Date: 1894. Long before cardiac bypass and open-chest surgery.

Once, in the dim and distant past, someone thought these were exciting and interesting and that the gentlemen of anatomy should be able to review them in the course of their daily work. But for generations now they have functioned as a simple and effective method of career selection. If you can make the long walk up to the lecture theatre on the top floor without reviewing breakfast *en route*, then there's a fair chance of surviving the real-life equivalents in the surgical theatre. Everyone else had better stick to medicine. This is the real reason Lee did anatomy and I did not. I could never make it past the Siamese twins with my eyes open.

It took me six months on the wards to learn the secret of the Anatomy Department myth. Anatomical variations are correctable by surgery. Even perfectly normal faces can be moulded to suit the fashion of the moment. The effects of gravity, time and over-indulgence vanish in a single, highly paid sleight of hand, leaving an entire generation with a permanently juvenile frown. It's the changes inside the head, the ones you can't see and can't get at with a knife, that make the nightmares real.

I think I could handle almost anything anatomy could produce these days, but as I followed the little man up the stairway, I kept my eyes on the pattern of the marble steps as a matter of habit.

The Anatomy archives are kept opposite the lecture theatres on the fourth floor in a vast room running the whole length of the building. McNeill wheezed and huffed his way to the door and bent down over the lock, rattling his keys noisily in case I should think the place unlocked, then pushed the door open and poked his head inside.

Nobody around. He coughed into the back of his nose and backed away.

'All the files are in here, Dr Culloch. If you need any help, I'll be at my desk.'

Which is four floors down and barely worth the walk.

'Thank you.' I flashed an earnest smile. 'If I need anything else, I'll call.'

That removed any inclination he might have had to hang around. He gave a single curt nod and vanished round the corner. I listened while his footsteps skipped down the stairs, half a flight at a time, then I opened the door, stepped inside and sneezed violently. It's the dust that does it, more than the smell. Formalin is everywhere in anatomy. Harsh, eye-watering and noxious, it seeps through wood and metal and human flesh and clings to the back of your throat for days. In the archives, it is mixed with the dust of centuries and the musty smell of old paper, crumbling in forgotten files, and it feels like walking into a room full of snuff.

I stood just inside the doorway, breathing shallow breaths through the floor of my nose, and let my eyes adjust to the gloom. They never believed in real light in Anatomy, it spoils the effect. They go for dark wood panelling and forty-watt bulbs that give out just enough light to illuminate the ubiquitous specimen jars so that they glow like giant, bulbous candles, lighting up their leering occupants.

The whole place gives me the creeps.

There was a lurid green glow on one wall, next to the skeleton of a giantess. I made my way over, skirting racks of files and tables with piles of index cards, and found that it was indeed the Anatomy computer. Or, at least, a terminal thereof; the mainframe sits somewhere in an underground cavern, powered by valves and steam turbines.

The log-in signal blinked sleepily, waiting for the next

enthralling set of instructions to wake it up. If McNeill had any initiative at all, he would teach it how to do crosswords.

I pulled out the file card Lee had given me and began to type.

For the next ten minutes I had a largely fruitless but very satisfying conversation with the skeleton regarding the parentage of the programmers, the archivists, the Anatomy Department and, most particularly, the motherless son of an unknown father who had removed Malcolm Donnelly's data from the file. I found his name and the date he had been transferred from Pathology to Anatomy, but beyond that nothing else. Somewhere in four floors of specimens and slides lay the disparate remains of Dr Malcolm Donnelly deceased, genetic engineer and friend, but without an identifying serial number to trace the various bits, I had no chance at all of finding him, or of finding how he had died.

The skeleton stood in polite silence while I invoked the aid of a number of ancient and malevolent deities and listened attentively while I described the hopelessness of the current situation. She heard me out while I ran through all the very good reasons why I could not possibly ask my recently departed lover for help, and understood completely when I explained what would happen to both myself and my close friend and companion Dr Adams if the forces of law and order were to connect us to the recent raid on a certain medical research establishment. When asked what she would do in my place, she obeyed the one solid rule of crisis counselling and left me to make my own decisions.

Everyone should have a seven-foot skeleton to talk to once in a while.

I left her in peace and went downstairs to find a phone. Before I left the room, I cleared a couple of desks out of the way so that she had a clear view through the window. It seemed the least I could do.

Janine was at work and not in the right frame of mind to talk over the phone, but she did agree to a lunch date provided I could pick her up at the office. I did some rapid mental arithmetic, calculating time and distance, and agreed when to meet her.

My paramour works in an open-plan office designed by an interior decorator on crack. Grey and pink geometric shapes on the carpet clash with the rigid black metal furniture which, in its turn, stands out brilliantly against mauve-on-white rag-rolled walls. Square white ceiling lights cut out all the nasty shadows that might otherwise render the overall effect somewhat less nauseating.

Everyone who works there keeps their eyes fixed on their computer consoles and all of them have tight crows'-feet at the corners of their eyes and the tense, nervous look that sells aspirin by the bucketload. Just walking in through the door is enough to inspire epileptic fits and I swore the first time I went there that I wasn't setting foot across the threshold ever again. Times change.

Janine has the only sane desk in the room. She sits next to a floor-to-ceiling window with views out into the real world of office blocks and tenements and passing buses in the street below. Spontaneous variety is supplied by a row of pigeons that sit on the sill just the other side of the glass. There were six of them when I arrived. Plump and bright-eyed, sheltering in the lee of the building, away from the rain and the hammering wind.

I sat on the edge of the desk and watched her work. The image of the office woman. A phone was tucked under her chin and she talked into it, staring blankly out at the pigeons while her fingers, independent life-forms, typed copy at several dozen words per minute.

A sideways flick of the head showed she had seen me. Her

fingers tapped at the screen and a message flowed up in mid-paragraph: WON'T BE LONG.

It stayed long enough for me to read and then disappeared, to be replaced by more crisp chunks of techno-copy.

I nodded and carried on counting the pigeons, wondering whether my epileptic threshold had changed since my last visit and how long it would take me to find out. All I needed was for a couple of the fluorescent ceiling lights to flicker and I would be on the floor, foaming at the mouth.

Two of the pigeons deserted, flying off to a more desirable sill. Four to go. If they all left, someone would have to go out on to the ledge to replace them.

Me, for instance.

We were down to three, all of them restless, when Janine finally hung up, laying the receiver off the hook on the desk.

It gave a high-pitched whine, the auditory equivalent of the office decor, and I felt the seizure patterns forming at the back of my skull.

I dragged my eyes away from the window to look at her. 'Lunch?'

'Good idea.'

If she was less closeted at work, I would have hugged her, but I settled for a stunning smile instead.

'How do you work in that hell-hole?'

'I know all the pigeons by name, rank and number. If they ever leave me, I'll go completely barking mad.'

'But will you notice?'

'That's what you're there for.'

'Thanks.'

We were sitting in a wine bar two blocks along from the offices. A journalistic watering hole, packed full of hacks talking shop, swapping stories, inventing new exclusives and reliving past scoops.

Janine was well known. Both barmen nodded as she shepherded me across the crowded floor to a quiet table at the back. A lass with a neat black uniform and neat black hair appeared as soon as we sat down and brought my other half a tall wine glass with a twist of lemon curved over the rim and tiny beads of condensation forming on the sides.

The girl raised her eyebrows ever so gently in my direction, I nodded and another glass with an identical twist arrived while I was still draping my jacket over the tall stool by the wall. Mineral water. Wonderful. A glance at the menu showed that it cost almost as much as the real thing.

'I ordered a couple of salads,' said Janine. 'Is that all right?'

'Sure. Whatever.' I looked around. Not one of the waiting staff was paying us any attention whatsoever. 'The barmen are psychic, right?'

'Ex-auctioneers.' She suppressed a smile and tipped her chair back against the wall, studying me and saying nothing.

We sat like that, watching each other in silence while the waitress brought us the salads. Executive lettuce torn into strips layered on neatly carved celery chips with wafers of tomato and mozzarella cheese. A meal designed to keep the mouth occupied without adding calories. I picked a particularly enticing piece of lettuce and nibbled it experimentally. It tasted much like ordinary lettuce. Disappointing.

Janine tipped her stool back to the ground and browsed methodically across the plate, hunting out the olives and piling them in a heap at the side.

It was the kind of meal that could easily have provided mindless distraction for the rest of the lunch hour and we would have been no further forward. One of us had to break the deadlock.

I put down my fork and pushed the plate to one side. Janine raised one eyebrow and savoured an olive.

'I need your help.'

184

The eyebrow slid higher. She selected a slice of tomato and studied it.

Malcolm's disks were in my pocket. I lifted the package out and laid it on the table.

'These came from the lab where Malcolm Donnelly used to work. They're protected and I don't know how to read them. Would you try? Please?'

She took out a disk and held it up to the light: a counterfeiter studying the latest foreign currency. To me, it looked square and black, like any other disk. She put it back on the table.

'How did you get hold of them?'

I shook my head. 'Pass.'

She speared a circle of cheese with her fork and ate it slowly. 'It's not legal to hack other people's disks. You know that?'

Neither is murder.

'I know. That's why I didn't ask you last night.'

'What's changed?'

'Someone is closing doors on us, fast. These are the only lead we have left. And the only one the opposition don't know about. The original is still in place. These were copied.'

'On Friday night?'

I studied my glass of water and said nothing.

'Look at me, Kellen.'

I looked. Her eyes were clear and self-contained. She lifted her drink so that it obscured the eye contact for a moment, then swirled the water slightly so that it fizzed in the glass. When she put it down, she had made some kind of decision.

'Give me one good reason why I should do this for you.'

I searched. There were a lot of reasons why she might want to help, but I wasn't sure that any of them could be classed as good. Especially not from her point of view.

It took me a long time. A lot more than the disks rested on the answer. The waitress came back and cleared the plates while I was thinking.

In the end, there was only one thing that really mattered.

'Because I need to know who killed Bridget.'

'So you can kill them too?'

Pass. An unanswerable question, even when one is not in a room full of active journalists.

'No. I only need to know. To make an ending.'

She nodded heavily, considering. Then she picked up a disk, spinning it over and over between her fingers.

'I really don't count in this, do I?'

Honestly?

'No.'

If she had walked out then and never come back, I would not have been surprised. But she didn't. She gave a small rueful laugh and threw up an arm to sweep a hand through her hair.

'It's honest, at least. If you had said anything else, I wouldn't have believed you.'

She sighed and shook her head so that her hair fell back down round her shoulders. 'Rae's right, you know. I really have to learn to let you go.'

'Really.'

'Yes, really. But not yet. I don't give up that fast.' She stood up, taking the packet of disks with her. 'I'll try and look at this today. I could meet you at Bee's after work?'

'Sure. If you think that's enough time?'

'It's enough.' She nodded, slinging her bag over her shoulder. 'Do you want to tell me what I'm looking for?'

'Genetically engineered eggs. There's something in them besides the yolk and the white. We need to know what it is.'

'Right. You'll be at the farm?'

'Yes.' I put out a hand as she turned to go. 'Jan?'

'Yes?'

'Thank you.'

'Don't mention it.'

I watched her leave, cutting a path through the jabbering

throng, red hair high above the rest. Then I ordered a coffee. When I went to pay, I found the price was already included on the bill, and it had been paid by Janine as she left.

The rain was easing by the time I reached the car and the drive back through Milngavie was pleasantly free of traffic. Too late for the morning commuters and too early for the mother-and-schoolkid shuttle. I switched on the radio and half-listened to the sledgehammer plot of the afternoon play, the other half of my mind spinning parts of the jigsaw, looking for more of the pattern.

At the farm, there were two sets of tyre marks, but only one car: an unmarked police Escort with a jacket draped across the back seat that was just the right size for a certain green-eyed WPC. The engine was still warm.

Inside, Caroline was sitting on the floor, her back against a fireside chair, with the dog lying peacefully beside her. Elspeth Philips was at the sink with her back to me, filling the kettle. She turned as I walked in the door and the usual wary animosity was, for once, gone from her eyes.

'White, no sugar, thank you.' I dropped my jacket on the window-seat. 'Where's our favourite Inspector?'

'Gone for the vet,' said Caroline. Her voice was tight, over-controlled.

'I'm sorry?'

The policewoman came over and sat in the chair, laying a protective hand on her shoulder, comforting the way she had done on the night Bridget died.

'The pup's poorly,' she said.

She looked very peaceful from where I was standing. I crouched down to have a closer look and realised, first, that Caroline was close to weeping and, second, that she had good reason. The pup wasn't just poorly, she was virtually comatose.

A cold, clammy, lifeless husk with a femoral pulse that pattered thinly under my fingers.

There are moments when medical instinct usefully takes over.

'There's a first aid kit in the glove compartment of the car,' I said. 'Get it.' I was talking to Caroline but Elspeth Philips was up and out of the door before I got to the 'please'. I suppose she was closest.

Caroline stretched the curled body out on the hearth rug for me to look at. There was a faint, unstable heartbeat palpable behind the elbow and when I opened the eyes, the pupils were wide and there was no response to light or touch. Every part of her was cold.

The first aid kit arrived. I slid the thermometer into her rectum, the way we did for the newborn kids and the geriatrics who can't suck a piece of glass without biting it, and ran a stethoscope across her chest and the rotund swelling of her belly. Breathing harsh, gut sounds minimal, temperature falling off the bottom of the scale.

A young dog, dying of whatever young dogs die of. Way out of my field.

I sent Caroline to find something warm to cover her and Elspeth to put the kettle back on. Both diversionary tactics to keep them busy until the Inspector showed up with the right professional person.

The fits began as we wrapped her in the blankets. Small twitches at first, then a tremor that started deep in her body and worked its way in spastic jumps down her legs. Within the space of five minutes, it had progressed to full-blown seizures, her head and neck arching back in a series of violent tetanic spasms.

A Land Rover drew up outside and a single set of footsteps ran for the door.

'Well?'

'He's out at a calving,' said a familiar West Highland burr from the doorway. 'They said he'd get here as soon as he can.'

'Shit. That's no good.'

'Aye.'

Inspector MacDonald stood in the doorway, his skin the colour of peat ash, the worn lines on his face giving him ten extra years.

I wouldn't have said he was the sentimental kind.

'Can you not do something, lass?'

'Christ, I don't know. It doesn't look like the average bout of neonatal gastric "flu", but I haven't a clue what it is.'

I ran my mind through the differential diagnoses for coma and symptomatic treatment for fits. Mostly the benzodiazepines: diazepam or midazolam. Or temazepam.

An idea grew teeth and gnawed at the back of my mind.

Caroline was sitting on the floor, staring fixedly at the twitching form, her head jerking fractionally in time with each spasm.

I covered the pup with one hand and lifted Caroline's chin up so that her eyes met mine.

'What happened, C?'

She shook her head free.

'Nothing's happened. She fell asleep and she won't wake up. That's all.'

Her voice was ice-cold.

I picked up a hand as cold as her voice and pulled her round to face me. 'Tell me what she's done since I left.'

'Nothing. She played with the cats for most of the morning till I shoved them out for a bit so I could feed her.' Her eyes came back to meet mine. 'You didn't feed her this morning, did you?'

I shook my head. 'Sorry. Forgot.'

'I thought you had. Anyway, I let the cats came back in again after she'd finished and the whole lot of them went to sleep on top of the Rayburn. When Elspeth and the Inspector arrived, I tried to move them off to make coffee, she just wouldn't wake up. She's gone to sleep and she won't wake up.'

'She's dying, lass,' said Stewart MacDonald simply.

A new corner of the jigsaw fell into place. Just one more piece to go and we have one whole edge.

'What did you feed her?' I asked.

'The eggs you got from the bantams this morning. I used up all the others yesterday. The meal list said to give her scrambled eggs once a day and . . . where are you going?'

'To my car,' I said from the doorway. 'She's got insulin poisoning. It's in the eggs. It's how they killed Bridget.'

Once in a while, I'm glad I did medicine. And I'm glad I stock up my car now and again with the kind of things wandering medics usually carry and members of the lay public do not. The medical kit in the boot is considerably larger than the first aid box in the glove compartment and very comprehensive.

I grabbed a bag of dextrose solution, a vial of diazepam, a drip set and a handful of catheters, and carried them back to the kitchen, telling myself that I did paediatrics once and a baby dog can't be that different from a baby human.

It's not true of course. Kids aren't covered in hair and they have nice blue veins on the backs of their hands and the tops of their heads. Dogs don't have either. I settled instead for the jugular vein and we shaved the hair off the side of her neck with a scalpel blade.

The years on the ward paid their due. Inspector MacDonald held the head still while I slid a catheter into a vein filled with sludging black blood. The dose of dextrose seemed fairly arbitrary. I guessed the dog's weight, pretended she was a five-year-old child, did some rapid mental arithmetic and opened the drip set to full bore. Half a cc of diazepam went in through the injection port and I watched it flow down into the vein before turning the drip rate down to a slow dribble. The Inspector held out a hand and took over as voluntary drip stand.

Time passed. The fits became more violent and ran closer

together. I gave her another half cc of the diazepam, praying hard that we were nowhere near the overdose rate. I shut my eyes. Prayers come easier that way.

'She's stopping,' said Caroline.

The shuddering spasms slowed to a standstill, leaving her deathly still.

I glued my stethoscope to the dog's chest and listened to the rhythm of her heart. It was there, but that was about the best that could be said for it.

'Diazepam's worked,' I said. Nobody gave me a gold star.

Caroline pulled the steaming kettle from the Rayburn and filled a hot-water bottle, wrapping it in a thick layer of tea-towels.

'She's cold,' she said simply.

It wasn't such a bad idea. We laid the pup on the warm towels and I eased the thermometer back into her rectum. Watching the mercury column edge upwards took our eyes off the slow, dysrhythmic rise and fall of her chest.

Time moved like a crippled slug. I remembered other eternities like this from the long, late nights on ICU. Poised for ever with one finger on the cardiac arrest alarm waiting for an erratic ECG trace to flatten out. Except this time there was no ECG and no crash team to call on with their advanced resuscitation technology. Just a mercury thermometer and a stethoscope and a dextrose drip.

It worked, but only just, and I have still got no idea whether it was the dextrose or the diazepam, or whether she would have come back on her own given time.

When it was obvious she was coming round, we sent Elspeth out to the butcher in the village for puppy meal and when she came back, MacDonald stoked up the fire, wrapped the pup in a blanket and sat with her on his lap, feeding her small warmed fragments with his fingers as a father would feed a sick child. I sat on the floor against the side of the chair, feeling worn out and useless.

Elspeth Philips came to sit opposite me, her hands wrapped round a mug of Lee's cat's-piss tea. She looked as tired as I did. Almost in the mood for a real conversation.

'What's the official treatment for insulin overdose, Kellen?' she asked.

I shrugged. 'Glucose infusion to correct the hypoglycaemia and an anticonvulsant for the fits. I only used diazepam because I had it in the car. Any of the others would have done.'

'Like temazepam?' she asked.

'Maybe.' I nodded, slowly.

'Bridget had temazepam in her stomach contents, didn't she?'

'I think so.' I tried to sound unsure. Suddenly it didn't feel like a casual conversation. MacDonald was still feeding the pup but I could feel his eyes on the back of my neck.

'Could she have eaten the eggs from the hens as well?'

'She did,' said Caroline. 'She had scrambled eggs for lunch. I saw the pan when I came in.'

Thanks, kid.

I watched the tumblers fall into place in Elspeth Philip's brain. She looked at me directly and I heard echoes of Laidlaw's size 14s tramping triumphantly across the yard. Very depressing.

'If the pup had died and we got a post-mortem on it now,' said the woman from SCC thoughtfully, 'it would look almost exactly like Bridget, wouldn't it?'

'Bride didn't have needle marks anywhere,' I said, 'but otherwise, yes.'

'So it's possible that someone gave her the sedative but not the glucose.'

'It's possible.'

MacDonald broke in. He laid the pup at his feet and turned his attention openly on his colleague. 'What are you saying, lass?' he asked.

'I think Bridget was murdered,' said WPC Elspeth Philips simply. 'Just like Caroline said.'

Inspector MacDonald looked up from the dog and smiled a little sadly. 'In that case, we'd better inform Chief Inspector Laidlaw that he has a murder in his patch,' he said, as if he had never considered anything else.

CHAPTER EIGHT

The telephone rang: a nasty insistent chirrup, invading the silence. Caroline reached it first.

She listened for a moment, then held it out to me, not bothering to cover the mouthpiece. 'It's Janine,' she said. 'She's waiting for you in town. You're late.'

I took the handset out into the hall, away from listening ears, and grovelled, promising to be at Bee's as soon as was humanly possible, allowing for the need to collect Lee on the way.

When I got back, Inspector MacDonald was still sitting by the fire, staring morosely into the flames. The pup looked better. She was sitting at his feet with her nose on his knee and he pulled absently at her ears.

I knelt down by his chair.

'I have to go out,' I said. 'Do you have to tell the Chief Inspector today?'

'We do,' he said. 'As soon as we get back to the office.' There was a tinge of regret there if you listened for it, but his face had closed over, all the conspiratorial friendship of the poacher washed to nothing beneath a smooth professional glaze.

'Chief Inspector Laidlaw's in Edinburgh for the Community Policing conference,' said a voice from the other side of the room. 'He'll not be back till tomorrow night.'

Elspeth Philips sat on the window-bench under the kitchen window, silhouetted against the ice-light of the dusk. Her face was unreadable in the heightened shadows and her voice held nothing more than mild conversation. She could have been reading the day's racing results and made it sound more interesting.

'I don't expect he'll look at his mail before Wednesday morning,' she said.

There was a brief silence while everybody avoided making eye contact.

Eventually, Inspector MacDonald leant down and pushed the dog gently off his feet.

'Right then,' he said, in a voice transparent with its lack of inflection, 'I'll write him a report tonight and put it on his desk personally in the morning.'

We stood at the door and watched them leave. Elspeth went first in her white, unmarked Escort, with Stewart MacDonald's Land Rover close on its tail. Five minutes later, when they were well clear of the drive, we turned the alarm system on.

Almost an hour later, Lee drove me to Bee's to meet Janine. We left the car on a meter outside the Botanic Gardens and walked the three blocks along to the café. The wind had died and the rain fell sluggishly, straight down, like drips from a cracked cistern, splattering noisily on the wet pavements.

Monday and Thursday are the 'women-only' nights at Bee's. It encourages a stable clientele when folk might otherwise stay at home to recover from the excesses of the weekend. Even so it was quiet as we walked in.

A dozen or so women sat scattered among the tables in twos or threes, leaning forward in muted conversation or sitting back in silence, listening to the piped jazz.

There was no sign of Janine. I left Lee on her own at a corner table and explored the bar downstairs. It was empty, except for a single woman, her face hidden behind a newspaper, sitting at the same table I had shared with mad Mhaire Culloch the previous evening.

Janine.

She lowered the paper as I sat down.

'Sorry I'm late.'

'You're always late.' For once, it didn't seem to matter. There was a tingle of excitement about her that took the chill off the words. She reached into the bag slung on the back of the chair and pulled out a handful of printed A4 sheets in a cardboard folder. 'I found out what's in the eggs,' she said.

'Insulin?'

'You knew?' She was disappointed. I should have kept my mouth shut and let her tell me.

'Caroline found it by accident.'

'Does that mean you don't need this?' She tapped the folder.

'No. We need it. What have you got?'

'Lots. Your friend was good. He had three different protection systems running together. The more interesting it got, the better it was protected. Letters and the like were easy, you could have opened them if you'd tried. The stuff in the middle was dynamite. Pure dynamite.'

'Tell me.'

'He took the gene sequence for human insulin and spliced it into the genes for the egg albumin. So he had hens that laid eggs with insulin in the whites. And it takes next to no processing to extract it and convert it into something injectable.'

'Hell. The medics would give their eye teeth for that.'

'Wouldn't they just? Take a look.' As she pushed the folder across the table, I saw the faintest shadow of a grin. Beautiful science inspires my beloved the way Ecstasy inspires the raver and if what she said was true, Malcolm had made some beautiful science.

The world is full of diabetics and each one of them has to

inject themselves twice daily with insulin. Modern insulin comes from cows. Tons of bovine pancreatic tissue are collected from the slaughterhouses and the insulin is squeezed out.

The problem is that once in a while someone reacts to the foreign protein in the insulin they inject and ends up with more problems than they started with. Human insulin would be infinitely safer, it's just that tons of human pancreatic tissues are hard to come by and the stuff has proved difficult to make. Until now.

Janine watched me from under lowered lids as I leafed through half a dozen pages of test results that listed the early experiments and purity of the compounds extracted. All very elegant. The kind of science I used to expect from Malcolm. In purely biological terms, what he had done was clever, even beautiful. In commercial terms, it was a licence to print money.

She caught on to the train of thought. 'It's a goldmine.'

'It is,' I agreed, staring blankly at the folder. There was no record of anything with a significant street value. No Hen's Teeth. 'But then why did they kill him? As I remember the story, it was always considered uncommonly stupid to kill the goose who laid the golden eggs.'

'Maybe it was an accident?'

I shook my head. 'Unlikely.'

'But not impossible,' She took the file back and pulled a single sheet from the bottom of the pile and slid it across the table. 'Look at this.'

It was a half-page memo, limited circulation, from Malcolm to the heads of research and development announcing the isolation of pure human insulin from the egg whites of the genetically engineered bantams. The last sentence was laid out in bold type and underlined:

NOTE: Work is continuing in an attempt to develop a form active only by the injectable route. In the meantime, the

clinical efficacy of the oral form carries significant health risk.
All effort is being made to alter the binding protein to avoid
this.

The memo was dated two days before he died.

Carries significant health risk. Oh, hell. Malcolm, you poor
bloody idiot, you even told them how to do it.

She looked at me, questioning. 'He means that eating the
eggs would give you an insulin overdose?'

'More or less.'

'Do you think that's what killed him?'

'I don't know. I think it's what killed Bridget. She had all the
signs of insulin poisoning on the blood results, but we couldn't
find any insulin. That's because we were testing for the wrong
sort. The tests are run for bovine insulin, not the human type.'

'Can you test for it now?'

'We could if someone hadn't destroyed all her blood samples.'

'Deliberately?'

'Yes.'

'Hell.'

'Quite.'

I watched her for a moment. She looked almost involved
enough.

'We might be able to test some of Malcolm's blood if we could
find the samples. Would you be interested in helping us take a
look inside another computer?'

'When?'

'Tonight. Now.'

'Is this legal?'

'Not at all.'

There was only the briefest hesitation before she stood up.
'Why not?'

Lee tailed us out of the upstairs bar, collected the car from the parking meter and picked us up at the traffic lights opposite the Underground station. From there, it was a bare five minutes' drive through the mid-evening traffic to the centre of town.

The Anatomy Department sat smothered in the shadows, at the end of the alleyway. A statuesque mausoleum with no lights visible at any of the windows. Anatomists are not renowned for working late.

Lee nosed the Saab gently into the small yard at the back, where the meat wagons from the mortuary park to unload their offerings, and flipped an official University Medical Authority permit on to the dashboard. It might have been legitimate.

She pulled a couple of pen torches from the glove compartment and handed one to me. 'We'll play it straight as far as we can. If there's a reception committee, we make our excuses and leave.' She passed me a spare car key. 'If it gets hot, you two get out. I'll see you back at the farm.'

'Right.'

Inside, the foyer was dead to the world. Cold, dark, creepy and inhuman. Still one of the most depressing places I have ever been. The darkness hid the monsters in their jars on the stairs and we were careful to keep the torch beams directed only at the steps. The giantess on her plinth in the corner of the archive room was more difficult to conceal, but the computer next to her proved to be enough of a short-term distraction.

It hummed to life and lit the gloom with a phosphorescent green glow. Janine pulled up the padded chair and began tapping keys.

'Password.'

'I'm sorry?'

'What's your password to open the system?'

'Oh. Here.' I passed her a file card Lee had given me with the jumble of letters and digits written on it.

'Thanks.'

More tapping. Lee backed over to the door to keep an eye on the corridor.

Janine dug a disk out of her bag and pushed it into the spare disk drive.

'What was his name?'

'Malcolm Donnelly.'

'Middle initial "D"?'

'Right.'

The disk drive whirred and chomped through blocks of data.

'Got it.'

'Christ, that was quick.'

'I know.' Her voice carried the edge of a smile. 'Hopeless amateurs.'

'That's handy. Can you tell when they stripped out the file?'

A pause and the rattle of keystrokes.

'Saturday morning.'

The morning after the night before. The night we raided the lab.

'Any idea who?' asked Lee from the doorway.

'Not a clue, sorry.' She opened the file and the screen filled with text. 'What do you need to know about Malcolm?'

There were two pages of text. At the top was the reference number we needed to let Lee find whatever was left of the body. The rest showed dates of processing and where the various organs had gone.

'This'll do.' I began to copy the number on to the back of the file card with the password.

'Hold on then.' The screen blanked out just as I copied the last digit of the number. More tapping, more whirring of disk drives. 'Right. Let's go.'

'Is that it?'

'Why not? I've shifted the stuff you need on to the floppy disk, we can go back to Rae's and print it out there.' The half of her face I could see in the torch beam looked very satisfied with life. 'It's far safer than hanging around here. And a lot more legal.'

Lee came over from the doorway and I handed her the card with the serial number. She seemed mildly impressed.

I flashed the light towards her. 'Coming with us?'

'Not yet. I've got someone to meet in town. I'll see you back at your flat later on.'

'When?'

'Eleven thirty. Leave a message on the answer-phone if you can't make it.'

'Right.'

Rae's flat was empty when we arrived. The fastidious tidiness made me as uncomfortable as ever. Not a fold of curtain or a tapestried cushion out of place. It sets my teeth on edge.

Janine, with the unconscious care born of natural instinct, shook the rain off her jacket at the top of the stairs and carried it through to the bathroom, where she hung it over the shower rail to dry. I flicked the worst of the rain off mine and hung it on a convenient chair in the hallway, where it dripped slowly on to the pastel wool of the carpet. Then I followed her into the spare room and found a piece of flash computer hardware that I had never seen before standing on a desk near the bed. I dragged the chair in from the hall and sat back to watch the technology at work.

Whatever it was, it came up with the goods. The disk disappeared into an internal drive and, three minutes later, a small ink-jet printer hidden under the desk spewed out a two-page history of the corpse of one Malcolm D. Donnelly, deceased. Useful as evidence if it ever came to that.

Janine lifted the sheets from the printer tray and held them delicately by the edges, blowing gently to dry the ink. Printer ink on carpets like these would be little short of catastrophic.

I read through to check the one thing I hadn't had time to

read over her shoulder in the dark of the records room: sometimes blood samples are taken and stored for later use in routine screening of population studies, especially if the deceased is fit, reasonably young and did not die of any contagious disease. It's the kind of thing that's so routine, it would be easy to forget to cancel it.

Half-way down the second page there was a check in the right box. If it was telling the truth, then there was a sample with Malcolm's serial number in the Anatomy freezers and we should have another piece of the jigsaw by morning.

I settled back in the chair to read the rest of the file, feeling more than usually optimistic.

'What do you think of Elspeth?'

'I'm sorry?' I looked up to see Janine staring straight at the screen, her face glowing oddly in the fluorescent glare, like a jaundiced vampire.

'Elspeth Philips. Do you like her?'

Hardly.

'She's in the police, Jan.'

'I know that. I hadn't realised that you discriminated against other women on professional grounds.'

'It's nothing personal. I just don't trust the police. Force of experience.'

'She likes you.'

I doubt it.

'How do you know? Has she asked you about me?'

This time she laughed aloud. 'If she was going to ask questions, Kellen, I don't think I'd be the one she picked first. Even a policewoman has more tact than that.'

'If she did, would you tell her?'

Wrong question. The amused animation in her face faded to nothing.

'You really don't trust me, do you?' she asked.

Pass.

Janine played absently with the function keys, and the ghoul-green glow of the screen transformed into a searing yellow. The question that was not a question hung in the air like an afterthought.

There is a time and a place for everything. I would rather it wasn't here and now.

I walked over to the window and opened it, letting in the noise of the traffic from the road below and the steady background splatter of the rain. A wall of cold, wet air pushed at my face, a sobering focus, like a bucket of river water. I turned back to face her.

'If I didn't trust you, I wouldn't have given you the disks and I wouldn't have asked you to help tonight.'

'Thanks.'

Irony, my dear, is a waste of time.

'I was going to ask you to do something else. Would you rather I didn't?'

'What is it?'

'I've got the number to a modem that's linked into Malcolm Donnelly's hard disk. Everything he ever did is on there. What we got on the floppies is the tip of a fairly large iceberg. I want to try to hack into the system and get the stuff out.'

'Is the modem switched on?'

'I have no idea. It was a couple of days ago, but it may have been switched off by now. There's only one way to find out.'

'Mmm.' She tapped again at the keys and the screen became a swirling red haze, washing out over her face in an angry rush of colour that was entirely at odds with her voice.

She turned to look me straight in the eye. It's not something she normally does outside the bedroom.

'Do you think you know me, Kellen?'

'More or less.'

'Do you think I know you?'

I stayed where I was, holding her gaze. 'I have no idea.'

Her eyes broke away and she looked back at the screen. 'No. Neither do I. Odd, don't you think, after two years sharing the same bed?'

Definitely a rhetorical question. I let it go.

She cleared the screen and began to open a communication file. 'If I do this for you, I want some real time to talk.'

'That's blackmail.'

'I know.' She smiled bleakly. 'I'm learning. Do I have a deal?'

I turned to look out of the window, watching the rain chase a teenage couple down the road to the bus shelter, and thought about what I had to lose. Everything or nothing, depending on your point of view.

She was watching me intently when I turned back.

'You have a deal.'

'Good.' Her smile broadened into something more real. 'What's the number?'

I gave her the phone number I had taken from Malcolm's desk and she keyed it in. The hard drive hummed and the screen generated a picture of a phone with a happy smile in the centre of the dial to keep us amused. Then it drew a cross through it. The smile drooped at the edges.

She swore and hit a few more keys but the picture stayed the same. 'No line. Either it's the wrong number or they're not on line.'

'It's the right number, we're just three days too late. Whoever reported the break-in to Laidlaw had switched the phone line off. I should have asked you on Saturday.'

'I don't think so. Saturday wasn't a good day.'

True.

'We need to know what's in there. If the line was reconnected, would you try again?'

'Tonight?'

'No. It's too late to set it up. Tomorrow evening.'

'Not from here. It's too easy to trace back to this address. It's not fair on Rae.'

'Could you bring the stuff out to the farm tomorrow night?'

She considered for a moment and nodded slowly. 'If you want.'

I did. I drew her a map, showing her how to get to the farm, and warned her about the alarm system. Then we sat together, on the bed for a while, talking irrelevancies and sharing fragments of gossip as if the earlier conversations had never occurred. Just after eleven, she saw me to the door with a promise to meet at eight the next evening, provided I could organise a link through to the computer at the other end.

CHAPTER NINE

Back in the street, the storm had blown itself out for the moment; the rain was sporadic and the wind had dropped to a mild breeze. It would have been a pleasant enough walk back to the flat if I had been feeling in the mood for solitude. I wasn't. I quite badly wanted people around me, company to keep me from thinking too deeply and I had half an hour before I was due to meet Lee. It's a long time since I rode the Underground for the fun of it.

I flipped a quick mental coin and then turned left along Byres Road, taking the long ramp down into the Kelvinside Underground station. The last train of the evening was due in and the Outer Circle platform was crowded with the dregs from the bars and pubs, leaning on each other or the back walls for support and understanding. The train rattled into view as I stepped off the stairs and I let the swaying herd siphon me in its wake on to the last waiting carriage.

A drunk lay flat on his back, snoring boisterously and taking up half a dozen seats on the main bench – four for his stretched-out form and one on either side where even the semi-inebriated chose not to sit. The rest of us crammed into the remaining spaces, or not, depending on relative stability. As virtually the only sober passenger, I saw it as my citizen's duty to stand at the doorway, holding on to the handrail for support and staring out at the darkness of the tunnels, listening to the various lilting melodies floating out into the ether.

George's Cross passed in a sodden flash. No one gets off at the dirty end of Great Western Road in the middle of the night unless they really want action. Even the rats carry bike chains as essential defence accessories.

Two minutes down the line, the train began to slow down for the stop at Buchanan Street and the more aware among my fellow travellers began to make their way up the carriage to join me at the doors. We could see the lights of the platform ahead of us when the rails rattled and the train speeded up.

'Wha' the . . .' asked a woman behind me, swaying backwards with the acceleration and missing a communion with the drunk only by a remarkable display of agility and balance.

The overhead speaker gave a feedback whine and broke into a rash of static.

'Ladies and gentlemen, this train will not be stopping at Buchanan Street station. All passengers for Buchanan Street, please disembark at St Enoch's Square. Thank you.'

There was a general rumble of disquiet.

A voice from down the train broke through the throng as Glasgow drunk, the original urban warrior, pronounced judgement.

'Fascist bastards.'

My sentiments entirely.

We sailed into the platform at speed. The night-darkness outside the window flashed into bright electric daylight, illuminating the crowd that gathered in a knot at the foot of the steps and highlighting the artery-bright streaks of blood that smeared out between a dozen pairs of booted feet.

Only one of the potential passengers was keeping aloof from the milling crowd. A lone figure in a Barbour jacket lounged back against the wall nearest the rails, watching the train speed past with the faintest of irritated frowns. Our eyes met and held as we passed each other and there was a brief moment of contact before the train hurtled into the tunnel at the end of the platform.

Every sense screamed danger. I craned my head back suddenly in a desperate and entirely futile need to see the body on the platform behind us. But the walls of the tunnel had closed in again and the outside world was blank darkness, leaving me only an after-image of a shadowed figure with hooded eyes and a mane of the brightest copper hair I have ever seen. And over and over at the back of my mind, I heard mad Mhaire's voice telling me that I had blood on my hands and not all of it was mine.

The five-minute ride to the next station took an eternity. Plenty of time for the street fighters and urban hell-cats sharing the carriage to agree on the political alignment of the Underground management and determine the only sensible course of action – verbal abuse combined with strategic physical violence.

I stood in silence, staring out at a vacuum, and held my brain on ice right at the point where it was about to tell me that the body on the platform was Lee.

A taxi driver circling St Enoch's Square accepted a tenner to jump the queue and drive me the quarter-mile back to Buchanan Street. He kept his mouth shut *en route*, which was little short of miraculous but did nothing at all to improve my belief in the inherent goodness of fate.

On the platform, the vultures still circled, oblivious to the sirens and blue flashing lights of the ambulance as it squealed to a halt behind me.

It was the first time in my life I used the 'Let me through I'm a doctor' line and it was worth every second of the five years' training. The crowd parted as the water before Moses and when it closed again I was in the centre, kneeling beside a body that was not, after all, Lee Adams.

It was a man: mid-height, Caucasian, short blond hair, dressed in a scruffy blue sweatshirt and old Levi's. He was curled up in a final spasm, one hand clutching at the small, reddening patch on his sweatshirt where the knife had gone in, the other reaching up towards his face, groping to protect a nose that had smashed as he hit the floor. When I tipped his head back to feel for the carotid pulse, the hand fell away, spraying another gout of foaming arterial blood on to the platform to cheer the vultures and revealing at the same time a pair of pale, cloud-grey eyes that stared out into a vacant world.

It was Danny Baird and he was dead. Professionally dead.

The wail of police sirens stopped abruptly at the north side. Too late to seal the station and far, far too late to catch a man with fox-red hair and murderer's eyes. But not too late to make life unnecessarily difficult for those of us still hanging around. I stood up carefully to avoid the blood and shook my head to confirm the worst. The crowd sighed in unison and parted to let me out as easily as they had let me in. There were enough of them to give me cover as I headed for the southern exit ramp.

I paused at the station entrance to check for blue uniforms and then, when I was sure there was no one hiding behind the rubbish bins, I wandered out to join the crowds weaving their unsteady paths out of the pubs on Sauchiehall Street and down towards George Square.

As I reached the foot of Buchanan Street, an ambulance coasted past me with its lights off and its sirens silent. The dead don't need speed.

Two blocks down the road there was single phone in a row of eight that accepted hard cash rather than plastic and was still working. I called the flat and heard my own voice telling me that I wasn't in to take the call but if I'd like to leave a message, I would phone back as soon as possible. Some hope.

I spoke to the listening ear.

'Lee. It's me. We have trouble.'

There was a barely audible click and she was there. 'What kind of trouble?'

'Were you meeting Danny Baird tonight?'

'I should have done, he didn't show. Why?'

'He's dead. He's on his way in to the Department now. The ambulance just left.'

Dead silence.

'You still there?'

'Yes. Are you sure he's dead?'

'Very sure. Single knife wound to the left thorax about the seventh intercostal space. Very neat. If he hadn't smashed his nose on the way down and sprayed blood all over the floor, he'd have passed as another unconscious inebriate till they cleared the platform in the morning.'

'Where?'

'Buchanan Street station. Eastbound platform. Are you on call for Pathology tonight?'

'No. Why?'

'There's a swelling at the base of his neck, left side. I felt it when I went for the pulse. It looks as if he swallowed something before he got hit. I think perhaps we ought to have a look before anyone else gets there.'

'Hell. All right. I'll go in to the department now. If I'm there when they get in, they won't bother to get anyone else out of bed.'

'I'll meet you there.'

'Right.'

The mortuary is the lowest of several underground floors in the Pathology building, although, obscurely, the lift button is marked with an 'A' and is at the top of the panel. If you turn left out of the lift doors and keep walking to the end of the corridor, you reach the frigid, white-tiled chambers of the autopsy suite. The dead are lowered down on hydraulic stretchers from the ambulance bay at ground level. Once in a while, one of the technicians has an extra drink at lunch-time and decides to try a spin in the body wagon. They don't often try it twice. The rest of us use the conventional route and are happy with it.

Lee was sliding what remained of Danny Baird from the stretcher cavity as I walked in. I lifted a plastic apron from the hanging rail behind the door, slipped my feet into a pair of oversized over-boots and helped her move the unwieldy mass on to the weighing scale and then across on to a stainless-steel autopsy table.

'Are we expecting company?'

'No.'

'Do you want a hand?'

'No. Thanks.'

She was in professional mode, her face closed in concentration, eyes searching and mind narrowed down to a single field. It's not a good time to talk.

I hitched myself up on to a nearby table and settled in silence to watch her work.

For someone who spends most of her life breaking most of the rules of man and a fair few of those set by the higher authorities, she can be unnervingly pedantic when it suits her.

Pathology as an art form undoubtedly requires a certain retentive streak. The difference between a good pathologist and a bad one is the degree of attention to detail, and Dr Elizabeth Adams is not one to do anything badly. Her post-mortems are methodical and meticulous and there's precious little left attached to where it used to be at the end.

It's worth bearing in mind that very few of life's deeper secrets do not show up on a detailed post-mortem examination.

If you're hit by a bus tomorrow, you can forget the clean underwear, it goes in a plastic bag before the body hits the table. It's the past several decades of medium-grade abuse of the flesh that are going to come to light under the steadily flaying scalpel.

If you dye your hair, it shows. If you bite your nails, it shows. If you pick your nose, it shows. Whatever you choose to do with a partner in the privacy of your own home leaves its mark and the marks show.

And if, as did Danny Baird, you choose to have tattoos from collar bones to ankle, they show too. For a time.

The mass I had felt at the base of his neck came to light fairly early on. Partly because she was looking for it, but also because whatever he had swallowed had not quite gone down. A short strand of something entirely unappetising poked out from between his front teeth when she rolled back his lips to check the state of his dental caries. Steady traction reversed its downward passage and brought it out into the light.

I craned over to look.

'What have we got?'

'It's a condom,' she said mechanically. 'It's the standard method of shifting drugs through customs.'

'Oh. Right.' I am probably the only woman in Glasgow over the age of fifteen who hasn't seen one out of the packet before.

She laid the sausage-shaped mass on a stainless steel tray and used a fresh scalpel to slit it open down its length, separating out the contents with a pair of tissue forceps.

Two plastic-wrapped mini-sausages opened out to reveal a gram or two of sulphur-yellow powder. Each also contained a slip of torn paper with the same toothed-hen logo as before, but this time the eye was drawn in more detail and had red '£' signs dripping out of it like tears. On the first slip, the hen stood inside a box with larger boxes drawn round it like a quadrilateral

Russian doll. Stick figures of sheep and things with long horns hung in the air around it. On the second, the hen had the figure 200 printed across its head and the tears ran down into a blue cross of St Andrew, swelling it and stretching the edges.

For a lad in a tight corner, they were as good as a half-page of text. He was brighter than he looked, Danny Baird.

'Cash Andrews?'

'Looks like it.' Lee stripped off her examination gloves and dipped a finger into the powder, sniffed it, then tasted it. Foul habit.

'You'll be sad if that's botulinum toxin.'

'No. I'll be dead. It isn't though.' She tasted again, to prove the point. 'It's powdered egg yolk.'

And doesn't everything just keep coming up eggs?

I shook my head. 'If it's worth £200 a gram, it's not just egg yolk.'

'Hen's Teeth.' She smiled for the first time that night. 'Whatever's in here is what Malcolm died for. All we need now is to find out who keeps the chicken run.'

'Cash Andrews'?' I asked, for the second time.

'It's the obvious place to start.' She put down her scalpel and I watched the pathologist in her retreat back into whatever recess it usually inhabits. It was replaced by something altogether more serious.

'If I were to decide to visit our friend Mr Andrews,' she asked carefully, 'would you want to come along?'

'Is it safe?'

'Not in the least.'

Surprise.

I nodded. 'Do you want a hand to finish this before we go?'

'No.' She stripped off her gloves. 'Give me a hand to get him into the cold. I'll do the rest in the morning.'

Cash Andrews, top-flight pimp, middle-range patron of the arts and award-winning horticulturalist, lives not far from the rural township of Kippen in a relatively discreet Georgian mansion surrounded by several acres of beautifully maintained gardens and a further hundred or so acres of prime farmland.

Rumour has it that friend Cash spent his twenties in Korea, learning to fight hard and to hate anyone with yellow skin. Other rumours, the ones circulated by his friends and given more credence by those in the know, said that he did time for possession. If the latter is true, then he learned enough from his spell inside to build a whole new empire when he came out. By the time he retired in the late 1980s, Cash Andrews had a controlling interest in virtually all of the prostitution, male and female, on both sides of the Clyde. He may have started off small, but he came out of it as one of the wealthiest and most influential men in Strathclyde.

Throughout his career, the grapevine stated quite specifically that he 'didn't believe in' drugs and that all of his 'field workers' were clean. Apparently, in spite of the fact that workers the world over turn to the game to fund their habit, and pimps the world over supply them, he was believed. When Cash cast himself in the Robin Hood mould with a sideline in Oriental martial justice, the various Sheriffs of Nottingham seemed happy enough to let him get on with the job, as long as he kept the body count down to a minimum and, one presumes, supplied them with the odd night's entertainment when required.

If Danny Baird's notes were accurate, then either rumour lied or Mr Cash Andrews had grown tired of his flowering azaleas and was back on the scene with something new.

The lights were on big time when we first cruised up to the gates of the Andrews residence. The house glowed like a lantern and halogen floods lit the gardens to daylight, casting quirked shadows on to the flapping canvas of a marquee. A string of chauffeur-driven cars lined the drive and music — live, professional and expensive – followed us up the road as we passed the walls and slid to a halt on the verge. Party time.

'Cash is entertaining,' said Lee, stating the obvious.

'Very.' I said. 'Shall we crash?'

'We could take a look, at least.'

We did. The wall surrounding the house and gardens was eight foot high with a flat top that glinted suspiciously in the light. Lee linked her fingers to make a stirrup and hoisted me up. A coil of razor wire lay in a bed of broken glass, both cemented into place. Peering at it from eye height, I thought I saw the thin thread of a movement sensor running lengthwise through the loops of wire. I hooked my fingers carefully over the edge to take some of the weight off Lee's hands and looked over on to the lawns beside the house.

It was the very tail end of the party and the remains of the guests had put on something warm and taken themselves out to the garden. A Rubenesque harpist in black satin stopped playing as I watched and accepted a drink from a woman in white. Butlers surreptitiously cleared away full bottles and empty plates, while straggling groups of guests poured champagne for themselves into wide-rimmed glasses. A cluster of those more sober than the rest watched as a powder-faced juggler in mime-artist black tossed a set of guttering fire clubs in flaring hoops over their heads.

A tall, angular, silver-haired man hefted an empty bottle and threw it, laughing a challenge, into the arc of the spinning flames. The juggler shone a set of teeth only slightly less white than the chalk of his face and the bottle wheeled high into the air with the clubs, twice, and then arced out at a different angle coming to land, upright, two feet to the left of the one who had thrown it.

Very neat.

The crowd applauded politely and a woman in blue with

shoulder-length dark hair moved up to speak with the man who had thrown the bottle, laying a restraining hand on his arm.

Shit.

I let go of the wall in a hurry and let Lee lower me to the ground.

'What's up?'

'Take a look. And mind the wire. It's live.' I braced my back against the wall and looped my fingers for her foot as she slid her rucksack to the ground, then stepped up for a quick peek and back down again in seconds.

'Laidlaw's there.' She wasn't pleased.

'Is he?' I wasn't exactly thrilled either. 'The floating piece in blue is Elspeth Philips. Busy earning herself the next promotion with everyday tales of country folk. Two-faced cat.' I spat at the ground. Infantile but satisfying.

Lee watched me fume, her lips compressed into a fine white line. 'Let's get out of here,' she said. 'Even if she's spilled every bean in the can, Laidlaw can't do anything with it till the morning. We've still got an hour or three to do something useful.'

'Like what?'

'Well, Danny didn't draw his sheep for their artistic merit. I think we should visit the farm.'

Why not?

In his guise as Strathclyde's foremost entrepreneur, Cash Andrews runs a hundred-acre farm as an 'educational centre'. The place is populated entirely by specimens of rare breeds on the edge of extinction, most of them hand-reared and child-friendly. The Highland cattle don't gore the passers-by, the Old Spot pigs can be persuaded not to rip them open with a quick flash of the tusk and the Przewalski's horses, if not exactly Pony Club material, are more or less stable in juvenile company. Bands of schoolchildren spend their holidays on the site learning that milk doesn't grow in Tetra-paks, that eggs grow into chicks if given the chance and that the smell of pig shit stays in your hair for weeks, especially if you've fallen into it.

The fact that the entire enterprise is built on the blood and body fluids of Glasgow's under-age whores and rent-boys is an irony that escapes the notice of the doting parents who make it their Sunday Afternoon Picnic Site of the Year on an annual basis.

Given the value of the livestock and the relative proximity to some of the less amiable areas of Glasgow, it's not entirely surprising that the centre and surrounding area are fenced, gated and padlocked when not open to the public. A solid pine stockade runs round the twenty or so acres of the main area and the gates look like something out of a fifties Western: wide, high and barred from the inside with poles made of rough-hewn tree trunks. It's all very rustic and it keeps out the lads with the motorbikes quite nicely, thank you.

Sadly, it also keeps out stray wandering medics with their hearts set on breaking in. A rapid investigation of the stockade revealed that only obvious entry point was through a small staff gate on the western side. It was chained and padlocked like the rest, but it had the advantage that there were no half-trees barring the inside.

'Shall we?' I asked.

'We can try.' Lee searched through the front pocket of her rucksack, brought out a loop of orthopaedic hacksaw wire and drew it experimentally across the padlock. 'Let me know if you hear anyone,' she said. 'I don't expect Cash is nice to his gatecrashers.'

It took longer and made more noise than I had expected. I stood with my back to the rough wood of the stockade, listening to the scraping whine of the wire on the steel hasp of the lock, trying to keep my ears tuned for anything bigger than a field vole coming our way. A conifer plantation ran parallel to the length of the fence, a hundred yards back. The trees scraped and whispered in the night breeze. Anyone using them as a cover could quite easily have got close enough to hear us without us hearing them.

I ran my fingers up and down the knotted pine at my back, watching my breath turn to steam before my eyes and listening to the lock, the trees and the thudding hiss of blood in my ears. My throat narrowed down to something smaller than a straw. Sweat dribbled in an itching line down the length of my spine.

Metal snapped. The gate swung open. Nobody stood there to greet us.

Life is not all bad.

'Shall we go?' Lee. Her throat was a dry as mine.

'Move.'

The gate closed behind us, I wedged it shut with the useless remains of the padlock.

'Where are the chickens?' Lee's voice in my ear.

'Pass.' How should I know? 'Try the stable block.'

The paddocks are fenced and full of dark shadows that huff and mumble at unwanted visitors. None of the shadows is a dog. Yet.

Everything is identified by scent and silhouette. Goats to the left. Horses to the right. Pigs somewhere else, too close for comfort. We don't want to go home smelling of pig shit; ruins the alibi.

No chickens.

Still no dogs.

The stable block is empty. All the horses are out in the paddocks. Behind it is the visitors' centre. Locked beyond anything we can do with a hacksaw wire and almost certainly alarmed. There won't be chickens in there.

'*Kellen*.'

Lee. Behind and to the left. Standing in front of a long, low hut.

Put an ear to the wood of the walls and knock, twice. Listen to the hens clucking back, sleepy and trusting. Lucky I'm not a fox.

The shadow that is Lee moves down the length of the shed, lifting up the lids to the egg boxes, feeling inside.

'Eggs?'

'Not yet.'

Try the other side. There must be fifty-odd nest boxes here. Imagine two or three hens per box. One of them must have laid since nightfall.

All the way round. Nothing.

Back to Lee. Puzzled. 'What now?'

Remember the pup. Remember Malcolm. *Significant clinical risk.* These eggs are lethal. They won't risk having them where Jemima Public and her kids could lay their sticky paws on them.

'Inside.'

Use the hacksaw again. Even slower this time, the wire's blunt. She should carry more than one. The lock parts in a millennium or two and the door opens.

Inside is not like outside. Outside, this chicken run is a rustic shell like the rest of the farm. Inside there is a small coop with half a dozen dozing chickens. If you didn't look hard you'd think that was all there was. If you are of a suspicious nature, you go through the coop, talking nonsense to the chickens and let your friend tap on the wall until she finds a way to open it. Then you pass through from the rustic rural idyll into the twentieth-century techno-farm.

Very neat. Very smart. Very, very soundproofed, with inch-thick claddings of cork and polystyrene to conceal the fact that the chickens here are factory-farmed and there are an awful lot of them. Rows of crates stacked from floor to ceiling. Five crates high, six hens per crate. God knows how many along a row. The eggs roll down angled ramps to collecting bays at the bottom.

Small, speckled bantam eggs. Just like the ones at Medi-Gen. Just like the ones at home.

Hundreds of them, easily. They won't miss one or two. My rucksack has our day clothes. Good enough padding for a couple of eggs. Double up for safety's sake. Make it four. There is no way we're coming back here for more.

Close the locks and slip the rucksack back on.

'Let's get the hell out of here, Adams.'

'After you, Stewart. Don't stop to talk to the horses.'

We reached the car just short of one o'clock, both of us breathing too hard and wet with sweat. The fear gave way to the surging, heart-pumping rush of triumph. Very addictive – like reaching the top of a climb and finding you didn't die.

The eggs went into the glove compartment, wrapped in my shirt and padded in place with the discarded masks and gloves from the night-gear. I sat in the passenger seat with my finger on my pulse, breathing slowly and deeply, trying to calm down before we got on the open road.

Cash Andrews' party was well over by the time we passed his mansion on the way home.

We cruised past the open gates. The floodlights were off, leaving the house in darkness save for a single light in a top window and a dim fire-fly glow from the conservatory at the back. As we watched, the upstairs light blinked into blackness.

'Who do you suppose went home with a tray of eggs?' I asked.

'Who do you suppose didn't go home at all?' Lee pulled the Saab over to the side, killing the lights and the engine together. 'Shall we look?'

I looked at her sideways. 'Do you want an answer to that?'

She smiled in the darkness. An adrenalin-laden smile. Too bright for safety. 'Not really.'

Mad. Quite mad.

Both of us.

I eased the gloves and the balaclavas out of the glove compartment, taking care not to disturb the eggs. 'Let's not hang around, huh? We can't even pretend to be gatecrashers any more.'

The night was getting colder. Every outbreath clouded the air around us. A light ground frost sparkled on the gravel of the drive and whitened the grey velvet of the lawns. The moon was nearly full and loomed high over the house, casting crisp, black shadows against the greys and whites of the garden. There is no colour with moonlight. Even the azaleas came out black.

Inside the wall, the gardens were relatively unprotected. The problem with having a garden party is that it's difficult to keep up a useful level of security. Guests, particularly those of influence and affluence, don't appreciate man-traps. It took the two of us less than twenty minutes to cross 500 yards of shrubbery protected by nothing more lethal than waist-high infra-red beams and the occasional pressure sensor.

Closer to the house it was more difficult. There was no obvious way to move quietly and invisibly. The gravel made too much noise and the frost on the lawns was the horticultural equivalent of fingerprint powder – everywhere we walked left a trail of black on white footprints that could have been seen from any window. The only alternative was to walk the uneven tightrope of the rocks that bordered the flowerbeds. We picked the ones closest to the house, relying on the shadow of its bulk for concealment.

Cash Andrews' home was better protected than his gardens had been. Looking up, I counted three different alarm systems and those were the ones I was supposed to see. The plants in the flowerbed to my left were not as aesthetically placed as they might have been and the soil was freshly turned. I would put serious money that there were pressure sensors under it, if not something more permanently damaging. Breaking in here isn't going to alert anyone except the occupants and then only to dispose of the bodies.

We edged a stone at a time along the border and I chose not to think of what would happen if one of the stones wobbled sideways on to the soft earth. By the time we reached the end of the border, I could feel my jugular pulse throbbing hard against the neck of my sweatshirt and my armpits were sodden. If anyone wanted to find us, all they needed to do was inhale deeply.

Twice in one night isn't just madness. It's certifiable lunacy.

I crouched beside Lee in the blackest shadows at the corner of the house, peering in through the glass of Cash Andrews' conservatory and held my breath.

No one came out. No one fired anything. No one stuck their head out of a window to ask us what the hell we were doing in their garden.

Vines and creepers looped crazy designs on the inside of the conservatory's domed walls but there was enough clear space to see through to the marble coffee table, the bottle of malt and the pair of squat tumblers standing beside it. And the single occupant sitting in the cane chair beneath an elevated basket of orchids. A big man, tall and carrying the unwanted weight of late middle age beneath the softening folds of a silk dressing gown. Angled lights behind his head cast odd shadows on the crags of his face and lit the white hair to the barley-gold of the Scotch. As we watched, he leant forward and topped up his glass, raising it appreciatively to the light. Cash Andrews, relaxing after a late night's entertainment.

I was about to edge round for a closer look when Lee's hand closed on my arm, her fingers tight like talons. The line of her gaze led through the clutter of greenery towards the back of the conservatory, where it joined the rear of the house. A figure in a body-tight black suit walked out through the doorway and paused in front of the table. A little figure. Fit and muscular and unmistakably male. His head and upper torso were hidden by a cluster of trifoliate vine leaves, but as we watched, he stepped forward and the chalk-white face was suddenly visible through a gap in the foliage.

The juggler.

An entertainer who had the basic effrontery to throw an empty bottle at a party guest. A circus actor who stood now in Andrews' private conservatory and poured his own malt as if he owned the place. Then he reached up to sweep both hands over his head, and his hair, freed from the close confines of the mime-actor's cap, was bright fox-red and it flared out round his shoulders like a mane.

Sweat prickled cold on the back of my neck.

Lee's fingers crushed deeper into the bones of my forearm.

Neither of us moved an inch.

The juggler stood ten feet away, facing us. Close enough to see the wind-browned skin and the thicker traces of chalk caught in the lines around his eyes. Close enough for him to see us if we moved, or if he caught a flash of white from an eye, or just chose to walk forward to the glass and look down into the shadows.

Very, very slowly, I closed my eyes.

Glass clinked on glass and malt flowed in gurgling bubbles.

'Satisfactory?' Andrews. He owns this man.

'Very. You have good taste.' A quiet voice but the edge is tungsten carbide. He doesn't believe he is owned.

'Naturally. I have the best to choose from. Did our young friend talk to anyone he shouldn't?' Andrews again. He's enjoying this. A game to end the evening.

'Not this time.'

'Any loose ends?'

'Of course. Why else am I here?' The juggler isn't owned and he isn't playing games. This one kills for the fun of it. Lethal.

'I'm sorry?'

'Baird shouldn't have started talking. Somebody sent him.'

'Then find them.'

223

'I have.'

'What? You can't think. Don't be ridiculous, man . . .?'

It was quiet then after all. In a crowded place, it would have passed for a cough, or a laugh perhaps, short and discreet at a private joke. The noise of flesh falling on wood carried further, but not enough to disturb the neighbours.

He walks in complete silence, the juggler. I never heard him leave. But I heard the tap of glass on marble and the gentle clunk as the door to the conservatory closed. After that, there was peace.

Cash Andrews' plants whispered in the wind; shrub to lily to monkey puzzle tree. Rodents dissected the debris of the party. A distant cat called insults at a neighbour. The juggler, if he was waiting, said nothing.

An age later, I opened my eyes and saw the single line of footsteps that ran across the frosted white of the lawn and into the concealing shadows of the conifer plantation.

Gone. Long gone.

Now I can be sick.

Lee moved forward from my side, heading for the door of the conservatory. I reached her before she opened it, got a hand on her arm, holding her back.

'What the hell are you doing, Adams? He's dead. Leave him be.'

'He might not be.' She removed my hand. 'Remember the dog?'

Oh, shit.

She pushed open the door. 'It won't take two minutes to check.'

It took far less than that.

Cash Andrews sat, as if asleep, on the cane chair of his conservatory. His hands lay, in careful repose, on his lap. His head lolled on one side, a silvered trail of saliva streaking down from one corner of his mouth. His glass of malt stood, half-full, on the table before him. A lone man, resting in peace after a night's entertainment. Except that his eyes were open and focused on nothing and where the front of his silk dressing gown fell sideways, an ink-thin line showed up black against the white bulk of his chest. Seventh intercostal space. Two inches to the left of the midline. Just the right size for a knife to go in and come back out again. Exactly like Danny Baird.

We must have stood there for all of thirty seconds, taking it in. Then Lee laid tight fingers on my arm and tilted her head to the door. 'Let's get out of here,' she said and this time, just this once, she didn't wait for an answer.

CHAPTER TEN

I woke at dawn with a scintillating headache and the taste of stale bile in my throat. Someone else was already up, rattling the coal in the Rayburn and clunking the kettle on the hot plate. I lay still for a while, trying, without success, to ignore the waves of nausea that came with the memories of the night before and to remember instead some of the deeper things that lay hidden beneath the clouding layers of dream and exhaustion and sheer bloody panic.

The blackbird started a fresh territorial war outside the window. Each trilling note drilled its way through the water-hammer pulse in my brain. I took a slow, steadying breath and got up.

Downstairs, the back door hung open and Lee was sitting on the step, staring pensively out over the limpid water of the pond.

'Want a refill?'

'Thanks.' Lee passed me an empty mug. 'Sleep well?'

'Lousy. You?'

'Not a lot.' She shook her head. 'This is getting out of hand.'

Tell me about it.

I made the drinks and joined her on the cold stone. We sat together, blowing clouds of warm steam out into the iced air over the pond and watching the sun grow up over the edge of the Campsies.

'Tod Andersen's dangerous,' said Lee quietly, staring out over the water.

'Who?'

'The juggler. Tod Andersen.' She grimaced faintly on the taste of the name.

Tod. Lowland Scots for fox.

Beware the fox.

'Does Mhaire know him?'

'She knows of him. He has a certain . . . reputation in town.'

'Professional?'

'Totally.'

'Did he kill Tan?'

'I should think so. It was his style.'

'And Bridget?'

'Doubt it. He only uses a knife. He wouldn't know about insulin unless someone told him.'

'Someone like Cash Andrews?'

'No. If Cash was giving the orders this time, he'd still be alive. This is someone closer to home.' Her eyes stayed on the water in front of us.

I know that. We both know that.

'Who?'

'God knows. I don't.' She picked a pebble from the gravel and tossed it into the pond, shattering the surface. 'We don't have any proof, or any real leads, and I don't think, frankly, that we have enough time to find any now.' She walked over to the gate, sitting down with her back to it, facing me, so that we could see each other properly. 'The doors are closing too fast. We need something to draw the bastard out.'

'Andersen?'

An image of a man in a Barbour jacket smiled a slow, vulpine smile at me from the surface of the pond. I shook my head, slowly because it still hurt, and looked away.

'We don't need to draw that one out,' I said. 'He'll be back soon enough. It's not as if he doesn't know the way. We just have to sit still and wait.'

'I know. So we need something to pull out whoever's at the top. Big enough to make sure they bring Andersen along too.'

Wonderful. So much for keeping things safe.

There was another long silence, punctuated by the sound of pebbles dropping softly into the water of the pond. In the barn, the bantams added a broody background clucking to the fluted song of the dawn. More eggs for the collection. More posthumous clues from Malcolm.

'If we know they're coming,' I said, 'it gives us an edge. It's better than nothing.'

'It's all we've got.'

'Then it has to be here.'

'Yes.'

'Tonight?'

'I think so.'

I stood up. 'Let's go and talk to the chickens,' I said. 'They're always good for ideas.'

We left the mugs on the step and wandered over to the barn together. Lee stood and talked to the horses, while I opened the various locks to the hen coop. Two fresh eggs lay warm in the dips in the straw. We carried them back to the house, one each, and as we walked, we sketched the outline of an idea.

She left soon after that with a pair of marked eggs, one from the barn, one from Cash Andrews' battery, each wrapped in its own fistful of toilet roll, nestling in the pockets of her jacket.

Back in the barn the air was horse-warm and smelled of old hay and fresh urine. Ponies shifted restlessly, kicking at the box doors, pushing anxious heads out into the passageway, seeking release from a day and a night's tedious incarceration. I took a hoof pick and a set of brushes from a tack box by the door and began to work my way down the line, cleaning out feet and scouring the worst of the mud from a succession of hairy backs.

Rain's filly, third in line, was skittish and foot-shy and had a bruised patch on the sole of her right hind that could have been the beginnings of pus in the foot. She objected, fast and hard, when I squeezed the hoof-testers across the bars of her heels, slamming me in a winded heap against the hard stone of the back wall with a hoof-shaped welt on one thigh. I cursed with feeling and picked myself up to try again.

'Were you needing a hand, lass?' The voice was familiar, if not entirely welcome.

Stewart MacDonald was standing there in the open doorway, one eyebrow lifted diffidently in an expression of mild enquiry that was entirely at odds with the spark in his eyes. He was dressed in the poaching gear again, although it hung better, as if there were perhaps no dead bodies in the pockets. His heavy leather boots were wet with melted frost from a walk across long grass. The dog sat by his feet panting happily. I hadn't even seen her leave.

I stood up and shoved the hair back out of my eyes. 'Can you hold feet?'

'I'll give it a try.'

He left his jacket by the door and took the filly by the head collar, talking pidgin Gaelic and stroking his hand down her neck and along her back to her rump. She arched her crest and turned to nuzzle the back of his sweater. He reached down and grabbed a handful of the long hair at her fetlock, lifting the afflicted foot into his hand.

'This one, was it?'

'Yes. Thanks.'

The pony stood like an angel as I squeezed her foot across

229

and across with the hoof-testers and then pared away the patch of sole over the bruise to let out the pocket of purulent fluid that had built up underneath. Then MacDonald led her out into the passage and stood feeding her horse nuts and little handfuls of wet sugar-beet pulp while I made a poultice and dressing for the foot.

'You should do this for a living.' I said when it was over and we had walked the pony back into her box.

'I nearly did,' he said. 'Father was a farrier.'

'But you chose the police instead?'

'Aye. There were two of us, the brother and me, and there's not enough work for us both with the horses. Duncan took after father and I went into the force instead. It wasn't a bad choice. I think, of the two, I got the better deal.'

He trailed off into silence and for a moment there was a distant look in his eye. Then he shook his head briskly and brought his gaze back into focus. 'Were you wanting a hand with the rest?'

'Thanks.'

I gave him the hoof pick and we worked the rest of the line together, him cleaning the feet since that was what he was good at, me on the manes and tails with the brushes.

He was bent double, hacking clotted mud and grit from Balder's dinner-plate feet, when he spoke again.

'I got a phone call from Mary Brower yesterday.'

'Really? Bridget's GP?' I finished the mane and walked round to the tail to hear him better. 'How's the baby?'

'Fine. She got home yesterday. She was a touch upset that no one had told her about the lassie dying. She only heard when she got back.'

'Why did she call you?'

'Ms Donnelly tried to phone her the day she died.'

'What for?'

'She was feeling poorly and she wanted advice. Dr Brower was waiting for a car to take her in to the hospital so she told the lass to call the practice.'

'And did she?'

'The doctor thought not. Your friend said she didn't like the new locum.'

'There's a surprise.' Bridget had better taste than that.

'Aye, well. Maybe if she had, she'd be better.' He finished the foot and let it drop, crossing to lift its partner. 'She called because she thought she had food poisoning after eating the eggs from the chickens.'

'Oh, hell.' I'm not sure I wanted to know that. 'You mean she knew? Bridget knew about the eggs?'

'No.' He straightened slowly, grimacing as his back creaked into line. 'At least, she didn't say anything on the phone about insulin. And even if she did know, it still doesn't tell us who it was pumped her full of temazepam afterwards.'

'Perhaps if we knew "why" we'd have more chance of working out "who".'

'Aye. That's usually the way of it.'

He's more friendly than he was yesterday. Less officious. I wonder if he knows Laidlaw's back in town.

We moved on to Midnight, last in the line.

'Could you check to see if Bridget phoned the practice after she called Mary?'

'I already have.'

'And?'

'The receptionist claims there were no calls logged to the practice from this number.' He helped me to put a head collar on to Midnight. 'I was wondering if there was another phone here that she could have called from. A mobile maybe?'

'Not that I know of. There's a cordless in the house but it's on the same number.'

'Then we have to assume that she never got a chance to make the call.'

231

'Or she changed her mind?'

'Maybe.'

We put head collars on the remaining ponies and led them out, eight at a time, to the paddock. Rain's filly walked out lame but not excessively so.

The gate swung solidly shut behind the last rump and I wound the new chain around the fence post. MacDonald picked up the padlock, examining it with a policeman's eye.

'Are you worried about someone getting at the ponies?' he asked.

I shrugged. 'It seemed like a useful precaution.'

'And the Fort Knox round the chicken coop in the barn – ' his voice completely bland – 'that's just a precaution too, is it?'

'Do you think it's unnecessary?'

'No.' He turned and hooked his elbows on the gate. 'But I think it won't be the chickens they're after when they come back next time. Nor the dog either.'

When. Not if. And there was a question in his voice.

I looked at him as he leant placidly on the fence, watching the dog quarter the field.

Somewhere, some time you have to trust someone.

'Wait there.' I left him by the gate and crossed the yard to the kitchen, where the growing collection of bantam eggs lay nested in toilet tissue in the cutlery drawer. I lifted one each from either side of the drawer, used a market pen to label them 'A' and 'B' and took them back to him.

'These are from the bantams,' I said, holding them out. 'One from each.' It was almost true. 'If I was right about the pup, they have the insulin in the whites. Human insulin. You could probably get them tested.'

'Aye?' He held one in each palm, rolling them speculatively, waiting for more. 'And why would someone want to kill your friend with these, do you think?'

'Pass.' That's what we're all here to find out. 'Perhaps there's more to them than that.'

'You reckon?' The dog put up a rabbit and we both watched as the pair raced for the fifty yards back to the warren. The rabbit won. MacDonald clicked his teeth in quiet disappointment, then brought his attention, with evident effort, back to the eggs.

'Suppose we were going to look in these for something else,' he said, 'where, in your considered medical opinion, should we look, Dr Stewart?' His expression was one of the mildest curiosity.

'I don't know.' I paused to give it some thought. 'Perhaps if there's insulin in the white then there might be something else in the yolk.'

'And what sort of thing might that be, do you think?'

'I have no idea. Whatever it is, if someone has gone to this much effort, it would have to be worth a packet.' I gave him my most helpful professional shrug. 'You're the policeman. I'm sure you have a better idea of the current market than I do.'

'Aye. Maybe I do, at that.'

He slipped both of the eggs into an inside pocket of the poacher's jacket, nodding quietly to himself and then turned to look out at the ponies as they browsed and rolled in the damp grass.

The dog put up another rabbit and made up more ground this time, coming close enough to graze its tail as it, too, sprinted for the sanctuary of the warren.

MacDonald's eyes creased in a smile and he sucked in a long-drawn sigh of appreciation. 'Man,' he said, 'but it's a beautiful morning.'

He turned down the offer of breakfast with the excuse that he was due in at work at nine and he had to get back home in time to change into his uniform. The fact that I was offering scrambled eggs on toast, of course, had nothing to do with the speed of his departure.

I hung on to the pup for a while after he left and then spent half an hour making breakfast, clattering around in the kitchen, digging out the old porridge pot that had been put away for the summer and searching the pantry for the tin with the oatmeal. The dog lay across the threshold with her nose poking out of the door, looking wistfully out across the fields at the footpath he had taken, which is, in a round about sort of way, a short cut back to the village.

Caroline appeared, wrapped in her blue towelling dressing gown, as I was pouring out the porridge. Her hair was stuck out at sleep-pressed angles around her head and there were shadows beneath her eyes. She looked much like I felt.

'Morning.' I held out my bowl. 'Breakfast?'

She took a look at the mess in the pan and winced. 'No thanks.' She dragged her fingers sleepily through the tangles of hair. 'I'll have some toast.' She dug out the three-day-old loaf from the pantry and began to saw off microtome slices, arranging them with care on the hot plate.

I tipped some salt in my bowl, sat down beside the fire and watched her making toast as a spinal reflex.

'Bad night?' I asked.

'It wasn't good.' She vanished into the pantry to get some butter. 'Did you know it was after three when you got in?'

Quite a long time after. 'Yes.'

'What were you doing?'

'Looking for bits of Malcolm, mostly.'

'Did you find them?'

'No. I have to go into town later on for another look.'

Caroline finished buttering her toast and took it across to the window-seat. Her hair glowed in the backlight of the morning sun and her face, in profile, lost years. Only her eyes, when they met mine, were still old. 'You had a visitor last night,' she said. 'Would you like to guess who?'

'The Tooth Fairy?'

'Better than that.' Her brows flicked upwards, suggestively. 'Elspeth Philips. She "dropped in" about one o'clock. We had tea until two and then she went home.'

Oh, joy. Bang goes the alibi.

'What the hell did she want at one in the morning?'

'Well, she *said* she wanted to warn you that her boss was back in town early, but I'd have said that was a pretty lame excuse myself.' There was a tinge of amusement in her eyes. 'I think you've made more of an impression than you might have wanted. She's coming back this morning.'

Some things are guaranteed to put me off my porridge.

'Why?'

'It's her day off, I've invited her for dinner. And I said we'd take her out on a ride to the waterfall first.'

You have to be joking. Somebody here has just lost all sense of perspective. I don't think it's me. Caroline looked at her watch. 'She'll be here in twenty minutes,' she said. 'If you don't want to end up taking her out, you'd better get out of here sharpish.'

Quite. Ten minutes later, showered and changed, I was in the car and heading eastwards along the Great Western Road with fragments of jigsaw migrating fast into the places I least wanted them to be. McNeill in Anatomy was expecting me. He spotted me as I stepped through the revolving door into the hallway and flittered out of his cubbyhole, nodding a greeting.

'Ms Culloch, good morning. You'll be wanting Level Two?'

I was. Like Pathology, the more interesting parts of the Anatomy Department are underground. The instinct for burying the dead, even when they are in pieces in small glass bottles, runs deep in the human psyche. The serial number from the computer printout said that the relevant parts of Malcolm were in the second floor below ground, the one reserved for student teaching labs and the histology research department.

235

McNeill led me down a series of subterranean passages, through rooms stacked with glass jars and plastic bottles where the very air was pickled with formaldehyde, and into the store-room. He twitched his nose in the general direction of a bank of freezers ranged along the wall.

'The blood samples are kept in there. If you take anything with you, sign it out with me at the desk before you go.'

Very likely.

I smiled acquiescent thanks and he left, blowing his nose briskly into a scarlet handkerchief.

Anatomists are retentive to a degree that makes the average pathologist look positively freestyle. Every body that slides in through the hatch is labelled and numbered and every piece detached thereafter is sub-coded and stored in order in the appropriate drawer or cabinet.

Malcolm's blood, a pint or two divided into ten-millilitre aliquots, was in the right place in the right freezer. I took two of the vials, slid them into an envelope lined with plastic bubble paper to keep them cool, and fitted the envelope into a slim Lycra body belt where it would be safe from McNeill unless he chose to perform a full strip search.

As an afterthought, on the way back upstairs, I visited the body racks on the first floor.

According to Malcolm's records, his body had been kept intact for the incoming year of students, preserved with one of the new phenol-based plastic resins that evolved after they discovered that formalin was carcinogenic. The racks fill two whole rooms, big drawers stacked from floor to ceiling in banks, like the ones in the Pathology mortuary, but less cold.

Dragging a set of mobile steps in from the corridor, I climbed up to the labelled drawer on the third row that should have contained the body of Malcolm Donnelly.

I stood there with my hand on the lock for a long time.

In anatomy, things have come a long way since the days of Burke and Hare. There is a general consensus that looking on the preserved face of one's loved ones is not necessarily a wise move and so, at the beginning of each new academic year, the records are checked and checked again to make sure that none of the new intake of students is about to come face to face in unfortunate circumstances with their Great-Aunt Hilda, deceased. It isn't foolproof, but at least they try.

Malcolm was once a very good friend and I owed him a lot. I thought about what he had looked like when I knew him, and all the images were active, vibrant, alive. I tried to imagine him dead, with the laughter lines smoothed out and replaced by the baby-doll face of the plasticisers and with the spark of understanding gone from his eyes and I knew that I didn't really want to look. Even so, I still had to make sure he was there. Somehow.

It's a very long time since I fluttered my eyelashes at anyone, but I made up for it all in the next five minutes. Every ounce of waning Stewart charm went into persuading Archie McNeill to accompany me back down to the vaults and up the ladder to have a look inside the cabinet. Even then, it took a while to convince him that I knew what I wanted.

He stood at the top of the ladder, his hand on the lid, and his drip was at eye height as he turned towards me. 'I don't see . . .'

'I just want to be sure that it's him.'

'Right you are.' He lifted the lid and frowned at the contents for a full second. 'Aye, it's Dr Donnelly, right enough,' he said. 'Why he would want to end up here is anybody's guess. You'd no catch me . . .' The lid dropped with a bang.

'Thank you very much.' I said.

'I'd say it's a pleasure, but I'd not like to lie to you.'

McNeill skipped the last three treads of the ladder and landed nimbly on the floor beside me. He turned so that the drip on the end of his nose was parallel with my eyes. 'I don't want to go setting a precedent, mind,' he said. 'It's no what I'm here for, you understand. There's too many folk coming here wanting a look at the bodies these days. It's not healthy.'

Red flares sparked at the back of my mind.

'Who else has been here, Archie?'

He set off back upstairs at a trot. I followed, waiting for an answer. Near the ground floor he paused for breath. 'Him with the fancy suit was in yesterday,' he said.

'Who's that?'

'I don't know his name. The one who reads the *Telegraph* and disnae do the crossword.'

'Does he not leave his paper for you?' I managed to filter a thread of shocked commiseration over the top of the unmasked glee.

'Aye,' He nodded sagely. 'He did at that. Do you want to see it?'

Do you think you could stop me?

'That would be very nice.'

I followed McNeill right into the inner sanctum of his cubbyhole and breathed down his neck while he dug out a copy of the previous day's *Telegraph*. There at the top, above the bold type of the title, was a newsagent's scribble: *Kemp*

Magic. If McNeill had less of a drip on his nose, I would hug him.

One more question.

'Who did he want to see, Archie?' I asked.

'What? Oh, the same as yourself. Dr Donnelly's the flavour of the month, right enough. I still can't think why he'd want to stay . . .'

'No. I can't either. Maybe he thought he'd leave something for posterity.' I smiled brightly and dropped the *Telegraph* back on the pile at my feet, but McNeill was already back in his seat, hunched over the latest, still unsolved, set of clues.

Kemp. The doctor with an urge to certify accidental death on no evidence. The kind of man who would sell his grandmother twice over if he could buy a bigger car on the proceeds. The man who is married to the professor's daughter and knows the department like he knows his own reflection. Once in a while, it's nice to have one's more consistent prejudices confirmed. Pity that in this case it's not the right piece for the right place in the jigsaw.

I rode the Underground to Kelvinside with my brain locked in circles, trying, without notable success, to fit the new piece to the old pattern. I wandered, still thinking, up the road to Rae Larssen's flat and dropped a brief note to Janine through the door, confirming arrangements for the evening and suggesting that she might prefer to arrange an alternative form of evening entertainment for Caroline and a certain green-eyed policewoman.

Myself, I wouldn't want anyone watching me hack into someone else's system, particularly not a paid-up member of the Strathclyde Central Constabulary, but then I don't have any faith at all in the integrity of the barriers between personal and private life.

The farm was empty when I arrived home an hour or so later. The back door was locked and, when I checked the barn, two of the saddle racks were empty. A note from Caroline, tucked under a mug on the breakfast bar, said that the pair had left at ten and taken the dog with them. Beneath it was a roughly sketched map of their route: out along the bridleway, up to the waterfall in the foothills and the long way back, with an estimated time of return in the late afternoon.

A whole afternoon to myself. Freedom.

If I was intelligent, I would have used the time to sleep and then perhaps the things that happened later would have been more lucid. But I was still stirred up after the nightmare of the previous evening and the odd conflicts of the morning. Sleep would have been hard to come by.

Instead, I raided the pantry for beans on toast and then changed back into horse clothes and went out to the barn to spend a happy hour venting frustration shifting barrowloads of damp straw and horse manure out to the dung heap at the back. It didn't change anything, but it made me feel a lot calmer.

When everything was tidy and ordered and, short of cleaning all the tack, there was nothing left to do, I pulled on a heavier jacket, filled the pockets with the things that I needed and went for a walk in the beech woods.

It was about five o'clock and the sun was low, sending horizontal beams out across the fields, lighting up the tall grass and the clumps of horse dung that were scattered randomly, like molehills, across the field. Wood pigeons cooed together in the background and the hooded crows squabbled over squatting rights in the uppermost branches of the beech trees.

The burn at the back of the field ran higher than it had done. Rain from the past few days poured off the Campsies, raising it temporarily above the winter level. The usual fording stones were awash with foaming white water and there were places where an inch or two of bank had crumbled away. A faint breeze picked up the mist rising from the water and pushed it in coiling tendrils between the trees, carrying the peaty scent of the hills with it.

I slid between the rails of the fence and walked upriver to the place where the stream takes a bend round a boulder. The turning force of the water undercuts the bank on the field side and leaves an overhang that bridges out across the water and makes a gap narrow enough to jump. From there another path runs straight through the wood to the clearing. Clear and narrow like a sheep path, except there are no sheep in the wood and never have been. Deer possibly, or foxes. I jumped across the gap and followed the track between the trees.

In the wood the air was electric. Some time after I crossed the river, the cooing and cawing had stopped, suddenly as if on command, leaving a raw silence. Even the rushing tumble of the water had died away. All I could hear was the crisp rustle of leaves as I walked.

Then, between the last pair of trees at the edge of the clearing, I stopped absolutely still, and the silence, like the vision on the mound, was perfect.

Mist, creeping in from the burn, met a stray strand of sunlight filtering through the trees to make a new, wavering floor to the clearing. The mound and Tan's grave were hidden under the blanket. Only the tip of the ancient cairn was visible, poking up like an iceberg from the sea, and there, on the flat, moss-covered surface of the roof stone, dark against the pale air behind, stood a wren. She eyed me sideways, bobbed once, tail up, and then lifted her head to sing.

Death, black and yellow and brown, exploded into the clearing.

A merlin, wings folded in a stoop, dropped into the gap between the trees and cut like a knife through the air above the cairn, twisting in pursuit of the lark she was chasing. The lark passed straight along the line of the mound, heading for the sanctuary of the woodland, and for a fragmented moment the two birds, wren and lark, were side by side at the top of the cairn. In that moment, the wren opened her throat in the first notes of the song and the merlin, caught by the noise, changed her aim.

Talons struck flesh in a burst of feathers and the song died in mid-note. The impact carried both birds half-way along the mound, then the falcon braked in the air, turned a tight half-circle and brought her prey back to the cairn to feed. She settled on the roof stone, less than fifteen feet from where I stood, and our eyes were level.

Black, black eyes glared at me across the white sea of the fog.

I closed both of my own down to slits so that there was no reflection and stood still as the rocks of the cairn.

The bird gave a high, tonal cry – of victory or annoyance – then bent her head to the wrecked body at her feet and began to pluck. It was swift and businesslike. Snowstorms of mouse-brown feathers scattered out with each angry twist of the head. Wing primaries and tail feathers spiralled downwards and vanished. The head twisted off and rolled over the edge of the flat rock to drop like a stone into the carpeting mist. In the space of a few hundred heartbeats, the falcon cleaned and ate her kill, pausing every few mouthfuls to wipe her beak neatly on the edge of the stone.

When it was over, she raised her head to glare one final time – a look that held pride and anger and defiance all in one. Then she threw herself up and out through the gap in the trees to the open sky.

I never really believed in omens. Bridget and Lee were more into that kind of thing. Both of them, at different times, spent patient hours trying to convince me that some things were worth listening to and some were mere noises in the wind. Later, professional training threw in texts of theory that spun a world of Jungian synchronicity in which nothing ever happens by chance. I don't believe any of it, but I know the theory and it still makes me feel deeply uncomfortable – especially when the messages are all of doom and gloom and I am expecting to die anyway.

I stood there, staring at the top of the cairn after the merlin had gone, and for a long time the only thing I could think of was that either Bridget or Lee should have seen it rather than me, because I hadn't got a bloody clue what it meant.

In time, I pulled myself together and walked forward to look at the cairn. The roof stone felt heavier than usual and the moss clung a little more tightly. It moved eventually, sliding sideways to reveal the hollow interior of the cairn. Without a torch or the angling sunlight, the cavity was impossibly dark. Whatever might have been inside remained invisible this time.

I lifted the plastic vial of blood from my pocket, prised the lid off with my thumb nail and reached deep into the depths of the cairn. I had imagined more of a ceremony than this, but the dead wren was a far more appropriate epitaph than anything the Stewart mind could ever conjure. The tube angled outwards in my hand and I ran it round as far as I could reach, tipping all that was left of Bridget in a crimson dribble over the inner surface of the stones. When it was nearly empty, I poured the final few drops on to the hard earth at the base and then drew out my arm, dragging my fingers tentatively past the sharp spur of stone that stuck out half-way up the near side.

My hand came up coated in cobwebs and small creeping things dangled from the cuff of my jacket. But nothing moved and nothing bit and the wind whispering through the trees said nothing I wasn't expecting. And Malcolm's watch, not at all surprisingly, had gone.

The midges came a short while later and drove me back home along the path through the woods to the burn's edge and from there across the field to the house, where the murmur of voices and the smell of cooking from the kitchen said that the riders were back.

CHAPTER ELEVEN

Later on, Inspector MacDonald appeared at the back door as I was setting the table for dinner. His grin had that harmless look to it that meant he was there for a reason, even if he was back in his moleskins again. There are times when I doubt if that man actually owns a uniform.

'Evening.' He looked around the empty kitchen. 'Are you on your own?'

'Kind of. Your young mole is out with Caroline, feeding the horses.'

'I heard you were taking her out on a ride.'

'No. I had to go to Anatomy. The lady of the house took her instead.'

'Very good.' He nodded amiably and perched on the arm of the chair nearest the dinner table. 'Fine evening for the time of year.'

Last time he said that, he dumped a dog on the doorstep. I looked at him sideways.

'Is this a social call?'

'No.' He shook his head. 'I just thought you'd like to know that Ms Donnelly did call your colleague Dr Kemp on the afternoon she died. The call was logged on his mobile phone.

The practice says he spent the afternoon playing golf with his father-in-law.'

'That figures.'

'Aye. They didn't think he would have missed a game for a case of food poisoning.'

'I should think not. He was only a doctor, after all. Why go out to see someone when they're ill? Did you ask him about it?'

'Not yet. He's not been in at the practice. I've been trying to trace him all afternoon.'

'He's probably back at the eighteenth hole by now. You'll just have time if you hurry.'

'Aye, you could be right.' He grinned affably. 'But it's the golf-club dinner this evening. Maybe I'll have to accept the invitation for once and go along for the company and the conversation.'

MacDonald in full dinner regalia. The imagination reels. I looked at him and rolled my eyes. 'Have fun.'

'I'll do that.' He eyed me curiously. 'What were you doing in Anatomy?'

Ever the policeman.

'Looking for blood samples from Malcolm Donnelly.'

'And why would you do that?'

Good question.

Remember the wren.

I took a deep breath. 'Because it's not impossible that Malcolm died of insulin poisoning too and if he did, there should be something to see in the blood samples now that we know we're looking for the human not the bovine type.'

I finished laying the places and turned round. He was leaning back on the table, watching me with the mildest interest. 'Were you thinking that perhaps the police might like to have a look too?'

'I was thinking that perhaps we could run the assays and then hand you the results. If we're wrong, then at least we haven't wasted your time.'

He chewed the edge of a fingernail abstractedly. 'Does the phrase "obstructing the course of justice" ring any bells, Dr Stewart?'

'Vaguely.' I counted four plates from the cupboard and put them in the lower oven of the Rayburn. 'As I remember, it was one of Chief Inspector Laidlaw's little runes. The kind of thing he chants before breakfast to keep the doctor away.'

'Aye. Well, I'd be a bit careful if I were you. Otherwise he might chant it out loud in court one day and then the doctor would be out of the way for longer than she might find comfortable.' He rubbed the side of his nose. 'Of course, if the blood samples were to be handed over to the authorities in the morning, then everything would be all right.'

'I'll bear it in mind.' I handed him a bottle of red wine and the corkscrew and left him to use them as he saw fit. 'Did you find anything in the eggs?' I asked.

He brightened. 'We did indeed. Human insulin in the whites. As you so rightly predicted.'

'Both of them?'

'Indeed,' He nodded cheerfully. 'And apparently the yolks are packed with stuff by the name of Hen's Teeth. Just the kind of thing the punters will pay through the nose for.'

'And kill for?'

'Maybe so. They'll kill each other, right enough. Your friend Dr Adams did a post-mortem on a lad called Danny Baird last night. He was one of their couriers before they cut him off short.'

I'll ignore that.

'Would they have killed Malcolm for the Hen's Teeth?'

'They might have done.' He frowned as if the idea were novel and not entirely savoury. 'I can't think why they would, mind you, but it's possible.'

He put the bottle down on the table and tossed the cork in the bin. A man of interesting habits. 'Chief Inspector Laidlaw came back this afternoon, a mite earlier than expected,' he said, appositely. 'He was reading my report when the lab rang in with the results of the samples. He's well pleased with that. Hen's Teeth's been something of an obsession for a wee while now. Now he's dead keen to go in and look at the place where Dr Donnelly used to work – since that's where the chickens came from in the first place.'

I stared hard at the centre of his forehead, where the eyebrows didn't quite meet, and avoided catching either eye. 'Is he going to look tonight?' I asked.

'He is.'

'Can they get a warrant at this time of night?'

He rubbed the side of his nose and gazed at a convenient horizon. 'Not in a hurry. It will take them a wee while to get the paperwork done. And there's a bit of a furore out near Kippen. One of the local dignitaries has died and there's the odd . . . irregularity that needs himself to sort out. He'll not be ready to go much before midnight, I shouldn't think.'

'Right.' I let out a long, slow breath. 'You're in for an exciting night.'

'It looks that way.' He reached into his pocket, lifted something out and laid it on the table. 'I thought you might be looking for this,' he said.

Malcolm's watch sat there between a knife and fork. There was the finest dusting of white powder caught in the cracks of the leather strap.

'Anything useful?' I asked.

'I don't think so. Nothing that would stand up in court.'

'Pity.'

'Aye.' He looked thoughtfully at the newly laid table, then slid off the arm of the chair and switched around one of the place settings.

'WPC Philips is left-handed,' he said, as if the previous conversation had never taken place.

He was gone long before the others came back in from the barn.

The dog knew that he had been. She followed his trail in through the door and dropped to the floor beneath the arm of the chair. Caroline was too busy rescuing the various pans on the stove from their state of impending incineration to notice anything, but Elspeth, looking at the cack-handed place setting, made her own deductions.

She watched me curiously as I went through the motions of cleaning the old silver cruet. 'Has the boss been in to see you?'

'He's just left.' I didn't look up.

'Any news?'

'He's planning to go to the golf-club dinner tonight.' I put the salt on the table and went to work on the pepper. 'Is that news?'

Curiosity gave way to doubt and then to a resigned amusement. She smiled slowly and it almost reached her eyes. 'Well, it's different, anyway.'

I looked up and smiled back. 'I bet he looks wonderful in a kilt,' I said. 'They'll love him.'

'They probably will. He's a good one with the pipes if you get him going.'

The mind boggles.

'The man's the original polymath. Is there anything he can't do?'

She smiled properly this time, a bright, eye-warming smile, and shook her head. 'He's not too good at playing politics with the men in grey suits,' she said.

'I can imagine.'

We were almost on the verge of our first real conversation then, but Caroline interrupted with a plea for help to dish up the meal and we settled down to a quiet family evening. The conversation was gently amusing and mostly involved a woman-by-woman dissection of the remainder of Rae Larssen's circle, spiced and improved by the gentle lubrication of the wine. I listened with half an ear and gave it little concentration. Most of my attention was focused hard on the phone, willing it to ring.

Lee finally called from a box on the other side of town as we were clearing away the plates. I excused myself and took the portable handset outside into the yard. The reception's better and there is less chance of being overheard.

'Hi. How's things?' Her voice, even on the phone, hummed with compressed energy.

'Everything's fine at this end but you might have problems. MacDonald called in earlier. Laidlaw's back.'

'I know.' Laughter rippled across the top. 'He's got half of the SCC flitting about like bats in a rainstorm. The road to Kippen's hellish busy for the time of night.'

'Very funny. Have you checked the eggs?'

'Not quite. The assay's running now. Why?'

'I gave a pair to MacDonald. One from here and one from Andrews' farm. He ran them through the SCC lab. They're packed with endorphins, both of them.'

'Fine. So we were right. What's wrong with that?'

'Laidlaw. He's read MacDonald's report and he knows about the Hen's Teeth in the eggs. He's planning a raid on the lab. MacDonald thought they'd get the warrant by midnight.'

'No problem. That's plenty of time.'

'Go easy, Adams. He could be wrong.'

'He could be lying, too. Don't worry. I'll keep my eyes open.'

If he's lying, we're dead. I don't want to think about that. Too late now.

'It really doesn't matter at this stage,' I said. 'We'll know who did what by the morning.'

'True. Is Janine all set?'

'She'll be here at eight.'

249

'Good. See you later.'

'Take care.'

'Sure.'

I called Janine straight after that to check that she had got my note. I was half-way through relaying a message to Rae Larssen's crystal-clear answer-phone when the woman herself picked up the receiver to tell me that my lover had already left, complete with kit. Much more importantly, she issued a personal invitation to the two extraneous members of the household, which meant that the second half of my note had also got through.

Some days the world is not as bad as I think.

Back in the kitchen, Caroline and Elspeth had moved on to the coffee. The conversation had progressed with the courses and settled into what sounded like a fairly intense discourse on the politics of outing. The kind of conversation that could run for ever if there was nothing else to talk about. I helped myself to a glass of water and sat down, waiting for a convenient break in the flow.

Caroline noticed me first. 'What's up, Kells?'

'Would you like the good news or the bad news?'

'Both.' Elspeth, relaxed and easy. 'First rule of policework. Don't underestimate the value of new information.'

That's nice. I didn't know she was working.

'But mustn't tell us which is which,' said Caroline, not entirely soberly. 'Bridget taught me. First rule of advocacy: never subscribe to your client's bias.'

This could become seriously wearing.

'Fine. If you insist. Undifferentiated news as follows.' I ticked them off on my fingers. 'One, Janine is coming here for the evening. Two, she wants to talk to me. Three, Rae has invited you two to her place for a genteele *soirée à trois.*'

Silence.

Caroline looked across at Elspeth. 'I think we have just been invited to take ourselves elsewhere.'

'It sounds that way.' She said it lightly, but Elspeth Philips was looking at me, not at her hostess, and her eyes were asking questions that were not in her voice. The wine glass in front of her was as full as when I first served her. And I thought I was the only one staying sober for the evening.

Caroline stood up and began to clear the table. Of all three glasses, hers was the only one that was empty. 'Do you want us to go, Kellen?' she asked.

'I'd appreciate it if you did.'

'Will you call us when you're finished?' asked WPC Philips.

Not the kind of question you would expect at all from a disinterested by stander. Or even an interested dinner guest.

Her eyes searched my face. Disconcerting. Too disconcerting for words.

'If you like,' I said. It seemed the best way to get them out of the house.

They left shortly before eight in Elspeth Philips' white Escort with a promise from me to call them as soon as it was safe for them to come back.

Janine arrived just in time to miss the washing up and brought a complete hacker's workshop with her. Computer, modem, disk drive, printer and yards of connecting cables.

We cleared the desk-top in the study and she set everything up, while I relit the fire and then sat on the floor, watching the flames, seeing images of the bird in the woodland flickering up to the chimney in the smoke. My mind wandered through the dark labyrinths of imagery and didn't like what it saw.

'You all right?' Janine spoke quietly from behind me. She was sitting easily in the chair by the desk, watching me with eyes like a hunting cat, pensive and not unfriendly.

I turned to face her. 'I'm fine. I was thinking.'

251

'Want to tell me?'

'I saw a merlin make a kill today, in the clearing in the wood. She had the choice between a wren and a lark. She killed the wren because it sang. I was thinking that life can be very unjust at times.'

'Only if you think like a wren.'

'True.' I stretched out on the floor, looking up at her. 'The difference between victim and hunter.'

'Very poetic.' She smiled. 'Which are you?'

'Tonight? Both probably. It's a very fine dividing line at times. If you can do what we need to do with the computer, it might swing the balance.'

She smiled peacefully and stretched out a leg so that her toe covered mine. 'I'll do my best.'

'I know.' I sat up and caught hold of the foot, squeezing her toes. 'It'll be over, one way or another.'

'Then we can talk?'

'Then we can talk.'

It didn't seem worth telling her that if the omens were right, I might not be around to talk to.

At nine thirty, Janine switched on the modem and dialled through to the number at Malcolm's lab. This time the phone icon smiled all the way and, when the screen cleared, we were looking at a replica of the screen on Malcolm's Macintosh.

'Got it.'

'Good.'

She plugged in the spare hard disk and began to transfer files. The principle was much the same as I had used on the first night in the lab, but orders of magnitude faster. Too fast.

I moved my chair in closer and put a hand on her shoulder. 'Hold on. Can we have a look at some of these?'

The tip of her tongue was caught between her teeth, her mind absorbed with the electronic processes on the screen.

I asked again and this time she heard me.

She shook her head curtly. 'It's faster this way. We can worry about getting into the files later. You don't want to have the line open too long.'

'I know, but I need answers now. Can we look at some of it. Please?'

She stopped, lifting her hands from the keyboard. 'Are you sure you know what you're doing, Kellen?'

'Very.'

Her eyes rocked up to the ceiling and back and she sighed pointedly. 'All right. It's your party. Just don't take me down with you when you go.'

'I won't, I promise.'

'All right. What are we looking for this time?'

'A name. There was something else in the eggs besides the insulin. I think Malcolm found out about it when he wasn't supposed to and he was either blackmailing someone or about to turn them in. Whoever it was had him killed to keep him quiet. The name will be in here somewhere.'

She tried again, one last time. 'There's almost a gigabyte in here, Kells. It could take us all night.'

'I know.'

Half an hour later, the phone rang twice, rang off and rang once more. I switched off the alarm system at the console over the fire and then switched it back on again a few minutes later when the black Saab rolled into the yard.

Lee.

I went out to help her put the car away in the shed.

'Everything okay?'

'So far. Laidlaw's racing in small circles and going nowhere fast.'

'Was he at the lab?'

'Not yet. He has a bit of a transport problem. I doubt if he'll make it for another hour or two.' She opened the boot and I helped her to haul out the rucksacks. As she swung the lid down and locked it, I saw the number plate: L999 SCC.

'Don't you want to change those?'

She looked at me, brow furrowed, as if the idea were all mine and not entirely sane. 'Not really,' she said, 'these ones don't change.'

And Chief Inspector Laidlaw is having a transport problem.

We gazed at each other in the darkness and the fake frown changed to a smile that was pure Lee: bright and savage. For a moment, everything felt very familiar.

'You're crazy, Adams.'

'I know.' She bounced the keys lightly on her palm and then hefted her rucksack on to her shoulder. 'Shall we go?'

I made tea and Lee dragged in spare chairs from the living room so that we could both sit and watch while Janine played with the software and prepared to commit act after act of electronic burglary.

Most of it was unspeakably tedious. Endless pages of data detailed the results of gene translocations; experiments failed outnumbering successes by about five to one. Whole folders full of half-written papers lay waiting for the other authors to complete their sections. Regular dated memos to lab technicians or the board of directors issued either instructions or explanations as appropriate.

Janine plugged on, hacking her way through a maze of electronic lock-outs with only the regular tapping of one foot to betray the frustration at so blatant an act of stupidity.

Some time around eleven, tired, bleary-eyed and with a communal headache, we struck, if not gold, then at least a possible productive vein.

Nested inside the personal correspondence file was a whole folder of letters from Malcolm to his sister. He wrote with unfailing regularity on the first and third Saturday of every month, until the week he died, when there were two letters dated less than twenty-four hours apart. Bridget never kept the letters, but Malcolm, with a scientist's need to retain order, had saved all the originals.

We read through the file in sequential order. Each one was neatly subdivided into personal relationships and work; Bridget's personal relationships and Malcolm's work. Never the other way around. Bridget worked, sometimes extraordinarily hard, and Malcolm, as far as I know, did have the occasional passing fling, but neither was of sufficient interest to make it to the letters.

The file began eight years previously, when Bridget and I were about to buy the farm together. I sat with Janine on one side and Lee on the other and all three of us read through a series of lengthy letters in which a man I regarded as close to being my brother reviewed my emotional profile and life history, and assessed my suitability as a past, present and future life partner for his sister. He was a rather better judge of character than I had thought.

The second half of each letter dealt with the progress of his career. In true Malcolm fashion, he was less than explicit about the exact technique he was developing, preferring instead to talk about the potential implications for the future of medicine when he had solved the technological problems.

Later letters followed much the same format, although after I left the farm, he never voiced an opinion of Caroline and most of his comments on the new relationship referred exclusively to specific meetings and events. Very disappointing.

Even when he began to move towards medical genetics and head his own project team, the scientific content of each letter remained consistently low and it was apparent that, for Malcolm, his sister was an ethical counsellor rather than a scientific adviser.

When the initial enthusiasm at the start of the new project gave way to frustration as funding body after funding body refused to provide further grants for the project, he used the letters to ask advice and to explore other possible avenues.

In the end, when he made the decision to approach the directors of Medi-Gen with an outline of the commercial value of the technique, it was with a heavy heart and much against his better judgement, but with the implicit support of his sister.

Subsequent correspondence had a different tone. He was clearly pleased with the facilities and revelled in the chance to prove his theories correct without the need to continually publish data to keep the university authorities happy. On the other hand, he found the atmosphere of commercialism threatening and hated the secrecy with which the whole venture was conducted, supposedly to avoid the inevitable industrial espionage. He began to spend regular evenings back at the university, communing with his erstwhile colleagues, trying to maintain a stable sense of perspective.

The eggs, and the note which went with them, had been dispatched in a hurry with no obvious motive, although he had followed them up the next morning by a more detailed, and very apologetic, letter. A letter which had never been sent, or, if it had, had never arrived, which was a pity, because if his sister had read it she would probably never have died.

In his final communication, Malcolm told Bridget all the things he had never told her before: the technique of genetic splicing, the idea of using eggs as a vehicle for producing proteins, the world-wide need for human insulin and how he was going to be able to supply the demand. And then, in bold type at the top of the second page, was a warning to Bridget that she should not, under any circumstances, eat the eggs from the bantams.

But the rest of the letter held the reason why it had never arrived. He told her about the Hen's Teeth, about discovering a different protein to modify the insulin which he could splice into the yolk gene, about his surprise at finding one already there, about the tests he had run to work out what it was and about the prospective meeting with the person he believed to be responsible at which he intended to confront him or her with the facts and force them to withdraw from the project.

It was naïve to the point of stupidity and he had paid for it. The letter was written and printed on the day of his death. Malcolm Donnelly had written and signed his own death warrant and, right at the top, he had put his sister's name and address.

The three of us sat around the console, each dealing in our own way with the facts on the screen. Janine broke the silence.

'Do you want me to copy this one?' She was looking at me.

'Yes, please.' I nodded, still trying to think it through. 'Can you copy the whole file, in case there's anything in there we missed?'

'Sure, if you want.' Her eyebrows travelled up a fraction. 'Do you want me to . . . edit them first?'

A week ago I might have done, but not now. Too late in the day for that.

I shook my head. 'No. Just copy the lot. Thanks.'

'No problem.' A red light blinked on the spare disk drive and it whirred into action.

I turned away to find the coffee pot by the fire and was brought back by a strained expletive from Janine.

'Shit. Kellen. There's someone there.'

The screen was blank, the text files and folder icons replaced by a uniform grey. As I watched, the telephone icon reappeared, smiled for a second or two and then reverted to the sad grimace with the cross drawn through it.

'What's up?'

'Someone's pulled the plug. We're off-line.' She hit half a dozen keys in rapid succession, swearing under her breath.

'Were we traced?'

She shrugged expressively. 'How the hell should I know? They could have been there for the last three hours or they might just have walked in the door. I told you this was crazy.'

Very true, but then we knew that already.

Lee looked at me across the top of the console and very slowly, out of site of Janine, she raised a thumb.

Janine, oblivious to the exchange, took it upon herself to explain, in words of one syllable, exactly what I had made her do, how absolutely unsafe it had been and how low her estimation of me had fallen as a result. Something like that.

I waited until she had blown of the worst of the steam, and then pointed out that, in view of all the foregoing, the farm might not be the safest place to stay in the immediate future. She calmed down sufficiently to accept Lee's offer to help her pack the hardware into the car and within ten minutes she was back on the road, heading for Rae Larssen's, secure in the belief that we were about to follow and with a request not to worry the others unnecessarily.

As soon as she had gone, we turned on the alarms and then changed into the clothes Lee had brought in the rucksacks – the same as before, but with the trainers swapped for something a little more robust, more appropriate for wandering about the fields in the dark.

I took a torch and made a brief and fruitful search of the loft for the one remaining piece of equipment that Lee hadn't brought. She produced a new saw-wire from her rucksack and set about the necessary modifications while I went through the house, switching off all of the lights and dousing the fires so that the only light came from the moon, full now and sitting high over the crown of the beech wood.

After that, all we had to do was wait.

Several lifetimes passed in the space of the next hour. Long enough for every creaking branch in the wood to change to an invading battalion and for each cat that stepped in through the cat flap to face death ten times over before it reached the sanctuary of the Rayburn.

We sat quietly together near the dead fire in the kitchen, sharing the peace: the silent centre in the eye of the storm.

At midnight, the clock on the upstairs landing struck the hour with nerve-jangling clarity. The chimes resonated round the house, so that when the red light blinked on the console for a moment it felt like an extension of the noise.

Lee stood up and handed me my rucksack. 'Time to go, Stewart.'

'Thanks.'

'Take care.'

'You too.' I found her eyes in the darkness. 'Don't go playing the hero, huh?'

'I won't. You neither.'

'Right.'

She touched my arm briefly, then I whistled Tîr to my heel and stood for a moment at the back door, listening for the sound of a car on the lane. It was there, a whispering crackle of gravel, and then, after that, the very faintest of sounds as a door was shut. He had parked in the same place as last time, at the bend in the drive.

On a count of five, I left the shelter of the doorway to walk across the yard, the dog a pale ghost in my wake. At the field gate, I waited for another count and then slid through the rails and ran down the line of the fence. The ponies huffed sleepy surprise as I passed and Midnight followed along companionably for a pace or two before turning aside to explore a new tuft of grass.

The river was running higher and faster than I had even seen it. It swirled in frantic eddies at the edges of the bank and white water foamed crazily across the line of the fording stones. It might have been possible to wade across, but not in a hurry. I turned upriver and jumped across the narrow gap at the bend. At the wood's edge, I waited long enough to hear the ponies move again before following the fox path, straight between the trees, to the clearing.

It was a bright, cold night. The mist had vanished with the falling sun and the few clouds left in the sky skittered across the bright face of the moon like tangled strips of tissue paper. The shadows of the tall stone cairn angled sideways into the clearing, like a sundial just off noon. The swollen belly of the mound lay beyond it, expectant and still, and the dried grass on the top ruffled in the breeze. The wood held its breath; the only sound was the steady rush of water on stone in the background and the scuff of dog's feet on the grass.

As we crossed the open ground, sliding in the shadows between the cairn and the mound, the dog turned, pressing herself against my knee, and then stiffened, nose forward and foreleg raised, like a gundog on point. I followed the line of her attention and felt, rather than saw, the movement in the wood to the north of the fox trail.

Time to go.

Hunter and prey. Cat and mouse. Fox and rabbit.

I would not, for choice, be either a mouse or a rabbit, but there are times when there is no choice. Then, the aim is to stay ahead as long as possible. I had the advantage that I knew the wood as well as I knew the farmhouse, possibly better, and I knew where I needed to be.

With the dog glued to my side, I dropped into a crouch behind the mass of the mound and then ducked sideways into the undergrowth. Using the moon as a compass point, I made a wide sweep, curving uphill to the east of the clearing and then back down again, south and west towards the starting point.

The route followed the rabbit paths that coursed between the thickets of beech saplings sprouting from the boles of the adult trees; narrow, winding paths littered with dead leaves and rotten branches and with the occasional root stretching across at ankle height as a trap for the blind or unwary.

We moved, almost as a team, me in the lead, the dog close behind and the man somewhere in the background, following each move as I ducked and squirmed through the undergrowth, pushing through non-spaces between clumps of beech saplings, twisting round the trunks of centuries-old hawthorns and, once, perilously close to a bramble thicket.

The wood found its voice again as we passed through: a muted groaning of wood moving on wood, a shuddering of leaves and a crackle of breaking twigs as the wind wove its own path between the branches. The nocturnal wanderers warmed to the glare of the moon and began a twittering chorus of high-pitched conversations.

For a while I felt the excitement more than the fear. The odd, light-headed exhilaration that comes from risking everything in a single challenge. The wood and the moon and the brooding mass of the grave mound were on my side and it was easy to forget the wren and the merlin and the fact that the man behind me was a paid killer with a long series of messy knife-kills to his credit.

I quickened the pace, moving steadily and as quietly as it is possible for anyone to move who hasn't spent their life in the forest. Not perfectly quiet, but enough to be difficult to follow. The dog, uncannily, proved to be a natural, stepping out soundless as a cat on velvet. Her pale coat glowed, almost white in the moonlight, but that was no bad thing.

Forty yards from the edge of the clearing, I slid down into a hollow beneath a fallen trunk and lay there, listening. He was there, just beyond the bramble thicket, moving slowly forward, hunting by instinct rather than by sound. I felt him behind me, a mind like a nightmare brooding on the edge of the night.

A cold, sharp mind. No anger, no venom, no blood-lust, just a single, inviolate purpose and the certainty of fulfilment.

Then I felt the fear.

I lay face down, cheeks pressed to the wet earth and every muscle, bone and tendon turned to water. Like a mesmerised rabbit, I was caught and the hunter knew it. A twig cracked on the path as he changed direction, bearing down on the hollow.

The dog was made of firmer stuff. She took hold of my hand and bit firmly, dragging me back to time and place and a reason to keep moving.

A tawny owl called once, not far away.

I shoved the dog away, pointing to where she should go, and waited long enough to see her move in the right direction before I, too, moved up and out, not so noiseless now, towards the trees at the edge of the clearing.

He caught up with me as I reached the big tree on the eastern side, just behind the great cairn. The leaves shivered slightly at my back and, split seconds later, I felt the touch of hand-warm steel at my neck.

'That'll do.' A voice like Malcolm's, as Caroline said, but harder and with an undercurrent Malcolm could not have dreamed up in his wildest nightmares.

I stood very still while his free hand slid up and down in a rapid, fruitless search. I had no weapons on me. I'm not going to carry something I can't use. Not with the real professionals about.

My skin tingled electric-cold as the small movements of his blade shaved through fractional layers of skin over the great vessels at my throat. By the end of the search, a thin dribble of blood ran down into the neck of my sweatshirt.

He shifted his grip on the blade and moved round slightly so that we could see each other face to face. He was in the juggler's outfit this time, not the oiled Barbour jacket, but the eyes were the same, and the tight line to the mouth. It was, without question, the man I first saw on Buchanan Street station the night Danny Baird died.

Tod Andersen. The red fox. Hunting.

He was not a big man, nowhere near as big as Cash Andrews. But where Andrews was old and his figure spoke more of the past than of the present, this man carried his life in the palm of his hand, and it showed.

Every line of his body exuded an easy, understated competence. A killer, fine-tuned to kill. And arrogant. So very arrogant. The superb, unsullied arrogance of one who knows he is the best simply because he is still alive to know it.

He stood there, balanced and relaxed, with his back covered by the trunk of the tree and his arm half curved to keep the knife at my throat, and he knew exactly what he was going to do and how he was going to do it.

Balanced, relaxed and entirely vindictive.

Bright laughter danced at the back of his eyes.

'Danny Baird died last night,' he said, and his voice ran neat acid beneath the surface.

I held his gaze and kept the expression out of my face.

'Really.'

The knife twitched and the blood ran a little faster into the neck of my sweatshirt.

'Yes, really. He was on his way to see your girlfriend. Didn't she tell you?' His mouth tightened in a vulpine smile and his voice feigned softness. 'Where's the new dog?'

I rocked my eyes across the clearing. 'Over there.'

Tîr slunk forward from the fox trail on the far side of the clearing and lay in the grass, watching us.

'Call it.'

'No.'

The smile stayed in place and the knife twitched. The wet patch on my sweatshirt spread down across my shoulder. He slid his free hand into his pocket and came out with another knife, shorter and balanced to throw.

'Call it.'

He spun the blade once into the air and I remembered a bird dying in an explosion of feathers.

No need to give him target practice.

I pushed away the memory and snapped my fingers. The dog edged forward, belly to the floor but only as far as the centre of the clearing. She stopped there and no amount of whistling, calling or snapping of fingers was going to move her.

I felt him pause, frustrated and then make up his mind. Moving round behind me, he shoved me forwards, out into the open.

'Make it stay.'

I did my best.

She lay still until we were almost on top of her, then scooted backwards and sideways, just out of reach. Cursing, I leant forward, away from the knife, to grab her.

He let me go, his eyes caught by the blurring movement of her pale fur across the grass, and as I moved off the edge of the blade, Lee stood up from the shadows of the old cairn and lifted the truncated barrel of Malcolm's shotgun to the back of his head and it was over.

Easy. Too easy. Such an old, old trick.

Disappointing that he should fall for it. He had seemed too much of a professional for that.

You don't argue with a sawn-off 4.10, however fit and well trained you are. He stood stock still with both hands in plain view as I removed the spare knife from the sheath at his back and then took the pouch from his waist. He sat down where he was told to, with his back to the great cairn and never moved a muscle while I used the cording from his pouch to fix his hands round the back. His eyes gave out nothing, or his face, except once, when I found the third knife taped to his shin, and then he looked, if anything, mildly peeved.

Lee looked at me and an eyebrow flickered upwards.

'Go for it,' I said and went to sit down with my back to Tan's cairn, feeling the rounded edge of the river stones dig into my back, and watched for the change, if it ever came.

Once, early on, I saw him tense against the cord, testing the ties that held him to the cairn and then scan round the rest of the clearing, as if checking for who was where. But after that, it was like watching the surface of an ice-flow; smooth, insensate and impervious to the relentless tide of questions. He knew, after all, that it was only a question of time. The only thing he didn't know was that we were waiting with him, and for the same thing.

I kept my gaze fixed on the set of his eyes and the pulse at his throat, watching for the change when his body said something different to his voice and I listened to him goading her.

'Who do you work for?'

'Cash Andrews.'

'Cash Andrews is dead.'

'So is Danny Baird. Was he good to you before he died?'

I wonder if he wants to die? Or perhaps there is some kind of killer's instinct that tells him she has no intention of pulling the trigger. Myself, I wouldn't be so sure.

Back to the questions.

'Did you kill Malcolm Donnelly?'

'No.'

'But you know who did.'

'I could guess.'

'Did you kill Bridget Donnelly?'

'Of course not.' A voice full of injured innocence. 'I didn't even kill the dog. It was still alive when I left.'

If I was facing a loaded 4.10, I really wouldn't push that close to the edge. We both saw Lee's eyes flicker and then calm down as she took a breath.

So now he knows what hurts and what doesn't.

Start again.

The change came soon after that. The moon had moved half-way across the gap, lighting up the clearing like a searchlight, bright-lighting the hair of the man seated against the cairn, leaving the side of his face nearest to me invisible in the shadows.

Lee was a silhouette, sharp-edged against the trees behind. She was back at the beginning: 'Who do you work for?' – no real answer expected and none given, except that the change was there.

This time, when the taunting voice said, 'Cash Andrews, who else?' the rest of him was somewhere else, searching for something beyond the edge of the wood. Or someone.

'This is it.' I stood up, feeling the cramp in my legs from too long in one place.

'What?'

'There's someone coming. Andersen's heard it. Time to move.'

He kept his face commendably still, but both of us knew it was true.

Lee didn't stop to ask him. She reached down to cut the cords at his wrist and, sliding the safety off the gun with an audible click, motioned him up and out of the clearing.

We moved in single file down the hunter's path to the river, Andersen in front, Lee following with the gun angled at the back of his neck, me behind, trying to feel what it was that was wrong. Something. The hush in the wood said that something was wrong, and the dog, who had melted into the undergrowth as we left the clearing and showed no signs of coming back to join us.

It occurred to me then, as I jumped third in line across the burn, that if I had guessed wrong and Inspector Stewart MacDonald was really the paymaster running Tod Andersen, then we were as good as dead.

He wasn't as it turned out, but there were moments later when I wished that he had been. As my feet hit the ground on the field side of the river bank, I heard a voice I hadn't heard since the days in the dusty lecture theatres of medical school.

'Good evening, Dr Adams, Dr Stewart. How very convenient. We were beginning to think we had missed you.'

A cold, uninflected, voice. Used to giving orders and having them carried out.

A tall man, angular and silver-haired, in full evening dress, as he had been at Cash Andrew's party. Totally out of place in a beech wood at midnight.

An indulgent smile under unsmiling eyes.

And a small, effete hand-gun held loosely against the temple of my lover, who stood stiffly at his side, her eyes dripping green dragon-fire over the top of an Elastoplast mouth tape.

'Professor Peter Gemmell,' said Lee from my side, and the words dropped like stones into the background noise of the river.

So wrong. So completely wrong. And too late to take anything back.

He smiled at us across the water. 'Sorry to disappoint you, Dr Adams. Don't let it upset you. We all make mistakes.' He transferred his gaze to the man behind us. 'My apologies for the delay, Mr Andersen. Nothing too inconvenient, I hope?'

Tod Andersen shook his head and smiled, and this time, the flat line of his mouth matched exactly the narrowing eyes and both of them said that the past half-hour was playtime compared to what was coming next.

I remembered Tan, lying alive on the flagstones of the kitchen floor, and my guts twisted hard and painfully.

The man on the other side of the river saw me and recognised the look. The sharp smile sharpened and he stepped forward to the edge of the river, dragging Janine with him.

'Your friend, I believe, Dr Stewart. It was extraordinarily good of you to show Mr Andersen the way to the flat this morning, Life would have been so much more complicated otherwise.'

He jerked Janine's arm out at an odd angle, forcing the elbow into rigid extension and laid the muzzle of his gun on the back of the joint. 'This is loaded, I promise you. I'm sure I don't have to demonstrate. The mess would be appalling. Mr Andersen, if you would relieve Drs Adams and Stewart of their weapons . . .'

If Lee had been on her own, the balance would have held. She had Andersen, still on the end of enough fire power to make permanent damage. Peter Gemmell had Janine. Neither was so attached to the other's hostage as to make any kind of meaningful trade-off.

But I was there, on the wrong side of the river, and it tipped the balance so far over that the bargain was made without any pause for discussion. Lee simply cracked open her gun, tipped the shells out into the river and handed it, butt first, to the man at her side. He dropped it to the grass at his feet and held out his hand for the blades; three of his own and both of Lee's. Quick, simple and efficient.

Across the river, Peter Gemmell murmured something barely audible about women and dangerous toys and then all three of us were over at the wood's edge and trekking back between the beeches to the clearing.

There was fresh blood on the cairn, stark black against the pale moss, where Lee had snicked the skin of Andersen's wrist while cutting the cords. Not an encouraging sight.

Gemmell held Janine with her back to trees at the place where the path opened out and Andersen took Lee over to the mound, to sit with her back against the cairn, in the place he had been less than five minutes before.

I stood on the sidelines, my back to a tree, unthreatened but manifestly not a threat, held as much by the knife at Lee's throat as the gun at Janine's, an unwilling witness to the wordless war of attrition about to take place in the centre of the clearing. Tod Andersen had several scores to settle and Gemmell, with the whole night ahead of him, seemed content to let him play for a while.

The only thing I could think of was to delay the start.

I sat down, keeping my back against the ridged bark of the beech.

'Does your son-in-law know about this, Professor Gemmell?' I kept my eyes off Andersen and let the tone of my voice divert attention to the side of the clearing.

He nodded, as he used to in lectures, a slow dip of the forehead to show he was aware of what I was doing but was prepared to let it happen. 'Not at all. David is one of life's less effective hangers-on. In the right circumstances, he could have been useful. As it was, he was an unqualified nuisance.'

'But he told you that Bridget was ill?'

'Not quite, I answered his phone for him. He was driving off the tee when the call came through. It seemed unnecessary, under the circumstances, to pass the message on.'

'So you did kill her? You killed Bridget?'

'I would dispute that. In effect, the lady killed herself by eating the eggs. I merely failed to administer all of the appropriate treatment and she died as a consequence. It was very peaceful, if that makes any difference to you.'

'Why did she take the temazepam from you? You weren't her GP?'

'No. But I was her brother's friend.'

'She trusted you.'

'Yes.'

You complete, unmitigated bastard.

'Why? Was she a danger to you? Did she have any idea of what you had done to Malcolm?'

'No. But she was asking questions and not all of them had easy answers.'

'That's it? You killed her for asking questions?' My voice was rising, losing control.

He sighed through pinched nostrils, his patience wearing thin. 'Dr Stewart, do you have any idea of the financial value of these eggs? In slightly under a year, we will have made returns greater than I have earned in three decades of medical teaching. That level of revenue is worth killing to protect, yes.'

'You're a medic, for God's sake. You don't do it for the money. What happened to the sanctity of life and the Hippocratic oath?'

'Don't be unnecessarily naïve, Dr Stewart. You worked in a hospital once. You know the things that tip the balance between living and dying. A great deal of them centre around money. I merely made the decision more obvious. The principle is the same.' He nodded across the clearing towards the cairn. 'And there are a lot of ways of living that are far less pleasant than being dead. As I suspect Mr Andersen may be about to demonstrate.'

Not yet.

'The police have the details of Malcolm's body, Gemmell. And the bloods from Anatomy. They can prove enough to pin you down with those. Especially if all three of us go missing.'

'No,' he said flatly. 'I don't think so. Grant us a modicum of forethought, Dr Stewart. You will not "go missing". You will merely be found to have died in a house fire. And Dr Donnelly's body is no longer in anatomy. He has, finally, joined his sister in the everlasting fires of the crematorium.'

'Did you kill him too?'

'Effectively. Again, he ate the eggs of his own accord, but I had impressed upon him the consequences for his sister and his immediate family had he refused to do so. The man was also asking questions of the wrong sort. It appears to be a family habit. As does wasting time.' He turned back towards the clearing. 'I believe we have one or two of our own to ask Dr Adams before we have to go into the farmhouse. Yes, Mr Andersen?'

The red fox smiled his slow, vulpine smile. A creature of very few words, the fox.

All attention focused on the cairn and on Lee sitting in front of it, her hands untied, the knife hovering loosely at her throat.

Gemmell moved Janine until he could rest his gun hand on a branch and have it aimed neatly at the small of her back. 'Very simply, Dr Adams, if you attempt to move, the lady loses her spinal cord. Is that clear?'

She nodded, tight-lipped. Her nostrils flared white at the edges.

'Good. Apparently a young man by the name of Danny Baird was trying to sell you information. We need to know who put him in contact with you. Would you care to tell us about it?'

The muscles on her jaw tightened fractionally and her mind moved behind a steel wall.

'No.'

And so the questioning began. Not because they really needed to know the answer, but because they had the time and the opportunity and they wanted to play. All I could do was watch and wait.

It wasn't pretty. Tod Andersen's understanding of anatomy was as comprehensive as it was functional and he was not constrained by the need to fake a legitimate death.

He kept the blade of his knife resting along the line of her jugular and dragged her left arm up on top of the cairn so that the hand lay, palm up, on the mossed surface of the roof stone with the fingers angled viciously over the edge. One knee came up to pin her wrist in place and he rested his free hand on the edge of the stone next to hers.

This is not the kind of thing I can watch.

Grinding my back hard against the tree behind me, I turned my eyes on Janine instead, willing her not to do anything to change the stakes. Neither Gemmell nor Andersen said anything more, but I watched as Janine's eyes stretched wide and bulged over the Elastoplast tape and I knew, without ever having to look, when it started.

Later, I watched her vomit into the gag and fight to swallow silently without choking. The faint acid smell of it drifted across the clearing towards me. I thought hard about the physiology of gastro-intestinal disturbance and very little at all about the possible causes of spontaneous emesis in an otherwise strong-stomached woman.

Later still, I felt something change and turned to look at the cairn. Lee's head turned towards me and her eyes met mine, wide, black and empty. An endless tunnel to nowhere. She shifted her gaze so that she was looking over my shoulder into the wood behind, then down to the grass at my feet and back up into the wood again in a single, clear message. Then Andersen had hold of the index finger and her eyes closed.

The wren died when it sang. I should have told her that.

For a single eternity, nothing happened. The silence was, in its way, more frightening than anything that had gone before.

I looked again and saw Tod Andersen bend to speak in Lee's ear. The bulk of his body hid whatever was happening on top of the roof stone but the joints of her arm were locked at impossible angles and he was braced as if weighting a lever.

I didn't hear what he asked but I saw her shake her head once, emphatically, and then, before he could move, she jerked round, twisting her neck sideways on to the knife blade that was still there, tight against her jugular.

Blood welled black along the line of the blade.

Gemmell shouted.

Janine passed out at his feet.

Andersen cursed and jerked his arm away, dropping the knife. Too late.

272

A life for a life. Maybe.

The noise in the clearing was enough to cover the noise of movement. I stood up and stepped back, sliding in between the trees at my back, crouched down and was invisible.

Through the undergrowth I watched the blood run free from the knife wound on Lee's neck. It wasn't flowing fast enough to be fatal. Neck wounds rarely are.

Good try, but not good enough.

Andersen had his hand in her hair, her head stretched back over the roof stone, and was leaning over, his eyes above hers. His lips moved but whatever he said was too quiet to be audible. He wasn't offering help.

I took another slow, cautious step back. Leaves moved underfoot.

Gemmell turned towards me, his eyes quartering the wood.

'Andersen. She's gone.'

The fox looked up and smiled.

Leaning back, still with one hand locked in Lee's hair, he lifted the 4.10 from the side of the cairn and held it against her skull, just behind the ear.

'Count of five,' he said, just loudly enough for me to hear him.

'One . . . two . . . three . . .'

'Drop it. We don't want her dead yet.'

Gemmell. He gives commands as a reflex.

The smile grew. The gun angled down until the mouth rested on her knee.

Lee twisted round against his hand, black eyes in a white face, voice raw. 'Kellen. No. Stay out.'

' . . . four . . .'

'No.' I stepped forward into the clearing, saw the smile stretch and, sickening, I saw his finger tighten on the trigger . . .

'No!'

. . . and heard the hammer fall on bare metal.

273

Lee had dropped the shells in the river. Andersen never reloaded.

He knew that and she knew that. Only I forgot.

I stood at the edge of the clearing, tasting acrid bile in the back of my throat, and knew that I had had my one chance and I had blown it very badly.

As the fox drew back the gun, still smiling, Lee pulled her hair from his grip and threw herself away from the cairn, towards the mound. Andersen sprang sideways after her in a one-handed tackle and they hit the barrow together in a bruising collision of flesh and earth. The momentum carried them over the ridge and down the other side, to land in a winded heap on the floor of the clearing.

The man recovered first. He rolled to his feet and stood over her, still holding the gun, teeth clenched and face contorted in a display of temper that was no longer under any control. Kicking her arm into extension, he trapped the wrist with his foot, pinning her hand to the floor of the clearing. Then he reversed his grip on the gun with an impatient flick and, holding the barrel vertically, he slammed the butt down hard on to her open fingers.

Her scream cut off as she fainted.

The silence was painful.

The moon slid the final inch down below the level of the gap and the shadows stretched like prison bars across the clearing. Only the river still moved. The rest of the wood watched in stillness, as it had since the first scream.

Andersen and Gemmell looked at each other across the open space. Both of them looked at me. I was shaking all over in a fine, uncontrolled tremor.

'Inside?' Andersen jerked his head towards the farm.

'I think so. And then Dr Stewart can tell us where she put her chickens.' Gemmell regarded me with a quiet loathing. 'We will need them, you understand, to rebuild a new flock elsewhere. The rest will, by now, have died in the fire at the farm of our late and unlamented friend, Mr Andrews. Unfortunate but expedient. It has the advantage that it will keep the emergency services occupied for quite some time while removing any significant evidence. I imagine a small fire at a farmhouse will attract minimal attention, although you would be amazed at how much damage a Rayburn can do if filled with the wrong fuel.' He grabbed the unconscious Janine by one arm and hoisted her up in a fireman's lift, gesturing curtly for me to walk in front of him.

'It amuses Mr Andersen to think of you taking the same route from this world as did your dear departed friends.'

On his cue, the unsmiling Andersen slung Lee over a shoulder and moved forward ahead of me out of the clearing.

We trooped in silence to the wood edge and stopped there at the river's edge to view the height of the water and the distance of the jump. Too high and too far for a man carrying an unconscious body.

Without a word, Andersen turned upriver and moved on along the sheep track towards the fording stones by the paddock.

It was dark on this side of the wood and old branches littered the path, making the walking treacherous. I kept both hands in view, kept my eyes on the ground and concentrated on staying upright. It seemed safest.

The river foamed white across the top of the stones and experience said that the carpeting moss on the surface, once wet, had a grip like oiled marble: treacherous underfoot.

On the whole, I would rather drown than burn and I can take one of them with me into the black water the other side of the stones. It's deep there and running fast enough to pull us under.

Me and one other.

Only one.

The red or the black. You can't have them both.
Mhaire. She never said it was Lee.
I hate that woman.

I bumped into Andersen's back and realised he had stopped. Stepping sideways, I looking past him and saw movement beyond the fence. Gemmell cannoned into me, cursed and pulled to my left. Cloth slithered on cloth as he lowered Janine to the grass. He stood beside me, staring out across the river to the field on the far bank. The ponies were there, herded in a crowd, like sheep at the shedding pen, stamping irritation. Balder shoved up against the fence and fly-kicked sideways, cracking an unshod hoof into the hard wood of the post.

A blur of white fur slid round the edges, holding the group together, as a sheepdog does. Tîr. As tricks go, it was amusing, but not, under the circumstances, particularly useful.

Andersen drew out a knife and tossed it thoughtfully, watching the dog circle back towards the fence.

He shifted his weight slightly, stepping back with his right foot to open his shoulder for the throw. Lee's dead weight on his other shoulder pulled him down, not quite on balance. The dog cast round wide, invisible behind a wall of horse flesh, sweeping in an arc towards the fence.

Only one.
Wait.
And wait.
No dog.

The herd parted and a figure pushed through between the crowding bodies: a man, mid-height, in full kilted evening dress. Ridiculous and out of place here in the wood. I couldn't see the hair.

Andersen altered his balance fractionally, aiming ahead now, not to the side.

The figure reached the fence and leant forward, resting both hands on the top rail, lazily, as if watching a dog hunt rabbits.

'That'll do, Andersen.'

A soft voice with a melting West Highland accent.

MacDonald. Alone. Unarmed.

'Kill him.' Gemmell, a reflex command.

Out of the corner of my eye, I saw him raise his gun arm to fire.

The red or the black? Do you think you can choose?

Yes.

'No!'

I kicked right, at the knee, pitching Andersen off balance, and then, spinning left, cannoned into Gemmell, wrapping my arms round his waist and carried him with me, deep into the swirling water beside the stones.

Water. Black water. Cold water.

Cold. So cold.

Black. Spiralling crazily behind lids held shut by the crashing water.

And red. Red fire, for the pain.

Then only black.

CHAPTER TWELVE

Black. Only black. And red, for the pain.

The metallic tang of old blood and the warm musk of horse hair.

The rapid insistent tick of a clock and water dripping on to stone: irregular, irritating, drawing me back.

A dog panting wetly close by and a warm weight on my feet.

Teeth, hard on my wrist.

'That'll do.' A woman's voice, almost amused. Warm and motherly. I should recognise that.

Teeth removed.

'Is she awake?' A steady voice with a melting West Highland burr.

'Close enough. Go easy though. Don't push.'

A hand on my forehead. Mother, I'm hot. And dripping sweat. The sheets are drenched.

'Kellen?'

That's the first time he's ever said my name.

'Yes?'

'Can you see me?'

I think so.

Daylight slanted in through the roof windows of the small room under the eaves.

Primroses pattern the duvet.

Rain splashes heavily on to the sill.

Eyes open.

MacDonald stood at the side of the bed, back in his full inspector's uniform, all sharp creases and shiny buttons. He looked gaunt and worried and tired past sleeping.

'Are you all right?'

Tîr lay across my feet, staring at me with her odd caste eyes. I remembered.

'Lee?' My voice was dry, like my mouth.

The hollows round his eyes deepened and panic wrenched at my guts.

'She's not dead?'

He shook his head. 'No. She's not dead. Not yet. But she's lost a lot of blood. Yon bastard had a good try at cutting her throat.'

'Andersen? But she wasn't bleeding that badly.'

'Aye, well, he had another go after you went in the water. She bled well enough when he was done.'

'Where is she?'

'In the Western. They're still transfusing her now. If she's fit tomorrow, they'll take her into surgery and have a look at her hands . . .' He frowned painfully and looked the other way.

Her hands.

I remembered and wished that I hadn't.

MacDonald saw it. 'She's a mess, Kellen. Her hands are a mess. What were they after?'

Dangerous. I nearly told him the truth.

I shrugged and then stopped, suddenly, as paralysing pain shot through me out of nowhere.

'Revenge,' I said, when I could speak again, which was true. And then, 'The others?'

'Yon lady friend's fine. Physically, anyway. Underneath, I would say she's seen things she'd rather not have seen.'

'She's not keen on the sight of blood.'

'No. Not when it's yours, at any rate.'

'The rest?'

'Andersen's dead.'

'How?'

'I shot him.'

What?

'But you weren't armed.'

'Of course I was. I just wasn't carrying it where it could be seen. And I still wasn't fast enough to stop him using his knife.'

Which is why his eyes look like that. He thinks he's responsible.

'Don't let it get to you, man. If you hadn't turned up, we'd all be a lot worse off.'

'Maybe.'

'Definitely. What happened to Gemmell?'

'He's still alive. Just. Neither of you quite succeeded in killing the other. Not for want of trying though.' He looked faintly exasperated, a teacher with an errant pupil.

'He didn't try to kill me.' Even to me, I sounded defensive.

'Is that so? What do you think this is, then?' He reached up and touched a surgical pad that was taped to my left shoulder, spanning from collar bone to earlobe. If I tipped my head on one side, I could feel the rough gauze of it against my cheek.

I moved my arm experimentally and laser points of sheer agony flared out in waves. The blackness rolled in again.

When I opened my eyes, he was leaning over me, pressing a wet hanky to my forehead. Even in the police they teach them more first aid than that.

I asked the question with my eyes because I still hadn't breath for speaking.

'Gunshot. Single wound, small-calibre. If you jump a man with a gun, Dr Stewart, you can expect to get shot at.'

Now he sounds just like my father, trying to be angry and not knowing how.

I tried to look contrite. 'Sorry.'

He shook his head. 'No, you're not.'

True.

'What happened to Gemmell? I wasn't trying to kill him. Really. Just stop him killing anyone else.'

'He's alive but he's not what you'd call *compos mentis*. He cracked his head on a rock on the way down the river. Apparently his brain looks like porridge on the scan and there are clots in places there shouldn't be. He's on a ventilator in intensive care. The doctors are being pretty coy, but I get the idea they don't think he's going to come round in a hurry. I've put a lad by the bedside in case he wakes up and wants to say anything interesting.'

He looked at me carefully and said nothing.

They can keep a man going on a life support system for years these days. He could be ninety before he dies.

That one lives for ever.

I shook my head, but carefully, because it hurt. 'Forget it. He won't wake up.'

'Aye, I thought maybe not.' He dragged his gaze away and looked out of the window at the rain. 'I'll leave the lad with him for a day or two anyway, just in case. It'll do him good to see the inside of a hospital for a bit.'

The room began to blur. I closed my eyes, trying to focus and failed. My mouth felt like old carpet. Somewhere, I could smell coffee.

'Is there a drink?'

He reached a glass from the bedside table. Water.

'Coffee?'

'No. Not yet. Doctor's orders.'

'But I'm a doctor.'

'That doesn't count. It's water or nothing.'

He held it for me to drink, rocking my head forward to the glass. He would have made a good nurse.

When I lay still again, he backed away until he was perched against the window-sill, a shadow against the wet grey sky. 'Can you hear me, Kellen?'

'Mmm,' I think so.

'Chief Inspector Laidlaw's assigned this end of the case to myself and WPC Philips.'

'Oh.' How nice.

'There isn't much left to do. We know more or less who did what. Ms Caradice has told us what Professor Gemmell said in the clearing. And the lab at Medi-Gen's been a goldmine.'

'The farm . . .' Wild smoke and dead horses loomed through the haze in my head.

'The farm's fine. The fire didn't take. They started it in too much of a hurry. Between that and the lab, there's enough there to keep the lads in white coats happy for years.'

'So . . .'

'There's just one or two loose ends . . .' His voice came from the end of a tunnel, a long away off. Like a dream.

'Mmm?' Not a bad dream. Just not very real. Difficult to hold on to.

'The Chief Inspector's car . . .'

Oh, bloody hell.

'He found it in the shed. Young Elspeth picked up some of Andersen's fingerprints on the wheel and she thinks he may have stolen it to use as a getaway car for afterwards.'

'She's a very . . . resourceful woman . . .'

'She is. Don't forget.'

'No. Thank you.'

I'm hallucinating. MacDonald's disembodied smile hovers over me like a rustic Cheshire Cat, while the rest of him floats backwards out of the room.

Sleep came in snatches, light and feverish. I dreamed of Mhaire Culloch taking me to her council flat in the South Side, to a big room with black curtains, and of me helping her to mend a set of tall white flag poles that had broken in the wind. We bandaged them tight with splints up the side and then she took the blood from my wrists and painted the bandages red, like maypoles.

Later, someone began to run a red-hot poker backwards and forwards through the muscles of my shoulder. Voices muttered in the background. I fought through the layers of hot, sweaty mist to the clogged air of the bedroom.

When I opened my eyes, Janine was sitting on the edge of the bed, holding my hand on her knee, peeling the pad away from my shoulder. The curtains were closed and the bedside lamp was on. Her hair shone oddly in the artificial light. A litter of dead mugs on the bedside table said that someone had been drinking a lot of coffee recently.

She looked up and saw me watching her.

'Good evening.'

'Is it? What are you doing?'

'Changing this.' She finished unpicking the micropore from the edges of the dressing. The final piece of gauze came off with a tug that made my eyes water.

By twisting my head carefully, I could see the hole. Angry and red, with burn marks round the outside. Close-range, small-calibre, high-velocity missile. Lucky it wasn't buckshot or I'd be dead.

Dead.

'Lee?'

'They're in theatre with her now.'

'Is she all right?'

'So far as I know.'

She fished a pad of damp cotton wool from a bowl by the bed

and wiped it smoothly around the edges of the wound. The poker changed to white hot and skittered across my back.

'That hurts.'

'I thought it might.' Her voice was brisk and businesslike. Not exactly oozing sympathy. Maybe I didn't deserve any.

She began to lay on a fresh dressing. It was cooler if nothing else. The poker became a small heated flat iron running rhythmically over the skin.

'Are you cross with me?'

'Not any more than usual.'

'Oh. Good.' I think it's good. I remembered the promise. 'Do you want to talk?'

'Not while you're still away with the fairies, I don't. We'll talk when you know what you're talking about, which isn't yet.' Leaning over, she kissed the top of my head. A sisterly kind of a kiss. The kind of kiss that leaves doors open for later. 'Just get well, will you? Then we can all go back to a normal life.'

Maybe.

She taped down the last edge of the bandage and then looped her fingers through mine to swivel my arm off her knee and back on to the bed.

The fire soared in tracks all the way from my fingers to my spine. I shut my eyes and watched comets flare across the blackness of the closed lids.

Later, a long while later, when my bladder had been threatening to burst for eternity, I hoisted myself out of bed and along the landing to the bathroom. It was further away than I had remembered.

The dog followed me along the corridor and sat outside the door, looking miserable.

'I think it's time you and me got some fresh air, dog.'

An ear twitched hopefully.

I found Bridget's cream dressing gown on the back of the

bathroom door and dug a pair of shoes out from under the foot of the bed, then the pair of us took the stairs, slowly, one at a time, to the bottom.

No problem.

There was no one in the kitchen and the back door hung invitingly open. I waited for a moment on the porch while the dog emptied a pint or three of urine into the gravel by the corner of the house, then I spotted Midnight hanging round the field gate, just asking for a visit.

The rest of the ponies were not particularly enthusiastic at my appearance, but they came over for a look and when it suddenly seemed sensible to sit down on the grass inside the gate, they managed not to tread on my feet as they wandered past.

Someone crunched up the gravel behind me.

The problem with a bullet hole in the shoulder is that it's difficult to turn your head quickly when folk sneak up on you like that.

'Kellen? What the hell are you doing here?'

Caroline. Sweetness and light. She's always somewhere, just round the corner.

'The dog needed a walk.'

'Bugger that. You're not supposed to be out of bed for weeks yet. Get up, woman.'

'Mmm. Good idea.'

'Can you get up?'

'I expect so, just give me a minute . . .'

'Oh, hell, Kells. Don't do this to me . . . Can you walk?'

'Sure.'

'Liar . . . You're a mess, Kellen Stewart, I should have let them take you to the hospital. At least they could keep you in bed.'

'I don't need to be in bed. I'm fine.'

'Just shut up and keep walking.'

'Thanks. I love you too.'

The kitchen, on the whole, was warmer than the field. I sat in the big chair by the fire and watched Caroline make a pot of cat's-piss tea.

'Here. It's good for you. And don't ask for coffee. You're not getting any.'

'Sadist.'

'Be grateful I haven't spiked it with anything. They've left me with enough tranquillisers to keep you in bed for the next month.'

'You wouldn't do that.'

'No. But I might if you don't behave.'

'You sound just like Mother.'

'Get lost. Do you want something to eat?'

'Mmm. Why not?'

I watched her embark on another culinary adventure and then edged myself down to sit on the floor and scooped a passing cat on to my knee for something to talk to.

'Why didn't they take me to hospital, cat?' I asked, running a finger along its back.

'Because one of your oldest and dearest friends put her foot down and wouldn't let them,' said Caroline's voice from the far side of the breakfast bar. The cat flopped on its side, kneading my good arm with sheathed claws.

'That's nice. Why did she do that?'

'Because you told me once that if you ever woke up and found yourself in hospital, you'd throw yourself out of a window. I didn't want to find out the hard way that you weren't joking.' She left a pan simmering on the Rayburn and came to sit in the chair opposite. 'Mary Brower was going completely berserk and Elspeth was threatening to have me on a murder charge if you died, but Janine backed me up. Between us we're the nearest thing you've got to a next of kin, so they couldn't do much about it. It seemed the right thing to do at the time.'

I looked up into a pair of wide green-grey eyes.

'It was. Thank you.' I felt the dog slide into the space between me and the fire and I let go of the cat. 'What about Lee?'

'Mad Mhaire's in there, sitting by the bed with a pack of twenty Marlboro, fending off all-comers. She's pretty protective. I don't think she'd let her chuck herself off a window-ledge.'

No. She wouldn't.

'Is she awake?'

'Sort of. She had a word with Elspeth and Inspector MacDonald this morning before they took her to surgery. I think it was fairly coherent.' The pan on the Rayburn rattled its lid and she went over to investigate. 'Soup?'

'Mmm. Thank you.' I waited while she loaded a tray with bowls and bread and came back to sit on the floor opposite.

My stomach registered the smell of food with an ambivalent lurch. I toyed with the bread, dunking bits of it in the soup to soften the crust. Just as I was about to test the first bite, Elspeth Philips turned up in the doorway. Her uniform looked as if she had slept in it. Her eyes didn't look as if she had slept much at all.

She looked me up and down, amused and appraising in one. 'The walking wounded, alive and well. I wasn't expecting to see you up yet.'

'That makes two of us,' said Caroline. 'She's on her way upstairs.'

'Is she really?'

'In a bit. I'd rather hear what's happening in the outside world first.'

'I thought you might.' Her eyes were warm and not at all unfriendly.

She looked at Caroline, who gave a resigned shrug and vacated the chair by the fire.

'Go ahead.'

'Thanks.' She sat down and kicked off her shoes. 'How much do you know?'

'Not much. Andersen's dead. Gemmell isn't. Jan's told you who said what in the clearing.'

'More or less. They tried to wipe the computer system at the lab but most of the stuff's still on the hard disks. Jan's been helping to recover it in return for an exclusive on the story when it breaks. The chickens at Andrews' farm were all alive and are laying nicely for the lab. We found the stocks of Hen's Teeth at Gemmell's house and turned them over to the lads in the vice squad. They should have gone up in smoke by now. If your Professor ever comes round, he's all lined up for several life sentences.'

'Who else was in it?'

'Besides Andersen? There were half a dozen distributors, most of them on a similar scale to Cash Andrews and all of them already known for dealing crack. On the scientific side, Gemmell used his daughter's research project as a cover. She was supposed to be finding out ways to protect the insulin from oral uptake. Her father passed on the genes she was making to Malcolm and he slotted them into the eggs at Medi-Gen. Neither of them queried whether the genes Malcolm got were the ones she had sent.'

'They wouldn't.' You don't question the given truth passed down from the professorial Ivory Tower. Especially not if it's inhabited by your father or your friend. 'What does the daughter say now?'

'She's devastated. Apparently she had no idea what was going on.'

'Do you believe her?'

'I think so.'

'And the son-in-law?'

'Your friend Dr Kemp?' She leant back in her chair and smiled, a proper smile that lit up her face and shone through her eyes. Green eyes. Like a cat. Still riveting.

I tried to focus on what she was saying.

' . . . he's being extraordinarily apologetic. We had to physically restrain him from coming in to visit you.'

'Bloody hell. I'd rather be dead.'

'Quite. We didn't think you'd appreciate it much. But you're going to have to see him some time. If he hadn't talked to the Inspector at the golf-club dinner, you'd probably be dead and Gemmell would be in the Bahamas enjoying the sunshine.'

'Are you telling me I'm expected to thank the man?'

'Something like that. You have to acknowledge that he worked out what was going on before the rest of us, he just didn't realise it was coming to a head quite so quickly.'

'Why? I mean, how?'

'He didn't like it when Bridget died without any reasonable signs. He called his father-in-law to try to get him to do the post-mortem and found Lee had already done it . . .'

'Didn't it cheer him up when Lee asked the Prof to sign it after all?'

'Hardly. He thought it was a blind. That Lee was trying to draw attention away from her part in it.'

'Mmm.' Brighter than he looks.

'That stuck you and Lee right at the top of the list of suspects. He had his wife give him the keys so he could go through Lee's room and found the eggs, but it took him a while to work out what was in them. He was planning on taking it all in as soon as Chief Inspector Laidlaw was back in the office.'

'So what made him change his mind?'

'He didn't. But he was trying to tell Stewart . . . the Inspector . . . at the dinner when the call came through about the fire at the farm and then Caroline and I called in to tell the boss that Janine had never made it back to Rae's.' She paused for effect. 'I told him there was no way you could have lit the fire because you were with me all evening.'

'Lee wasn't.'

'No.'

'Did you tell him that?'

'No.'

'Why not?'

'Because you might have let her light fires, but I knew you wouldn't have let her do anything to hurt Jan.'·

Observant as well as resourceful. 'Thank you.'

'You're welcome. Anyway, you had set everything up to draw them here.'

'Was it that obvious?'

'Of course. Why didn't you ask for help?'

I shrugged. 'I didn't think about it. I suppose there's a tendency to think we should be able to sort things out ourselves.'

'I noticed.' She accepted a mug of tea from Caroline and they exchanged a look that spoke volumes about friends who think they can sort things out on their own.

The need for sleep began to drag at the edges of my mind. The soup was cold and the bread had turned to the consistency of sodden blotting paper. I put the bowl on the floor and began to think of the climb back up the stairs. 'No loose ends?' I asked.

'None that matter.'

Only one last question before I sleep. 'How did you know about the car?'

She observed me peacefully from beneath lowered lids. 'I don't know what you're talking about,' she said.

'Fine.'

They steered me upstairs and somewhere along the line, someone mentioned a bath.

Sheer heaven. Like floating on the sea in the sunshine, listening to the water washing round in the rock pools.

Bed was the same. Someone else had changed the sheets for something in cool green without the bloodstains and there was a towel for the dog to lie on so she wouldn't shed hairs all over the place.

Thoughtful, on top of everything else. She didn't learn that in the police.

Sleep was a deep, dark space and the dreams were inhabited only by the dead.

The scent of fresh coffee drifted through the dreams, enticing. It overlaid the medical smells of bandages and wound ointment and fulminant pus that were beginning to overtake the room.

'Ready for some fresh air?' A voice near my feet.

Lee.

It can't be. Lee is in hospital with a tube in her throat and drips in her arms and the surgeons have played with her finger bones. I opened my eyes.

Lee sat on the end of the bed balancing a tray across her forearms. Her left hand was fixed in an orthopaedic splint and it was impossible to see the fingers. Plasters criss-crossed the radial veins where the drips had gone in. As she turned her head towards me, I saw the suture lines along both jugulars. Neat, cosmetic, subcutaneous stitches closing a pair of parallel incisions, one longer than the other. Both looked half-healed: pink, rather than bright red at the edges, the way wounds do after a week or so.

There were two mugs on the tray. She blew gently across the tops and the mixed smell of coffee and cat's-piss tea floated confusingly between us.

She smiled and nodded as I reached for a mug. Nothing was really different.

'Good morning.'

'Is it?' The coffee sang through my brain.

'It's not bad. The rain's stopped and the sun's up. Caroline's

291

taken the assembled guardians, which is to say herself, Janine and Elspeth Philips, on a ride. I thought perhaps we could make the most of the freedom. Your dog would appreciate a walk if nothing else.'

'Sounds fine by me.'

'Good woman. I knew you weren't dying really.' She looked at me rather more intently than usual. 'There's a thermometer on the bedside table. It might be worth having a quick suck just to check you're not about to fall over unexpectedly.'

'Is that likely?'

'I don't know. According to Mary Brower, they took a swab from your shoulder and you're growing every species of Proteus known to medical science. The bacteriologists are ecstatic but from a physician's point of view, it's less amusing. I gather it's not being entirely amenable to antibiotics. Possibly if you're much over the lethal limit, we ought to switch to Plan B.'

'Which is?'

'I bring Mhaire up for a chat.'

'Oh, give me a break.'

I found the thermometer, cleaned it carefully on the edge of the duvet cover and sucked on it for the required sixty seconds, wondering why I had no memory of my temperature having been taken at all in the recent past and not particularly wanting to know the answer.

It came out at 103, which is reasonably far below the lethal limit. I held it out for Lee to see, angling the glass in the light from the window so she could read the height of the column.

'It's not too bad. Can we stick to Plan A?'

'Yup.'

'Are you going to tell me what it is?'

'Uhuh. I was thinking we could walk up to the waterfall, it's not too far. You need something more sensible to wash your shoulder. Mhaire says it will work.'

'Great.'

She smiled cheerfully. 'I knew you'd appreciate it. There are clothes in the cupboard. I'd wrap up warm if I was you, it's fairly brisk outside.'

It was, unquestionably, brisk. But it was glorious to be outside in the sun again, to watch the dog exploring the far reaches of the field and to talk to the ponies as they followed us across the grass in a loose-knit huddle. Midnight had gone and Balder and the leggy dun Highland pony that had kicked Bridget on the first day we bought it and then turned to be the steadiest schoolmaster of them all. Perfect for a beginner and just about the right size for Janine.

Rain's filly followed us for a couple of hundred yards, walking almost sound and with a neat new bandage showing white on her foot.

Beyond the fence at the end of the field, sheep tracks push out through the bracken, then the gorse, then the heather, winding round solitary rowan and hawthorns in a random quest from here to anywhere higher up. One or two of them are wider than the others and have bootprints and hoofprints moulded into the springing peat between the heather roots.

The widest path follows the line of the river, back up towards its source in the high granite of the peaks, and I knelt to check the prints as I followed Lee away from the field. None of them looked particularly fresh.

'Do you know where the others went?' I asked.

'They're doing the circuit round the western edge of the Ben. They'll be away till dusk. We'll be back by then, don't worry.'

'Should I be worried?'

'No. But if I don't have you home in time, Janine will probably send me back to the ICU for life.'

'She wouldn't do that.'

'You haven't seen her when she thinks I'm responsible for killing you.'

'Is it bad?'

'She's a lot more frightening than you are when she's angry.'

'Oh.' That's bad.

The river ran lower than it had done when I last saw it, less savage, less desperate to make it to the sea. Instead it ran as a bright, living thread, weaving a way round the solid chunks of silver-grey schist that litter the higher land. Two-thirds of the way up, the edge of a basalt cliff stands out starkly against the heather and the path follows the stream as it cuts through the western side into a small hidden corrie.

This is the second secret of the farm. Unlike the clearing, there is no cairn or burial mound to render it sacred, but the beauty is completely breathtaking. Even with a temperature of 103 and a hazy grasp of reality, it hit me, as it always does, as I squeezed through the gap between the rock and the hawthorn that guards the entrance.

Sixty feet away, at the back of the corrie, the river launches itself off the polished stone of a cliff edge and tumbles crazily down in a rushing, spuming waterfall to plunge deep into a wide basin carved out in the rock below.

The corrie faces south and, in all but the shortest days of winter, the sun reaches over the southern wall to light the water as it falls and fills the pool. Fish flash silver across the warmed rock of the shallows and the kingfishers stare for hours at the water's edge. It's the kind of place you might expect to see otters if you were feeling particularly romantic.

I was feeling decidedly unromantic by the time we reached the pool. My shoulder burned and I could hear unnerving liquid gurgles from beneath the bandage, as if the flesh had melted and been replaced by a pint or two of pus.

Mary Brower's comment about the Proteus infection ate at the back of my mind. The bits I remembered from my bacteriology classes were not altogether reassuring, particularly not the paragraph relating to systemic infection from a single-point source. I've watched people die of blood poisoning before and there are better ways to go.

The sight of the waterfall worked as it always did and, for a moment, I forgot the pain and the ugly images and lost myself in the magic of sunlight and green grass and the music of the water as it sang its way down the cliff face. Lee eased her way out of a rucksack and unbuckled it single-handed, taking care not to stub the fingers of her left hand on any of the straps. She tipped it up, dropping out a pair of bath towels and an industrial-sized plastic lunch-box that proved to contain a selection of sandwiches and a couple of apples. A flask of coffee emerged from one of the side compartments of the sack. There are times when it is really useful to have entirely predictable tastes.

We laid the towels on the dark rock at the edge of the pool and began, very carefully, to undress. It took a long time and a lot of swearing and the air, when we were done, was not nearly as warm as it had seemed. I pulled the towel up round my good shoulder while Lee exercised her clinical discretion and began to remove the bandage from the other one.

'Have you seen what it's like under there?'

'Yes. You might not want to look, it's not that encouraging.'

'It looked fine last time I saw it.'

'Aye. Well. That was a while ago.'

'Really?'

'You've been out of it for almost ten days, Kellen.'

'Shit.'

'Mmm. I think it's probably easier that way.'

'When did they let you out of the Western?'

'A couple of days ago. They're short of beds on the ortho-paedics ward and they weren't doing anything I couldn't do at home. Besides, Mhaire can be very persuasive when she tries.'

I can imagine.

'Was Caroline happy to have you at the farm?'

'She wouldn't have let me go anywhere else. She wanted me somewhere she could keep an eye on me. If you had died, I'd have been the wood that lit your funeral pyre.'

'She doesn't mean it. It's just an over-developed sense of guilt.'

'Maybe. I don't want to find out.' She finished unpicking the micropore from the edges of the bandage. 'Hold tight. This is going to hurt.'

It did. It hurt a great deal. I lay back on the towel and stared at the sky, counting backwards from 100, in threes. By the time I got down to single figures, I was feeling well enough to have a look.

The wound was every bit as bad as she had said. The nice neat puncture wound had transformed into a gaping cavity with an interesting purulent discharge that coated the dressing and spread out over my shoulder.

Almost as bad as I had imagined and I thought I was being pessimistic. I looked away.

Lee was watching me. 'Nasty,' she said.

True.' I looked at the languid water of the pool. It looked pleasantly inviting. Like a siren-mirror calling me in. It didn't promise to let me out again. 'Is washing it going to help?'

'I think so.'

'Okay.' I stood up, slowly. 'Shall we go?'

We stayed a long time in the water, walking out under the waterfall, letting it cascade over us like a living shower, scouring off the waste and the debris and the smell of death that clung, unnoticed, as a second skin. After the first shock of the cold, the anaesthetic effect on the wound in my shoulder felt as if someone had removed a spiked vice from the skin. Wonderful. I leant over backwards and let the water jet in, like a power hose, or a surgical irrigation, abrading all the dead flesh.

Afterwards, we lay back on the towels and toyed with the

food, watching the wind ripple the fringes of grass at the top of the cliff and keeping an eye out for imaginary kingfishers.

Lee rolled on to one side to look at me. 'How's your shoulder?'

'Better. How's your hand?'

'Okay.'

'Was the surgery all right?'

'Reasonable. Marje Stevens did it. She's as good as they come.'

'All in one piece?'

'It's all there. It might not work quite as it used to.'

'Do you mind?'

'I'm still alive. In the scale of things, it could be a lot worse.'

'Mmm.' I stared at the clouds for a while and thought about how much worse it could have been. I rolled over to see her better. 'Andersen's dead, did you know?'

'Yes.' She kept her face to the sky. 'Gemmell isn't.'

'We can't leave him like that.'

'No. But we'll wait till you're better before we do anything heroic.'

'And if I don't get better?'

'He can stay where he is.' She sat up and reached for a pocket in the rucksack. 'Here. It's time we were going or the others will be home. Do you think you could stand another bandage on your shoulder?'

'Do you think I need it?'

'I think it would look less suspicious if you had one.'

'Fine. You're the surgeon.'

We made the descent a lot faster than we had climbed up and I was back in bed, coffee mug removed, by the time the sound of voices and hoof beats rattled into the yard.

* * *

Three months later, around midnight on hogmanay, a white-coated clinician made an unscheduled visit to the Intensive Care Unit of the Glasgow Royal Infirmary.

Some time later, the night nurse in charge of Peter Gyton Gemmell, noticed a change in the stable rhythm of his heart. In the time it took her to call the emergency team, the dysrhythmia had changed to overt fibrillation and the doctor in charge, who was a humane man, elected not to initiate resuscitation.

In due course, the ventilator was disconnected and the body transferred to the Pathology unit, where a brief post-mortem examination confirmed the cause of death as cardiac arrest.

A small private service, for close colleagues and members of the immediate family only, was held the following week at the local crematorium.

Also of interest:

Val McDermid
Booked for Murder
The fifth Lindsay Gordon mystery

**From the massively acclaimed winner of the 1995 Gold
Dagger Award for Best Crime novel, her superb new
book.**

Why would anyone want to kill bestselling author, Penny
Varnavides? It can't have been the freak accident it first appeared
– Penny's death was an exact replica of the murder method in
her forthcoming book. Apart from Penny, only three people
knew the plot: her agent, her editor and her ex-girlfriend,
Meredith. In memory of her old friendship with Penny, Lindsay
Gordon agrees to investigate. And as her investigation reveals an
incendiary mixture of soured relationships and seething rivalries,
Lindsay must face the frightening truth. Someone in Penny's
literary or love life must have been driven to murder . . .

**'Move over V I Warshawski . . . Pacey and wittily written
. . . bound to make McDermid one of Britain's favourite
detective writers.' Options**

'Move over Morse . . . a refreshing detective story.'
New Woman

'Plot, characterisation, pace are all first-rate.'
Sunday Telegraph

'Tough, exciting, moody and unpredictable.' The Times

Crime Fiction hardback £15.99
ISBN 0 7043 5071 8

Hannah Wakefield
Cruel April
A Dee Street crime thriller

Dee Street doesn't want to fall out with her old friend, Janey
Riordan. After all, Janey has just found her a key defence witness
for an upcoming murder trial. But Janey still owes Dee's law firm
a lot of money and no amount of favours can replace the cash.
Now Janey's refusing to pay and, even worse, is risking their
friendship with a nasty, and very public, argument.

Then Janey is found murdered – and all the evidence points to
Dee . . .

'Excellent and original.' *Daily Telegraph*

**'An engaging first-person heroine with real depth and a
distinctive voice.'** *Time Out*

'Lively, entertaining and legally accurate.' *Guardian*

'Riveting.' Patricia Craig, *London Review of Books*

Crime Fiction £6.99
ISBN 0 7043 4475 0

Meg O'Brien
A Bright Flamingo Shroud
A Jesse James mystery

Jesse James has learnt never to rely on the men in her life. When the going gets tough, they're sure to leave. Just like the grandfather she never knew. But now her grandfather is back – if the man who knocked on her door is who he claims to be.

He's a down-and-out conman, a liar and a thief, but he needs Jesse's help. 'Gramps' has swindled a dangerous man and is in hiding for his life. Against her better judgement, Jesse allows herself to get involved. But once the man who claims to be her relative is safe, Jesse herself becomes the target of a vicious, cold-blooded rage . . .

'**A wise-cracking, street-smart heroine in the V I Warshawski mould . . . Fast-moving, feisty and fun.**' *Sunday Times*

'**A verve and naturalness unmatched since Sue Grafton teamed up with a Gatling gun.**' *Clues*

'**A cracking story.**' *Guardian*

'**Meg O'Brien is a real find. Credible characters, wonderful dialogue. A bestseller.**' **Ted Allbeury**

Crime Fiction £5.99
ISBN 0 7043 4463 7